LIKE
JOYFUL
TEARS

LIKE JOYFUL TEARS

DAVID STARR

RONSDALE PRESS

LIKE JOYFUL TEARS
Copyright © 2019 David Starr

RONSDALE PRESS
3350 West 21st Avenue, Vancouver, B.C. Canada V6S 1G7
www.ronsdalepress.com

Typesetting: Julie Cochrane, in Caslon 11.5 pt on 15.5
Cover Design: Lisa Canzi
Paper: Ancient Forest Friendly 55 lb. Enviro Book Antique Natural,
    100% post-consumer waste, totally chlorine-free and acid-free.

Ronsdale Press wishes to thank the following for their support of its publishing program: the Canada Council for the Arts, the Government of Canada, the British Columbia Arts Council, and the Province of British Columbia through the British Columbia Book Publishing Tax Credit program.

Library and Archives Canada Cataloguing in Publication

Starr, David, author
  Like joyful tears / David Starr.

Issued in print and electronic formats.
ISBN 978-1-55380-565-6 (softcover)
ISBN 978-1-55380-566-3 (ebook) / ISBN 978-1-55380-567-0 (pdf)

  I. Title.

PS8637.T365L55 2019   C813'.6   C2018-906370-X   C2018-906371-8

At Ronsdale Press we are committed to protecting the environment. To this end we are working with Canopy and printers to phase out our use of paper produced from ancient forests. This book is one step towards that goal.

Printed in Canada by Marquis Book Printing, Quebec

for Amel and Rose,
sisters in struggle

"A real friend is one who walks in when the rest of the world walks out."

– WALTER WINCHELL

I

1

RUMBEK, SOUTHERN SUDAN
SEPTEMBER 1983

VICTORIA DENG WALKED toward St. Matthew's Anglican Church, under a sky swollen black with thunderheads, clouds full of the rain that was turning the dirt streets of Rumbek to mire. Before the door closed behind her, Victoria heard the *adhān*, the Muslim call to prayer, as it echoed from tinny speakers hung high in the minaret of the small mosque down the sodden road.

Allahu Akbar, God is greatest. Ash-hadu an-la ilaha illa llah, I bear witness that there is none worthy of worship except for Allah.

St. Matthew's Anglican Church was a squat, brick building with a high steeple rising from its peaked zinc roof. Since its construction in 1935 — one of the last investments in Sudan by the British colonial government — the church had managed to survive season after season of blowing dust storms and monsoon rains with hardly a leak. It was a solid building, no doubt, but attending services within was not a comfortable experience for even the most devout parishioner, and Victoria, who endured the weekly ritual at the insistence of her father and mother, was hardly that. Sunday morning was her least favourite time of the week.

Even at this early hour, with rain drumming on the metal roof, the heat was insufferable inside. Electricity in Rumbek was scarce, unreliable and expensive. Certainly, it was not something to waste on powering air conditioners in a church. So with the heat and humidity climbing rapidly, the sweating worshippers inside, all dressed in their Sunday best, baked as if in an oven.

Victoria and her family took their familiar places on a hard, wooden pew in the third row from the front. A few moments later the priest began to speak. He was an old, leather-faced man, the priest, with a shock of white hair and a simple black cassock.

The old man looked out at the expectant crowd. "Today I shall talk to you of the delivery of Moses and his people from the subjugation of the Pharaoh of Egypt." It was a good choice, and timely. The congregation murmured in approval. That particular sermon from Exodus was always a favourite in Rumbek, even more so in light of recent events.

The service at St. Matthew's was by tradition delivered in English, but it could just have well have been preached in Dinka, the language spoken by most of the residents of southern Sudan.

Or even in the country's official tongue, for that matter. After all, even the poorest of residents in Rumbek spoke at least a smattering of Arabic, although the language of the north was not a welcome sound these days.

As the sermon began, thunder echoed outside, raising the drama within. He railed, the preacher, against the excesses of the Egyptians and their king, and though the Bible spoke of people and events two thousand years past, they knew he referenced more contemporary issues.

The old man's voice rose both in fervour and volume, his arms gesturing grandly as he preached behind the wooden pulpit at the front.

His audience listened intently, all in rapt attention save for Victoria who stifled a yawn, wriggled uncomfortably and whispered conspiratorially into her younger sister's ear. "I'm sure it wouldn't have been so difficult to convince Moses to leave Rumbek," she said in Dinka. "It's so boring here."

Her sister Mary hissed angrily back. "Victoria! Hush! You're going to get us into trouble — like always! When are you going to start thinking before you open your mouth?"

On cue, Victoria's parents cast disapproving glances her way. Her father, Peter Deng, was headmaster of St. Matthew's School. He took the Sunday service at the namesake church very seriously and did not tolerate misbehaviour from his children. Victoria was thoroughly chastised, her cheeks burning from the rebuke, but not before Mary shot her an "I told you so" look.

Unaware or unfazed by the family drama unfolding in the third row, the priest carried on, reaching the climax of the sermon where Moses was finally convinced by God to stand up to the Egyptians. "And he lifted up the rod," the old man said passionately, "and smote the waters that were in the river, in the sight of the Pharaoh and his servants . . ."

The door of the church flew open. Gabriel Yuot, a friend of Victoria's father and the editor of the *Rumbek Times* newspaper, staggered in, walking as if drunk. Drenched from the rain, Yuot made his way toward the front of the church, a paper clutched tightly in his hands.

Victoria watched silently as Yuot approached the preacher, stepping up onto the small stage. With shaking hands, the man lifted the paper into the air. The headline was written in English, in thick black letters large enough for all in the church who could read to see.

SHARIA LAW DECLARED FOR ALL SUDAN. KHARTOUM
ORDERS SCHOOLS IN THE SOUTH TO TEACH KORAN

The congregation gasped. Some swore in disgust, language most unseemly for a house of God. Others cried openly. "And all the waters in the river were turned to blood." The priest finished the verse in a trembling voice. "The service is over," he said, struggling to be heard over the angry rumble in the church. "Go home and pray."

The rain stopped as they left St. Matthew's. The Deng family walked home, passing a group of barefoot children playing soccer with a ball made from bundled rages and twine. Five minutes farther on, they came across a man begging against the side of a brick wall, his face horribly disfigured by leprosy. "*Salaam Alaikum,*" the man said respectfully.

"And peace be with you," Victoria's father replied easily in Arabic, placing a five-piaster coin into the beggar's crippled hand as he did.

The man quickly slipped the brass coin into his tattered trousers. "Thank you, headmaster," he said. They continued the walk home to their comfortable two-storey brick and tin-roofed house on the north side of the city, a house that once belonged to a mid-level functionary in the British colonial government.

"*Wa*, why do the Muslims hate us so much?" Victoria stopped and studied her father carefully, finally daring to broach the question that had been on her mind since leaving the church.

"And why do they hate God?" Mary added, to Victoria's agreement. At fourteen, Mary was a year younger than Victoria, shorter, skin more chocolate-brown than black, with a round moon face.

Mary didn't resemble her sister. She hardly looked Dinka at all for that matter, and that was not the only difference between them. Younger or not, Mary was by far the more mature and sensible, watching out for Victoria, often getting her out of the mischief she constantly seemed to find herself in. Two girls, so close in age, yet so different in both looks and disposition. It had always been a source of wonder for some. When asked about the subject, Victoria knew it was because of the Nigerian.

The girls' great-grandfather on their mother's side was from Lagos, a sergeant in the British Colonial Army who'd come to Sudan in the dying years of the nineteenth century. His mission had been to regain control of the country for the Empire after General Gordon lost Khartoum, his army and his head at the hands of the rebellious Mahdi. The British retook the city, and the young Nigerian stayed on in Sudan, retiring from the army, eventually marrying a young girl from Rumbek: Victoria's great-grandmother.

Victoria never met him. The Nigerian died years before she was born, just before Sudanese independence, missing the chaos of the civil war that ensued. By all accounts, her grandfather was a serious and responsible man, and judging by her parents' memories and the faded black-and-white photograph that still hung on the wall of their house, it was easy to see that the Nigerian's genes lived on in Mary.

"Who told you that, children?" asked her father. "Who told you the Muslims hate God?"

"Everyone." By the look on Peter's face, Victoria saw the question had deeply unsettled her father. "In the market, at church, everyone says so."

"At school as well? Your teachers?" Their father pressed and the girls nodded in unison. "I see. Perhaps I should come and have a talk with your teachers tomorrow." The headmaster put his hand on Mary's shoulder. "Listen to me, children. Jew, Christian, Muslim: we are all People of the Book. We share the same God, although we use different names for Him. This current situation isn't about religion at all and it will pass."

Victoria's mother had different thoughts on the subject. "No, Mr. Headmaster," Alek Bol said cynically. "It will not pass. This is the price southern Sudan continues to pay for your precious England abandoning us. Twenty years of war, do you remember? Blood will be spilled again because of Sharia, you mark my words."

Despite her harsh comments, Victoria knew her mother cherished her father dearly and this was the only thing they disagreed on. Her family connections to the Empire aside, it was well known to Victoria and Mary that Alek Bol had lost a brother in the carnage of the Sudanese Civil War, and that she strongly believed Africa would be far better off without European interference.

Peter turned to his children. "We all know your mother's opinions on the subject. Yes, there were troubles in the past when independence from Britain was declared. It is also true that southern Sudan is Christian, the north Muslim and that tensions exist between us, but Sudan is a civilized country. We are capable of solving our problems with words instead of guns. There'll be no war. Not again."

Victoria's mother had heard the speech before and was unmoved. "I love you, my *mionyde*, but you are naïve. You underestimate the hate men carry in their hearts for each other. This is the start of something very bad. I just know it."

"If it isn't about the Muslims, what is it about, *Wa*?" Victoria heard the rare sound of fear in her mother's voice and worried.

Before her father could respond, a loud rumble and the sudden honking of a horn forced them off the road. A dark green Sudanese Army transport truck, full of heavily armed soldiers, sped past, followed closely behind by an oil tanker. They gazed at the passing soldiers — boys really, hardly older than Victoria.

As the trucks drove by, one of the soldiers stared back. He pointed his rifle at them and pretended to fire. Despite the mercury pushing thirty-five degrees Celsius that day, a chill ran through Victoria's body, one that remained until the trucks disappeared, leaving only muddy tracks and a small pool of thick black oil behind in their wake.

Her father bent down and put his finger in the viscous fluid that had pooled on the road. "No, children, this current situation isn't about God at all, no matter what His name is. It is about what problems in our country are always about: land, water, cattle — and other more recently discovered treasures."

It was raining again when Peter Deng tucked his daughters into bed that night. Lightning, though far away to the west, flashed brightly in the darkened sky, filling their small bedroom with light. "Don't be worried about all that talk at church today," her father said, kissing Victoria on the head. "Six months from now, it will all be a distant memory."

"You're certain of that?" Victoria asked.

"Absolutely. Things will be fine, I promise you. Now go to sleep; you have school first thing in the morning."

Her father repeated the ritual with Mary, bid them good night once more, then shut the door behind him with a gentle click. "I knew things would be fine," Mary said, once her father's footsteps had disappeared down the hall. "Mother overreacts, she always does. Do you remember how angry she was when you broke that stupid old vase by the front door? Go to sleep, Victoria. I don't want to hear any more about it."

Victoria stared out the mosquito-netted window to the distant storm. "The rain's falling harder," she said. "I don't think I can."

Ahead in the distance, an old wooden bridge crosses a wadi. Victoria scrambles down the bank to the dry riverbed, ignoring Mary and the lightning that flashes across the black sky overhead.

"You know what Father thinks about this place," Mary says, her eyes everywhere, looking for danger. "We've gone too far from town."

"I know what Wa says," Victoria tells her, "but I want a lizard, and the best ones live here in the wadi."

A lizard basks on a rock. Until now the creature has stood motionless, but as Victoria approaches, the reptile darts away. She squeals happily, chasing the lizard as it scurries toward the old bridge.

"Victoria! Don't! We aren't allowed to go past the bridge! It isn't safe! Don't you remember? There's been lion sightings. And hyenas. We're not allowed to come here by ourselves."

"And hippos and dinosaurs too," Victoria laughs. "Come on, Mary. It's the middle of the day. It's perfectly safe."

Before Mary can respond, a little voice pipes up. "Wait for me, Victoria!" Her little sister Alexandra is just a few months past her sixth birthday. Alexandra loves everybody, but she and Victoria are connected in a way nobody else can understand, and she follows her like a puppy anywhere.

Without another word, Alexandra climbs clumsily over the rocks, making her way down to Victoria. Mary yells for them to stop, but Victoria ignores her, takes her little sister by the hand and walks down the wadi toward the bridge, stalking their prey.

Victoria woke up, crying. Outside, the wind had picked up. The storm, which seemed so far away just a few short hours ago, had descended with a fury onto Rumbek. Mary jumped into Victoria's bed and hugged her tightly. "It's the dream, isn't it?"

Victoria didn't reply, weeping instead as her sister gently stroked her hair. "It's not your fault, Victoria," Mary whispered.

But Mary was wrong.

Victoria knew it was.

2

RUMBEK, SOUTHERN SUDAN

NOVEMBER 1984

THE WET PASSED and for five months southern Sudan baked in the searing heat of the Dry. Lakes evaporated, the marshes and rivers retreated from the heat, and as the waters receded, *haboobs*, unpredictable vast choking storms of red dust and sand, stalked the countryside. The sandstorms covered everything in their path, making going outside risky and, at times, impossible.

And then, in its time, the Wet returned, running its course through summer until November neared its end and the skies dried up once more. This season, however, the Dry brought with it something else, a storm far more dangerous than any *haboob*.

In late November 1984, twenty bored students, dressed in the crisp white-and-green uniforms of St. Matthew's, sat lined up in neat rows, in the same old desks their grandparents used when the school was new and "God Save the King" was sung at the start of classes. "So, when the British left Sudan in 1956, it ushered in a period of uncertainty that led our country down the path to civil war," droned Mr. Ibrahim, the school's history teacher.

Mr. Ibrahim was a tiresome, skinny old man with a bald head and ears that flapped like bat wings. Victoria tried her very best not to fall asleep as he talked about ancient events she cared little about, but it was hard to focus and her eyelids grew heavy.

Suddenly, an engine roared, brakes squeaked and the air outside the school filled with the harsh sound of clanking metal and voices shouting in Arabic. Mr. Ibrahim looked out the small, open window of the classroom, annoyed his lecture had been interrupted no doubt, judging by the sour look on his face.

Gunfire erupted. "What in God's name?" Mr. Ibrahim said, wincing as the first screams reached the classroom. Victoria peered out the window to see what was happening. She wished she hadn't.

The view was horrific. Dozens of green-clad soldiers streamed from the backs of transport trucks, assault rifles clenched in their hands. They fired upon the street, shooting indiscriminately. Victoria heard strange whooshing sounds and watched as three houses hit by mortar shells erupted in flame. Thick plumes of black smoke from the flaming thatch quickly spiralled into the deep blue sky.

On the street, bodies of perhaps half a dozen people lay still as dozens more wounded civilians, including small children, screamed in pain as they struggled to get away from the shooting. "Away from the window! Now!" Victoria's father ordered as he entered the class. Sweat glistened on his head and fear burned in his eyes.

"Sir, what's going on?" asked Mr. Ibrahim.

"It's the army. That's all I know. Wait here with the children until I come back. Shut the blinds, stay away from the windows, sit on the floor and don't panic. That includes you, Victoria," her father said sternly.

"Can't I come with you, Wa?" Victoria begged. "I'm scared. I don't want to stay here."

"You'll do as you're told, and at this school you will call me Sir!" he snapped.

"Sorry, Sir," she said, meaning it.

His voice softened. "Good. You'll be safe here, Victoria. Don't worry. I'll be back shortly. I promise."

He left. From the doorway Victoria watched her father enter each of the other rooms on the second floor, issuing no doubt the same order he gave Mr. Ibrahim. Then he reached the last class in the hallway, the room where Mary was studying maths with the other fifteen-year-olds. Victoria jumped at the rattle of machine gun fire close by and then, despite her father's direct command to stay, ran after him.

Several girls in Mary's class were crying. "It will be all right," Victoria heard her father say soothingly when she reached the doorway.

"Mr. Dau," Victoria's father commanded the maths teacher just as he did Mr. Ibrahim. "Close the window, draw the blinds and bring the children to the centre of the room."

Despite the urgency of the situation, Victoria took a second to admire Mary. She was the first to react, taking the hand of a sobbing, mousy-looking girl, leading her to the middle of the room. Then Mary looked up to the door, saw Victoria and called her name.

"Damn it, Victoria!" her father cursed. "I told you to stay with your teacher."

"*Wa.*" Victoria said from the hallway. She had never heard her father curse before, had never seen him anything but unflappable. "I'm sorry, I wanted to be with you."

Victoria knew her father was as scared as she was in his own way. Victoria ran over and hugged him tightly. Her father relented and enveloped her in his arms. "All right, you can stay with your sister."

A loud explosion shook the school. Smoke drifted into the class. "Mr. Dau! I thought I told you to close the window and draw the curtains!"

Victoria's father let her go then strode quickly toward the still open window. "The next time I tell you to do something . . ."

He never finished the sentence. A short burst of machine gun fire erupted through the open window. Heavy-calibre bullets slammed into him, ripping open his chest. Shocked, Victoria watched her father spin awkwardly and thud to the floor. He lay still, a mess of blood and gore on the hardwood.

The same spurt of bullets hit Mr. Dau. One cleaved off the top of his skull, sending a spray of bone fragments and chunks of brain across the room, covering the students. With a surprised look in his eyes, the teacher fell silently to his knees, slumping lifelessly onto Victoria's father's body. The children were too shocked to move until two small green metal objects flew through the window and scudded across the wooden floor.

"Run!" Mary shouted the warning and rushed to Victoria, who stood motionless. She grabbed Victoria's hand, pulling her roughly out of the room into the corridor behind the cover of the thick wooden walls.

The grenades exploded. The concussion blast sent a wave of noise and pain through Victoria's head, stunning her, knocking her to the floor as thick, acrid smoke billowed out of the classroom.

Fragments of shrapnel and wood and body parts hurtled into the hallway, as a sound like church bells echoed in Victoria's head. Coughing uncontrollably, ears ringing, barely able to breathe, Victoria pushed herself up to her knees.

She felt something soft and wet. Through the dust and smoke, Victoria saw remnants of a small, bloodied arm, jagged wet bone sticking out from the flesh. On one of the fingers was a familiar gold ring with a little heart on it. Victoria pulled back her hand in revulsion and retched.

She knew that ring. Her friend Sarah had been given it by her mother for her birthday last year. Sarah had shown it to her friends at school so often that they'd all grown quite bored with it. Secretly, Victoria had prayed that she'd lose the thing — if only to shut her up.

Turning away from what was left of Sarah, Victoria lifted her head to see that the classroom had become an inferno. Flames lapped up the walls, consuming the student work that Mr. Dau had so proudly displayed. The floor inside the room was littered with bodies, some whole, some ripped apart by the force of the explosions, pieces hardly recognizable as human. The world spun. Victoria threw up once more.

"Victoria?" Mary's face was covered with soot and tear tracks ran down her cheeks. She helped Victoria to her feet as students poured out of the other classrooms and stampeded past them, shrieking in terror as they tumbled toward the stairs.

"Stop! Don't go outside!" cried Mary as an older girl brushed past the sisters, nearly knocking them down in her mad rush to reach the stairwell. Mary's warning was ignored and the panicked exodus from the burning school continued as student after student fled into the corridor and down the stairs.

"*Wa?*" Victoria's voice was weak and hollow. "Where's *Wa?* I want *Wa*."

"*Duet nyankäi*, dear sister, we have to go," Mary tugged on her arm, urging Victoria to move. Victoria remained stuck in place, her wide eyes not comprehending what they had seen.

The air outside filled with machine gun fire and screaming. The school would be overrun with soldiers soon and that they had to flee.

Or die.

The fire had spread from the classroom. The old polished wooden walls in the corridor burned and the sounds of shooting and shouting from the streets grew louder. "Hurry, Victoria," Mary repeated, shaking her sister. "We can't stay here. Not anymore."

"We're going the wrong way," Victoria mumbled as they ran, her head swimming, legs unsteady beneath her. "The stairs are behind us."

"We're not going down those stairs," said Mary. The machine gun blasts and the screams that had followed served as more than enough warning about joining the children who'd tried to seek safety down that particular stairwell.

They walked, stepping over bodies, edging around others. Mary led them to an entryway at the other end of the hallway. Victoria knew that door. Behind it was a set of steep metal steps used exclusively by the school's janitor and groundskeeper. Students at St. Matthew's were strictly forbidden to use it, although Victoria had broken that rule many times.

The last time was three weeks ago. She'd run into a workman carrying a mop and a full bucket of water, nearly sending the poor man flying down the stairs. The incident was quickly reported to her father, the transgression resulting in a week's worth of detention. Daughter of the headmaster or not, all students obeyed the rules and were treated equally when they broke them.

Victoria objected, the irrational thought of causing her father more unhappiness made her hesitate, as if he were still alive to discipline her. "But father said . . ."

Mary pushed open the door. "Father will be fine with it — just this once."

Sobbing gently, Victoria took Mary's hand. They descended the rusting metal stairs to the main floor and the service entrance to the school grounds. Victoria watched Mary put her ear to the door, listening for any noise. Hearing nothing, she carefully cracked it open, squinting as sunlight flooded into the dark landing.

Mary slowly pushed the door open a little wider, poked out her head then stepped carefully out onto the gravel path beside the school.

"There's no one out here, Victoria. Let's go home."

Home.

Their mother would be heartbroken about their father, but she was a strong woman. She would know what to do. Victoria found the tiniest shred of comfort in that thought. Her world was upside down, ripped apart, blown to shreds, but through it all, this much Victoria still understood: her mother would keep them safe, and Mary would find a way to get them home.

They came to the corner of the school and peered cautiously around the wall out onto the street. It was then Victoria realized with a sickening feeling in her guts that going home would be no simple matter. Soldiers patrolled the front of the school, guns raised, but the shooting in the immediate vicinity had stopped. The reason was obvious: there was nobody left alive to shoot.

The red dirt road they'd walked a thousand times between school and their house had been transformed into something unrecognizable. Smoke poured from the entrance of the school, shrouding the torn bodies of their classmates who'd escaped the fire, only to run into a wall of machine gun bullets.

Dozens more lay twisted and bleeding on the ground, whole or in pieces, alone or in twos and threes. Mothers who'd tried vainly to protect their babies. Husbands with lifeless arms around their dead wives. Dead children. Dead students. Dead friends.

Overhead in the black sky, vultures flew in lazy arcs, waiting patiently to feed on the carrion below. Houses and businesses, familiar landmarks and people, demolished, blown to pieces, gutted by fire, by shrapnel, by bullets.

Victoria fell to her knees, letting out a choking cry as the enormity of what she saw, of what had happened, crashed down upon her. Mary clamped her hand tightly over Victoria's mouth as she did.

"Be quiet! The soldiers are still here! Do you want them to shoot us too? Do you want to end up like our friends? Like Father? Be silent!"

"We're not going home, are we?" Victoria asked when Mary removed her hand. It was not a question, not really, with the road blocked with rubble and bodies, and the army patrols everywhere.

Victoria fought an overwhelming urge just to lie down and wait for the earth to swallow her up, but then a loud crash startled her. She turned quickly, heart racing, expecting to see a soldier, gun raised at her head.

Instead, Victoria watched as the far end of the school collapsed into a pile of red brick, a thick column of black smoke and flame billowing up into the sky.

Mary pulled Victoria to her feet. "We can't stay here. The rest of the school's going to fall down on top of us if we don't move."

"So where are we going to go?" Victoria winced as a fresh flurry of gunshots echoed somewhere in the distance.

Mary took her hand as they stepped gingerly over blackened bricks, away from the front of the school.

"Anywhere but here, Victoria. Anywhere but here."

3

A DIRT PATH led them to the far corner of the school grounds, to a small shed nestled in the shade of a grove of acacia trees. The little hut was the domain of St. Matthew's head groundskeeper. His name was Lucas, an old Nuer man with a shiny bald head and no surname, not as far as Victoria knew.

Lucas had been at the school for more than forty years and was well into his seventies, a neat, methodical man and the shed reflected his personality. Always one to enjoy chatting with the students, and never without a bag of sweets or a cup of tea to share, the old man had spent considerable time chatting with the girls.

Lucas was long past the days of hard physical labour, but Victoria's father and the headmasters before him for decades now had kept Lucas employed, and for good reason. The old man knew every inch of the grounds and seemed to have an almost magical touch with the school's temperamental plumbing and wiring. That, and his gift of keeping near-derelict equipment working that would have otherwise been junked, made the few pounds a week he earned well worth the investment.

Hiding in the shed with Lucas certainly seemed a better idea than being on the streets. "We can stay here until the soldiers leave," said Mary. "Then we can go home. Lucas will help us."

Mary pushed gently on the wooden door that hung half open, creaking gently on its rusted hinges as she entered the shed, Victoria walking closely behind. "Lucas? It's Mary Deng. Are you here?"

There was no answer. Rakes, shovels and all other manner of tools hung neatly on racks on the wall, but the old man's rough-cut wooden table — the same table Victoria had sat at a hundred times before — was flipped on its side, the chairs smashed.

Victoria's pulse raced when she saw the old man's teapot and cups in shards on the ground. This mess was not something the fastidious groundskeeper would have let happen willingly. Victoria took another, more tentative step inside, sticking like a shadow to Mary. "Lucas?"

As Victoria's eyes adjusted to the gloom, she saw something glitter dully in front of her feet. It was a machete, its blade stained a dark rust. She stepped further in, the sound of blowflies buzzing in the still air.

"Lucas? Are you here?" Victoria heard nothing in response save the flies, her own ragged breath and the blood pounding in her temples. Then Victoria's foot hit something solid. She looked to the ground and was unable to stifle her scream.

Lucas was dead. He lay on his back, eyes open, the grimace on his face mirrored by a deep slash across his throat, the force of the blow so strong that the old man's head had nearly been severed from his neck. The sisters turned and stumbled to the door and out into the light. Beside the shed, a gate in the wrought iron fence that encircled the school opened up toward the south.

"There's still one place we can hide," Mary said, catching her breath. Without another word, she took Victoria's hand and pulled her through the gate.

The soldiers had now passed the southern outskirts of Rumbek. Left in their wake was a city littered with the smoking husks of brick and thatch homes. A ruined city. A dead city. A city of corpses bloating in the afternoon, food for the legions of vultures in the air above.

Some braver birds already sat, wings folded, on the ground. Others waddled awkwardly among the dead, beaks full of carrion. "Where are we going?" Victoria asked.

"Someplace safe where they can't find us." Mary pointed across the street where three hyenas strolled amid the dead, heads bobbing leisurely from side to side, snouts stained red with blood. Hyenas were not an uncommon sight on the outskirts of Rumbek, but to see the spotted carnivores stalking so brazenly in the middle of town was something altogether new. The hyenas stopped and stared at Victoria curiously then carried on their way. With so much food readily available, they had no need to chase down the living.

In the distance, a small wooden bridge crossed a dry wadi. Beyond it, a narrow dirt road slashed southeast through the scrub and savannah toward the small village of Billing. Victoria knew this place. "No! I can't! I won't!" She stopped, refusing to walk one step further.

"Victoria, we can hide under the bridge and go home tomorrow," pleaded Mary. "I don't like it either, but there's no other place for us to go."

"No! Please don't make me."

Mary grabbed Victoria roughly by the arm. "Do you really think I'd have brought us here if there were any other choice? You saw what happened to our school, our friends and to our . . ."

A gunshot rung in the distance and Mary flinched. "I don't want to be here any more than you do, but nobody will find us under the bridge."

Victoria stood, motionless, staring at the wadi and the old wooden bridge above it. Water from a November downpour puddled in the shallow depression. By the looks of the black clouds forming in the late afternoon sky, more rain was imminent. Mary pressed. "It's just for the night. We can go home in the morning. The soldiers will have left by then, I'm certain."

Still, Victoria refused to move. "I don't think I can."

"Then stay here by yourself!" shouted Mary. "I don't care. I want to go home when things are safe and see Mother. If that means I must stay in this place until then, I will, with or without you!" With that, Mary turned her back and marched away.

There was no escape for Victoria from the awful truth. Her sister was right. "Mary! Wait!" Victoria spoke in a voice she didn't recognize as her own. With eyes half-closed and feet moving slowly forward as if they had been set in concrete, Victoria Deng walked toward the bridge. "Wait. I'm coming."

Victoria stared up at the bridge. Dust covered the beams and supports of the underside of the wooden structure, and rays of pale afternoon light streamed through the gaps in the decking.

"Up here." Mary indicated a small recess where the bridge deck met the road. After carefully checking for snakes and scorpions, she crawled into the narrow space then looked at her sister expectantly. "Hurry, Victoria. It's safe."

Victoria scrambled up the bank and sat next to her sister. The air here was musty and hot. Victoria started to gasp, chest constricting as if she'd fallen into quicksand. Mary stroked Victoria's hair, calming her down. "Shut your eyes and breathe slowly. In the morning, we'll go home."

"Did *Wa* suffer?" Victoria asked after a few moments. "And Mother? What's happened to Mother?"

"I'm sure Mother's fine," Mary said, not answering the first question. "I promise you she is. We'll go home tomorrow. You'll see. Get some rest. Things will be fine tomorrow."

As they waited in silence, in the narrow confines under the bridge, the sun lowered in the sky, the shadows lengthened and the long day ended. Somehow, Victoria slept until the sound of a hyena laughing in the distance jolted her awake. For a second, she was confused until the events and images of yesterday hit her like a flurry of punches.

Victoria reached for her sister, but Mary wasn't there. Victoria panicked and scrambled down out of the dark place where she'd hidden, like a mole, like a rat. Her heart raced, and Victoria was about to cry out when she saw Mary, standing on the road beside the bridge.

Victoria breathed again then climbed up out of the dry riverbed and stood next to her sister. She placed her hand in Mary's. Her throat was parched and as she gulped in the cool night air, Victoria wished it was water. The hyena cackled again, farther away in the darkness.

The sky had cleared. The storm clouds had gone and overhead in the purple black sky, impossibly bright stars twinkled. A faint lightening on the eastern horizon indicated that dawn was only a short time away.

"It's going to be light in twenty minutes. Are you ready to go?" Mary asked. Ready or not was irrelevant to Victoria. Travelling under the cover of what little darkness remained was safer than risking the roads in daylight.

"Go where?" a man's voice came from behind them. Victoria stifled a cry and turned around. A few feet away in the gloom she made out the form of a young man, nineteen, maybe twenty years old, dressed in army fatigues, a khaki, long-sleeve shirt and a New York Mets ball cap. An assault rifle dangled casually in his hands, the barrel pointed at the ground.

"You don't look much like a soldier," Mary said, recovering her composure, facing the man — boy, really, hardly older than she was. The soldiers Victoria saw yesterday wore red berets, proper uniforms and spoke Arabic, but this one talked to them in Dinka, the language of the south. Their language.

His teeth flashed brightly in the dawning light. "Neither do you."

"Who are you?" Mary demanded.

The armed man was tall and slender, with high cheekbones and bright eyes. "Jacob Bok," he said, switching to English. "What are the two of you doing out here? It's not safe."

Before Mary could answer, another man, shorter, heavier, a year or two older, emerged out of the darkness and lit a cigarette. Like Bok, he had an assault rifle, but this one also carried a long, wicked knife that hung in a sheath from his belt.

"You've a gift for finding lost sheep, Jacob." The man stared at Victoria in a way that frightened her.

"It isn't hard when there are so many of them about," said Jacob. "This is William Chol, my comrade in arms. We are both members of the SPLA, the Sudan People's Liberation Army. We fight the oppressors from Khartoum."

Chol spat with disgust. "Fight? We're little more than babysitters these days, and you know it, Jacob."

Behind Chol a small figure moved. Victoria squinted in the predawn light and saw a boy, perhaps eight years old, shuffle out of the darkness.

Behind the boy other shapes emerged, and as the sun broke the plane of the eastern horizon, dozens, hundreds more children were visible, standing huddled in clusters.

They had been silent, the children. Victoria had no idea they were there in such numbers. Some of them were her age, but most were younger. Some, hardly more than toddlers, nervously held the hands of the older ones.

"We've been walking for five days now," said Jacob. "These children came from Kashwal, from Mokwi, from a dozen other burned villages to the west. We came to the wadi looking for water but found you instead. Now get your things if you have any; you're coming with us."

Victoria was repulsed at the idea. "No, I'm going home! Mary promised we would go home. I want my mother!"

Jacob shook his head. "Look toward Rumbek." It was lighter now and Victoria saw that smoke hung thick over the city, fresh columns rising from newly burned buildings. Tiny specks of black floated above the haze. Vultures and other carrion birds, in numbers far greater than yesterday, surveyed the city, searching the streets below for a meal.

"Listen to me," Jacob said, though not unkindly. "Sudan is at war with itself. Towns are burning throughout the south and Rumbek is gone. You have no home, not anymore. Your mother's either fled the city or she's dead. In any event, you won't find her in there."

William finished his cigarette and tossed it to the ground, crushing it with his boot. "Let them go, Jacob. What do we care? They'd die before they took ten steps and then we'd have two fewer mouths to feed. Don't take my word for it, girls. Go. See what's waiting for you."

Mary put her arm around Victoria's shoulder. The soldier was right, and Victoria knew it. "What do we do now then?" she asked.

"Now?" Jacob replied, slinging the rifle over his shoulder. "Now you join our little flock."

4

LIEUTENANT COLONEL MOHAMMED Suleiman, commanding officer of the Sudanese Army's First Division Jihad Brigade, stood in the back of his Land Rover, surveying with satisfaction the devastation he had brought to Rumbek.

At forty-five, the lieutenant colonel had the physique of a man half his age. Not quite six feet tall, he was short by Dinka standards. But Suleiman was not Dinka. He was a northerner, an Arab with little love for the infidel cattle farmers of the south.

Heavily muscled, square-jawed and with the black whiskers of his short beard flecked with grey, Lieutenant Colonel Suleiman was well known in army circles, and long ago he'd earned both the respect of his superiors and the fear of his men.

It was hot for so early in the morning. Humid, too, he thought with distaste. The dry heat of the northern desert he could handle, but Suleiman loathed both this God-forsaken, swampy corner of the country and the people who lived here. In truth, Suleiman hated everything about the south. The people, their infidel religion, the weather, the swamps and the clouds of malarial mosquitoes that sent dozens of his men to the infirmary. As glad as he was to be out of the barracks, he was done with the field as well. A man of his talents was better put to use at army headquarters — or perhaps even on the president's staff.

Before that could happen, however, Suleiman had been given the task of eliminating the SPLA and all who supported them in this remote backwater state. And, God willing, he would do it well.

Suleiman's hand strayed to his shoulder patch. There was only one lone star below the secretary bird insignia now, but he had every intention of earning two more, or perhaps even the crossed sword and baton of a major general before he retired.

A sergeant approached nervously, waiting as Suleiman took a Cohiba from his shirt pocket. One of these coveted cigars cost more than most Sudanese made in a month, but the lieutenant colonel had a friend, a Russian major, stationed at the embassy in Khartoum, who'd introduced him to Cuban cigars several years back.

Suleiman allowed himself the Cohiba. Discounting his pistol and his fondness for the Land Rover he'd taken from a hapless British aid worker who'd made the mistake of crossing the border from Uganda without paperwork, cigars were his only weakness. "How many guerillas have you killed?"

The subordinate squirmed. "Sir, I'm sorry, but we haven't found any rebels. Not that we haven't been looking," the nervous non-commissioned officer added quickly as Suleiman scowled down at him. "We've torn the city apart, brick by brick, and interrogated dozens of civilians, but it seems Intelligence was wrong. The SPLA aren't in Rumbek after all."

Suleiman drew deeply on the cigar and exhaled, focusing his attention down the street to where a dead woman, in her early twenties perhaps, sprawled twisted on the ground beside the body of a dead infant.

The woman was naked from the waist down, raped a hundred times by his troops, no doubt, before she was killed. The damage done by shrapnel and the vultures made identifying the gender of the child impossible. Not that Suleiman cared either way. One fewer infidel, boy or girl, was a good thing.

"No matter. They'd have come here sooner or later, finding men for their cause. We have left them fewer recruits."

"What are your orders, Sir?" The sergeant was grateful his commander hadn't flown into a rage. He'd seen what happened to messengers before when Suleiman was given bad news. It wasn't something he cared to have happen to him.

"If the SPLA aren't in Rumbek then they're in Bor, or Tonj or some other place nearby. We will find them and eradicate them and those who protect them from the face of the earth. Finish our task here and move on."

Another vehicle, a sand-coloured Walid armoured personnel carrier drove up and stopped beside the Land Rover. A short, wiry officer stepped quickly down from the passenger seat and approached. "Yes, Captain Soulu?" asked Suleiman to his second-in-command.

"Sir, a patrol on the southern edge of the city reports seeing a number of footprints leading away from Rumbek, across country toward the east."

"You've been wasting your time chasing cow-herders?" Suleiman asked, underwhelmed by the report.

"Not farmers, Sir. The men saw hundreds of different sets of footprints. Most were small, children or women, but one, maybe two sets belonged to adult men in boots. They found this as well." The captain opened his hand and held out a cigarette butt. "Nyala brand. Ethiopian. Locals wouldn't smoke these, but the SPLA?"

Suleiman rested his cigar carefully on the roll bar of the Land Rover then reached for the large gold-plated pistol at his hip. Both Soulu and the sergeant winced at the sight of the gun. Suleiman smiled at the response. Fear, he knew, was a good thing. Suleiman ignored his subordinates, focusing his attention back to the corpses of the woman and her child and to the vulture that had clumsily landed beside them, looking for an easy meal.

Suleiman raised the pistol, an Israeli .50 calibre Desert Eagle. Not that any would say it to his face, but Suleiman knew some of his men disapproved of the pistol he'd obtained while on a course in Baghdad with the Republican Guard.

Suleiman cared little about what they thought. Made by the Jews or not, the pistol was one of the finest weapons on earth, and Suleiman knew his guns. Besides, a smart warrior studied his enemies, and there was much to learn from the Israelis. They may be infidels, but the Jews deserved to be observed and respected. Only then could they be obliterated.

Lieutenant Colonel Suleiman saw something of that same character in the southerners. There were some on the general staff who discounted the tribes of southern Sudan as little more than half-naked farmers, but Suleiman knew his history. These people fought the better armed north to a standstill in the decades-long first civil war.

Fighting was in their blood, after all. When they weren't ambushing government troops, these people were entangled in bloody tribal fighting or cattle raids, and the recent provocative moves from Khartoum were sure to enrage and unite them. Dinka or Nuer, man or woman, rebel or civilian: the southerners were not to be taken lightly at all.

Suleiman aimed carefully, and with the bird in his sights, he pulled the trigger. The vulture exploded in a puff of blood and feathers. Suleiman grunted in satisfaction, slipped the large-calibre weapon back into its holster, and addressed his troops.

"Despite your assurances to the contrary, it seems the rebels were here after all, recruiting the next generation of fighters."

"We'll find them, Sir," Soulu vowed. "They won't get far. Those dogs will never live to take up arms against us."

Thunder crackled across the sky and large drops of rain pelted the Land Rover. Suleiman looked at the rain in disgust. The Wet was supposed to be over by now.

"Whatever tracks they may have left will be gone within minutes," said Suleiman. "And thanks to this damned rain, we wouldn't get one hundred metres off the road without bogging down in the mud."

"There are hundreds of them out there," said Soulu. "They're children after all. How hard can they be to find?"

"Some of these SPLA rebels are deserters from the army. They have military training, and this is their country. It won't be as easy as you think, but yes, we will find them. Some fledglings may have escaped the nest, but we will ensure they don't fly far."

5

THE WALK HAD routines, rules. They began marching an hour or so before the sun went down, travelling at night to avoid the heat of the day and not to betray their position with a telltale dust cloud, easily seen by those hunting them on the ground — or from the air. Jacob was terrified of aircraft finding their trail. He ordered them to walk no more than three abreast to cover their numbers and obscure their footprints, quite visible in the dirt and marshy soil of the countryside.

The children were responsible for finding their own food and water. The Wet had ended, but there were still some pools and temporary creeks that twisted across the countryside, though they were drying rapidly. Wild food was also available if you knew where to find it. Even people in the cities had that gift, Victoria knew, to find food in the least likely of places, a lesson learned from tragic experience. In Sudan, fields of wheat, millet and maize were fragile, precious gifts. Gifts that often failed.

Sometimes, swarms of locusts descended upon the harvest, consuming crops in a matter of hours, the insects blocking out the sun through their sheer numbers. Other times, too much rain fell, drowning the fields, washing away the precious seeds. But worst of all was when the annual rains came too late. Or not at all.

Then the tall, green stalks of sorghum and the white kernels of millet burned away in the relentless sun, turning to dust, burned to their roots in the fissured dirt, as hard and lifeless as the surface of the moon. In those years? Famine was sure to follow.

They had names, the worst of famines.

Obuor Hotio: White Bone All Over.

Tombi: Famine of the Locust.

Nyengthiec: Do Not Give Whoever Asks Assistance.

Ruon Makerup: The Year of Massive Death.

Now, however, bush food was plentiful. Groundnuts were everywhere, as were the starchy *kei* and *athon* roots. The baobab produced a large edible seed as well, and almost everywhere was the small round fruit of the Christ's Thorn Jujube, a food since biblical times.

But still, Victoria was hungry. Her body missed protein, missed meat. As they walked, their way illuminated by a moon that hung impossibly large and silver in the night sky, their eyes constantly scoured the bush for mice or lizards, searching for anything to eat.

On the fifth day from Rumbek, as the sun dipped in the west, Mary and Victoria walked beside another child, a young girl, at the back of the column of children. This girl — Victoria didn't know her name — had stepped on a thorn or some such thing. Her right foot was infected, the swelling slowly crawling up her leg, and she could not move quickly.

The girl needed help and food, and Mary, as was her way, climbed a small tree to get the girl some fruit. Half an hour later, with dusk upon them, the girl stopped suddenly, grabbing her stomach, doubling over in pain. "My belly! Wait for me!" she begged.

"Do your business where someone can keep an eye out," Mary said. The three girls had fallen some fifty metres behind the main group.

Victoria knew Mary worried that they were exposed and too far away from the rest, but the girl ignored the warning, stepped into the tall brown grass that waved lazily in the wind, and hiked up her skirt.

She didn't see the lion.

None of them did. The cat had been stalking the children for quite some time, camouflaged perfectly in the tawny grass alongside the path, invisible in the gathering dark. It was a young male, though big for its age, recently chased out of its pride no doubt, forced to fend for itself.

There were a great many small, two-legged creatures. In a herd they would have seemed too much for the juvenile lion to attack, but when one separated from the rest, the lion recognized the opportunity and took full advantage.

There was no roar, no loud announcement, just silent footfalls and the soft sound of crushed grass and rushing wind as the lion launched itself into the air and onto the crouched girl.

Too late she saw it. The girl screamed, a cry quickly cut off as the lion took her head into its jaws, biting down hard with a sickening crunch, dragging her away into the bush. Mary and Victoria yelled out for help, voices rising together.

Jacob and William sprinted toward the lion. It was now some twenty metres away in the knee-high grass, its muzzle red, strips of black flesh dangling from its teeth.

The girl lay still between its paws. The cat stood protectively over her, growling as Jacob and William approached. Ten metres away from the lion, they opened fire, short quick bursts erupting from their assault rifles. The animal reared once as the bullets slammed into it then fell dead.

William fired one more round into the cat's skull to make sure, his face set in a grim smile as if he enjoyed the act. Then he and Jacob pulled the heavy animal off the girl to see if by some miracle the child was still alive.

She was gone. The animal's fangs were long and gently curved like a sword, like a crescent moon. They had crushed her skull and ripped a gaping hole in her neck. William made Mary and Victoria look at the wreckage of her face. "This is what happens when people fall behind."

Mary was unapologetic. "She was hurt. We were helping her!" Victoria didn't speak, numbed by what she had seen.

William's anger was palpable. "Fall behind again and I'll kill you myself, you skinny cows! We can't afford to help those who can't keep up."

Mary was in no mood to be lectured by this sour-faced boy. "Who's asking you to? We didn't want your help in the first place!"

William raised his gun, the barrel pointing squarely at Mary's chest. "Maybe I should just shoot you myself. Look at you, already skin and bones. You won't last another week out here."

Jacob stepped in between Mary and William. "There will be no more shooting." His was tone calm but forceful. "William's right," he admonished. "You shouldn't have fallen behind. There are bound to be others who die, and we can't afford to linger. Stay with the group from now on."

They left the girl where she lay for scavengers and pushed on, walking silently toward the east. As they travelled, Jacob proved to be a prophet. Others did die, the next one four days later. He was a boy of ten, skinny even by the standards of the Walk, with hollowed cheeks and a rattling cough that shook his tiny frame with every spasm. He was sick and had lagged since the day Victoria and Mary left Rumbek.

With the morning sun burning fiercely in their faces, the children stopped to rest in a small grove of acacia trees. The boy with the cough slumped wheezing against the stem of the tree, shut his eyes and fell asleep.

They all did, the three hundred or so. Nobody noticed when the boy's gasping stopped, and his small eyes rolled up to stare blankly at the spiny branches above and the endless blue beyond them. They left him where he lay and moved on, before the telltale flocks of vultures appeared.

A week later, two dozen more had died, two or three a day. Some were bitten by the poisonous snakes that hid in the grass and branches. Others, too sick or too tired to continue, simply stopped walking and collapsed to the ground.

Those who lived continued walking, looking sadly over their shoulders to their abandoned brothers, sisters and friends until their small bodies disappeared like ghosts in the waves of heat that bounced off the rust-coloured rocks.

To Jacob and William's consternation, vultures and other carrion-eaters constantly followed. Hyenas and jackals skulked silently in the dry grass along the path as well, waiting patiently for their next meal. William hated those birds above all else, above even the fear of aircraft. "These damn vultures will give away our position, Jacob. You can see them from kilometres away; they're going to lead the army right to us."

"Perhaps if we find a way to keep these children alive, the vultures will go away," Jacob replied. "If they have nothing to eat, they may leave us alone."

"Or maybe we should get back to fighting the Arabs and leave these brats to their own devices. Let them all get eaten, I don't care. I just don't want to die alongside them."

This was not the first time Victoria had heard this complaint. It was constantly on William's lips, as familiar to her now as the hot wind blowing through the desert.

"You know as well as I that the leadership of the SPLA has ordered us to get these children to safety," Jacob said.

But William would not be mollified. "Bah! Everyone else is fighting for the future of our country while we babysit. Look at them, Jacob. It's pointless. Half will die before we reach our destination."

It was hard to disagree. In the shade of rocks, emaciated children rested or grubbed through the dirt hungrily, searching for insects, nuts and berries. Once plentiful, food was no longer easily found as the Dry deepened. They'd not had anything to eat for two days, and their bellies had started to distend, mouths slack-jawed and open, gaping like fish left behind when the water in a stream receded.

"But half won't, William, and that half will be our future. They're the reason we fight. We can never forget that we will need them to lead our new country when all of this is over."

Victoria listened to Jacob speak in defence of her ragged life and her ragged country, and as she heard his passion she somehow felt, through the thirst and the hunger and the sadness, hopeful. The sun disappeared. A cloak of purple spread across the sky, sparkling now with the stars of early night.

William shook his head. "These children are to lead our new country, Jacob? There will be nothing left of them except bones within a fortnight. Us too, most likely, but since I'm a good soldier, I will obey and carry on with this mission. Round up your flock, shepherd. The sooner we reach our destination, the happier I'll be."

6

IT WAS CHARITABLE to call the miserable collection of thatch-roofed huts a village. Lieutenant Colonel Suleiman wrinkled his nose in distaste as the Land Rover entered the settlement, stopping next to a small well and an acacia tree, scattering in its wake a handful of clucking chickens scratching for food in the dust.

An old cow, one scimitar horn broken, ribs poking through its skin, looked up at the approaching vehicles, then put its head back onto the ground, relaxing in the shade of the tree, tail flicking the blowflies away.

The unnamed hamlet seventy kilometres east of Rumbek was connected to the rest of Sudan by nothing more than a sliver of dirt track. Impassible in the depths of the Wet, the road was barely navigable now, even after weeks of little rain.

The interrogations were quick, the devastation complete. After Suleiman obtained the information, sparse though it was, every man,

woman and child was shot and either thrown into the flaming wreckage of the huts or tossed down the well, contaminating the water
supply for years.

The last gunshots still echoed across the plain when Captain Soulu,
his green uniform stained dark with sweat and blood, approached
Suleiman. "Sir, there are tracks several kilometres north of the village,
but it's impassible for any vehicle to get there. Hills, marshes, rocks:
there's no way we can follow them."

The slight twitch of his cheek was the only thing that gave away
Suleiman's displeasure. Finding the escapees was proving harder than
he'd anticipated, and the thought of a bunch of shoeless children, led
by a handful of terrorists besting his troops, was infuriating.

They'd been searching for weeks and were always two days late or
ten kilometres short. They found footsteps and the remnants of the
occasional small corpse, torn to pieces by scavengers, but the main
party had managed to elude them.

Suleiman had scheduled three days at most to mop up this mess.
He was now into his second week of searching for the children, and
his commanding officer back in Juba was getting impatient with the
lack of results. Suleiman knew all too well that the general did not
appreciate delays.

As much as Suleiman hated to admit it, he needed assistance. "Get
me the air force on the radio," he commanded.

"Sir?" said Soulu quizzically.

Suleiman took the radio and spoke quickly. When he was done he
put the mouthpiece down and adjusted his beret. "Help is on the way,
Captain."

"Help, Sir?" Soulu had difficulty believing his commanding officer
would ever ask for such a thing.

"Yes, Captain," said Lieutenant Colonel Suleiman. "There are
times when even a lion must rely on the vultures to show him where
to find prey."

7

THREE WEEKS INTO the Walk more than fifty had died. The children, sicker and more exhausted than ever before, no longer stopped when one stumbled, fell and lay still on the ground.

Nor did they look back as the vultures circled downward. All that mattered to their desperate, parched throats was water, a precious resource becoming rarer by the day.

The Wet had long ended. The countryside was drying quickly, and it was with a sense of relief that bordered on hysteria when Victoria saw a small pond shimmering ahead in the morning sunlight. Her elation vanished as they reached it. Two weeks had passed since the last rain and what little water remained in the pool was stagnant and stinking, full of leeches, tadpoles and other crawling things. As thirsty as she was, Victoria recoiled in disgust.

"Drink, don't drink. I don't care," William sneered. "It's the only water we're bound to see for days. The choice is yours."

Jacob reached into his backpack, pulled out a long piece of gauze and carefully wrapped it around Victoria's mouth. "Drink through this. The mesh will filter the water and keep the bugs from your throat. If we had time, I'd boil it as well to be certain it is safe. As it stands, this will have to do."

As Victoria drank, William approached, a scowl set firmly on his face. "Tell your sheep to hurry, Jacob. We're far too exposed out here."

"He's an angry man," Victoria said as William stomped away to round up the others.

Jacob tucked the gauze back into his rucksack. "William has his reasons. He was a farmer, out tending his cattle when the soldiers came to his village. He returned home and found his wife and baby dead in the charred ruins of his house. There was nothing left for him except the SPLA."

"But you're kind and he's a —"

Jacob interrupted. "It's neither your place nor mine to judge him. William is my brother-in-arms and I trust him with my life. While it's true he resents being here and wishes he were on the front lines, he will carry out the mission."

The mission.

That question had been burning in Victoria's mind for days. "What is your mission? When are you going to tell us where we are going? I thought maybe you were taking us to Juba, but now I don't know."

As far as Victoria could tell, they'd been travelling almost due east, but Juba, southern Sudan's largest city, lay to the south. Mary and Victoria had been there with their father on several occasions, and although she didn't know how many kilometres there were between Rumbek and Juba, she was certain they would have reached it by now, even on foot.

"Juba's fallen," Jacob said. "There's no safe place left in Sudan for Dinka children, but we still have some friends. The Government of Ethiopia has established refugee camps just across the border. You'll be safe there."

"Ethiopia?" Victoria could hardly believe the words. "How on earth are we to get to Ethiopia?"

Jacob shouldered his rifle as the sun crested the eastern horizon, lighting the way forward. "How else?" he said. "We walk."

Several hours later, with the sun climbing rapidly in the cloudless blue sky, William ordered them to stop under a large grove of baobab trees. Victoria was exhausted. After checking the grass for snakes — an act as commonplace in the bush as taking your shoes off before entering a house — she lay down beside Mary in a shady spot near the thick base of the tree and fell asleep.

Sometime after noon by the look of the sun almost directly overhead, Victoria woke up. She was famished. She left her sister to sleep and went off in search of food, but what few baobab seeds she found had already been eaten, with nothing but empty pods strewn upon the ground.

Victoria saw some familiar plants. She dug up a handful of small, bitter tubers, wiped away the red dirt from a root and bit into the thing, a tasteless, dry stick that helped fill her guts but did little to satisfy her ravenous hunger.

Not long after, Victoria's stomach cramped. She barely had time to pull up what was left of her skirt when her bowels loosened, a thin spray splattering on the ground between her legs.

Victoria looked down self-consciously, first at the mess on her feet then at her belly protruding through her filthy and ripped school blouse. Food did this to her now. She wondered why she even bothered eating.

Kwashiorkor. Meat hunger.

Victoria learned the term in school. She'd seen the swollen bellies and pallid look on many of the poorer children back in Rumbek, children whose diets consisted of little more than grain and roots, with none of the protein of the more expensive nuts and meat. She had never experienced such a thing before. Until now. It was a hunger that spread to her bones as each cell and every atom of her body screamed for protein.

In Rumbek, she ate meat at least two times a week. At the thought, Victoria suddenly tasted her mother's roasted chicken, juicy and delicious, covered in peppers and other spices. Her senses were overwhelmed by the phantom scent of chilies cooked in chicken fat, rising from the stove in the kitchen. Tears welled. Victoria was surprised to learn she had enough water left in her body to cry.

Home.

Victoria hadn't given herself the luxury of thinking of her family for days. One foot in front of the other. One seed. One small piece of fruit. A sip of water from a hole in the ground, sucked from a stalk of grass. Nothing else mattered. Rumbek, her school, even her parents were little more than dreams now, shades of a life almost forgotten.

Victoria recovered her composure and cleaned herself up as best she could with some leaves stripped from a nearby shrub. She was alive and relatively healthy. So was Mary, which made them more fortunate than most.

Victoria looked at the children, most still sleeping in the shadow of the baobabs. Their group was two thirds the size it had been that first night at the wadi, and those who remained were sick and starving.

"Where are we now?" she asked Jacob.

"Not quite halfway to Ethiopia yet. We haven't yet reached the Nile River."

The Nile. The thought of all that water tormented Victoria. As bad as the hunger was, it was her thirst she hated the most. As if he could read her thoughts, Jacob handed Victoria a length of rope. "Tie this around your belly. It will help with the thirst and the hunger pangs."

She took the rope and did as he suggested, cinching the cord tightly until it hurt. Victoria winced, and Jacob smiled. "See, it's working already. You're not thinking about food anymore, are you?"

"Where did you learn this trick?"

"Fighting the government soldiers. We often went several days without eating. You learn ways to deal with hunger."

Jacob unshouldered his rifle and backpack. He lay them on the ground, the gun resting on top of the pack, action and barrel safely out of the dirt. He opened the flap of his pack and pulled out a long, coiled length of rope and a folded canvas bag.

Victoria watched Jacob eye several of the baobabs carefully. After a moment, he walked over to one of the shorter trees. "Hungry or not, water is more important than food," said Jacob. "You can last two weeks without food. Three days without water? The hyenas will be fighting over your bones."

Jacob tucked in his shirt and bent over to pick up a rock the size of his fist. He stuffed the stone into the bag, then pulled himself up onto a thick limb, climbing nimbly until he reached the cleft of a tree branch and the massive trunk. "I thought as much!" he shouted triumphantly.

Curious, Victoria watched Jacob tie the bag securely to the end of the rope and lower it into what must have been a hole in the tree. A few seconds later, the bag emerged. To her amazement, it was swollen full, dripping with clear water.

"Drink, but take small sips," Jacob instructed, passing the bag down. "You've not had much water for a long time; your stomach won't be able to handle it."

Victoria had never tasted anything so sweet, so delicious in all her life. Despite Jacob's instructions not to, she drank deeply, her body quivering as the cool water washed down her throat.

"How on earth did you know?" Victoria asked, tearing her face from the canvas sack, but before Jacob could respond, she vomited. The water, still cool, poured back out of her mouth, soaking her tattered shirt.

Jacob shook his head as Victoria retched. "I told you, just a few sips. Now wait until you stop throwing up, take a breath and have another drink. A small one this time."

"How did you know I'd be sick? Did you learn that in the army too?"

Jacob smiled bashfully. "In medical school. As I said, your body's been without adequate water for days. This is a standard response."

"Medical school?" Victoria's curiosity grew. This boy, this ragged guerrilla, not much older than her, was studying to be a doctor? Victoria asked more questions. Reluctantly, almost embarrassed, Jacob answered.

"My father was a cobbler in our village. He saved every pound he could to help pay my tuition. He wanted more for me, wanted me to go to school and get a good job. I was studying to be a doctor at Juba College of Medicine. I was in my second year when it happened."

Jacob's face clouded over as he spoke. "I was on my way home for a visit, but the army got there first. Three brothers, my parents. No one was left. I couldn't go back to school after that. There was nothing for me to do but join the SPLA. That's where I met William."

Jacob pulled the bag back up, took several small gulps himself then lowered it back into the depths of the tree. "The baobabs are aboveground wells. The trunks collect water in the rainy season and hold it. Nomads and others who know the bush find natural holes in the trees or make their own so that even on the driest day they can find water. Now wake the others; no doubt they're as thirsty as you."

Jacob sent the canvas bag time and time again into the depths of the tree. It was more than an hour before all the children drank their fill, and when he was done, Jacob's fingers and palms were blistered and bleeding from the rough hemp rope.

Jacob grimaced in pain, but instead of climbing down, he took out his knife, clamouring higher up the tree, cutting down as many seeds as he could see for the children to eat.

He also seemed to be gathering something else, something Victoria couldn't make out from the ground, small things that he tucked into his shirt. As he climbed, she watched Jacob scan the baobab carefully, looking, she was sure, for venomous snakes.

On the Walk, Victoria had seen more than enough snakes. Thick puff adders — snakes as common as they were deadly — were virtually everywhere, almost invisible amid the stones. The adders alone had killed more than a dozen, but they weren't the only danger that lurked along the path.

Any number of cobras, a particularly ill-tempered snake, slithered through the grass or over the diminishing waterways, flaring their hoods, striking, spitting venom at anyone unfortunate to cross them. They had bitten children as well. All had died, screaming in agonizing pain as the poisons in the venom spread through their small bodies, turning their flesh rotten.

Victoria watched Jacob shimmy from branch to branch, his eyes darting everywhere. A sheen of sweat covered Jacob when he finally climbed back to the ground, his shirt stuffed full of something. He opened his hand and Victoria saw several large, grey-white grubs about the size of her little finger crawling about in his palm.

"Caterpillars. They live on the baobab leaves. They're not exactly roast sheep, but they're quite edible and very nourishing, believe me." Jacob looked critically at Victoria's distended belly. "And you need the protein. We all do."

There was a time, not so very long ago, when Victoria would have recoiled at the prospect of eating grubs, but those days had died back in Rumbek alongside her father. Victoria stuck out her hand hungrily, but Mary stopped her. "There are others in worse shape than us."

Chastised, Victoria pulled back her arm. Mary was right; the few younger ones who remained wouldn't last much longer without a meal. Jacob undid the top button of his shirt to reveal a squirming white mass tucked underneath. "Don't worry. Everyone will eat today."

Mary accepted the grub. Following her lead, Victoria took her own large caterpillar, biting into it without hesitation as the grub wriggled in her mouth. The caterpillar's juices and guts splashed onto her tongue in a way that was surprisingly pleasant. It tasted nutty and Victoria smacked her lips when she swallowed it down. Jacob laughed and handed her another. "Eat. There's at least two for everyone."

They rested under the baobabs for the night and most of the next day as well, although the decision was not without discord. Jacob was adamant they remain, eating seeds and the protein-rich caterpillars, drinking their fill of the cool, clear water.

His decision was both strategic and compassionate. Without rest there would soon be precious few, if any, children left alive to make it to Ethiopia.

William held a different perspective, one made abundantly clear when he stomped his feet and waved his arms in disgust, trying to change Jacob's mind. But Jacob was in charge and would not bend.

They were both the same rank, the equivalent of privates in the SPLA, but while William was two years older, Victoria knew that Jacob had served longer. He had almost completed his training in Gambela, across the border in Ethiopia, when William, still burning with anger over the loss of his family, joined up.

Besides, Victoria knew that Jacob had been placed in command of the mission by the leader of the SPLA himself, the famous Colonel John Garang, a former Sudanese Army officer, but more importantly, a Dinka, a southerner.

When government troops attacked Bor, Garang rebelled against Khartoum in a fantastically public fashion, becoming a folk hero in southern Sudan because of it. Jacob almost worshipped Garang. He had told Victoria so a dozen times, a hundred maybe, as they walked together through the scrub. She knew Jacob would die before disappointing Garang, so if that meant listening to William rail for a while then so be it.

The matter ended when William stormed away. "It is settled. We'll stay the night," said Jacob as William disappeared behind the trunk of a baobab to sulk. "The rest will do us all good."

8

A LOW BUZZING noise rose gently above the breeze. "That sound. Do you hear it?" Victoria asked Mary as they lounged under a baobab. Jacob had collected more caterpillars and water from the tree, their thirst was slaked and all had eaten well. For the first time since leaving Rumbek, neither hunger nor thirst gnawed at Victoria's belly.

Her eyes closed, her body contented, Mary was somewhere between sleep and awake. "The only thing I hear is the flies."

"Seriously, Mary. Listen. I hear something. Up there." Victoria looked anxiously skyward.

The sound grew steadier, closer. Jacob heard it too. "Stay still and do exactly as I say," he ordered, his eyes scanning the horizon. "Stay close to the trees, under the cover of the branches. Do not move, no matter what happens."

A few of the rags the children wore were red, blue or yellow, colours that would stand out in the dust and scrub, even under the trees. "All of you with bright clothes, take them off and cover them with dirt," Jacob ordered. "Now."

The children did as they were told and pressed their naked, skinny frames to the large trunks of the baobabs, acting as if, through the sheer force of their resolve, the trees would extend their protective bark and envelop them.

The sound was now quite recognizable. Not the whoosh of a jet engine nor the rhythmic whopping of a helicopter blade, but the whir of a large, propeller-driven aircraft. Louder and louder it grew, though still invisible in the dying light of the sun. Nobody saw the plane until, twin engines deafening them, it appeared, rumbling slowly over the trees, barely one hundred metres above.

"Don't move! For God's sake don't move!" shouted Jacob over the noise of the engines. Victoria held her breath, frozen as the plane flew over the baobabs. She stood rigid against the tree, watching as the wings, then the fuselage and tail appeared through the branches.

Then Victoria saw a flash of movement on the ground. "Stay still!" Jacob screamed as a naked boy, one of the youngest children still alive, panicked and sprinted away from the trees, crying hysterically. For a few seconds, Victoria thought perhaps the pilot hadn't see such a tiny figure. But then the plane banked tightly, carved an arc in the purpled sky and slowly returned.

From the shadow of the baobabs, Victoria saw small, grey things plummet to the ground. "Don't move!" Jacob cried, but his voice was drowned out by the explosions that tore through the grove. The bombs slammed into the trunks of the trees, ripping apart leaves and branches, but through some miracle, Victoria was unhurt.

Perhaps this was little more than a fishing expedition, Victoria hoped, an attempt to flush them out, to see if the children were even here. Perhaps had they all stayed put, the air-crew would have chalked up the running child as a lone nomad. But, as the bombs continued to fall, two small girls screamed and bolted out from under the trees, setting off a stampede. Two dozen or more followed them. In the sky, the plane banked sharply again.

Within seconds half of those still alive followed, sprinting out from shelter to the open plain, packed together like antelope hunted by a pride of lions. They were now easy targets, and Victoria watched with horror as more bombs landed among them.

What, Victoria wondered, will she remember about the human wreckage strewn across the plain, of the trunks of children and of trees mown down like so much wheat? She had no words, no way to articulate what happened. But Victoria believed she would remember the boy who first ran, the boy who broke from the safety of the trees and disappeared into the scrub.

His name, she recalled, was Rual — she knew him from Rumbek, one of the few other children who made it out. Rual was of the Shilluk tribe, though he spoke Dinka well enough. He was skinny and had large ears and a nose that seemed made for another's face. He didn't attend Victoria's school, any school in fact, but worked fixing bicycles alongside his father, outside their mud and thatch hut.

He was a sad-looking man with one leg, Rual's father. Victoria's mother told her that he'd lost the limb in battle as a young man, fighting in the first civil war. A badge of honour, her mother said, and she would take their bicycles to him twice a year whether they needed fixing or not.

If Rual's father was sad, he had his reasons. His wife and daughter died years before of one thing or another, and Rual, with his oddly shaped nose, was all he had left. Victoria remembered seeing the two of them working side by side, Rual's father patiently showing his son how to patch a tire or fix a twisted handlebar for a few brass coins, looking down at his boy with quiet pride as he worked, the faintest crease of a smile crossing his lips.

It was Rual who brought the bombs down upon them, but Victoria didn't blame him for that. After all, who was she to judge, to say how a person should act when they break?

Victoria pretended that Rual didn't vanish in the scrub, dying of exposure and thirst, his bones drying to dust. Instead, she chose to believe he found his way home, back to his father and his bicycles.

She imagined seeing him as he emerged safe from the desert, his father pounding out the bent rim of a wheel by the door of his hut.

She saw his father look up as Rual approached, drop his hammer, take his wooden crutch and pull himself up, hobbling quickly down a street untouched by fire or mortar shells. She saw them embrace, the two falling to the street in each other's arms.

She saw Rual help his father up. She saw the two of them walk home, arms around each other's waists, three legs of flesh and one of wood, walking back to the small thatch hut with the bicycles out front.

That was how she would choose to remember Rual, and that was how she would remember the day the bombs fell.

Safe.

Together.

Home.

9

FROM THE TOP of the small rise and far to the east, Victoria saw the river, a thin strip of blue meandering through the brown of the surrounding plain. It wasn't what she thought it would be, the Nile. Victoria had pictured a sharp blue line, cutting a wide swath through the desert, but here its path was undefined, little rivulets branching off the main stem, twisting through the swamps, running playfully like errant children, dutifully rejoining their mother after a few hundred metres of freedom.

"Bahr al Jabal," said Jacob reverently. "I was born on her banks, in a place just like this. Seeing the river makes me think of home." Victoria leaned into him, her thin body resting on Jacob's arm as they looked at the small village on the riverbank below. The two stood there in silence, watching the smoke from the breakfast fires curl over the sparkling surface of the river.

"Time to go," he finally said. "We need a place to stop for a few hours, some food and a favour; I'm hopeful these people will help us with all three."

The group was met by an armed delegation on the outskirts of the community; a dozen men with long-shafted spears and cudgels surrounded their leader. One even had a gun, an ancient rifle that could have come to Sudan with General Gordon and Victoria's great-grandfather.

Victoria could tell their chief was not impressed to see such a shabby procession of children approach his village. "*Mëëth kith*. A lot of mouths to feed."

"*Bäny*-chief. We are only passing through," Jacob replied respectfully, "but we would be grateful for a rest, a meal and passage across the river."

Several long dugout canoes were pulled up onto the bank of the river, and Victoria understood the favour Jacob referred to. There were no bridges over the Nile, not for kilometres, and they would have to cross the river if they wanted to reach Ethiopia.

The chief said nothing, eyeing the assault rifles slung over William and Jacob's backs suspiciously. A short distance away was a woman. She was intensely beautiful: tall, slender, skin the colour of jet with long knotted hair, her forehead marked with the dotted tribal scarring. She wore a long red scarf draped over her head and held a baby in her arms.

"I'd like to think if your children needed help, someone would look after them," Jacob said, as much to the woman as the chief. He had read this situation well. The woman said something to the chief in a dialect Victoria didn't understand. The chief scowled at her in response, but she held her ground, gently stroking the face of the baby that cooed in her arms, its small hand playing with the hem of the scarf.

"You'll leave before nightfall," he said finally in Dinka. "And you will tell no one you were here."

The children bathed in a backwater of the Nile, and though the villagers assured them this particular eddy was safe from crocodiles, the man with the old rifle stood guard anyway. Victoria nearly cried in relief as the dust and dirt of a month in the wasteland washed away, carried off by the lazy current of the river.

Despite the chief's reluctance, the women of the village seemed thrilled to have the children. They took to them as if they were their own, tending to their numerous cuts and infections, feeding them armfuls of warm, freshly fried *kissra* bread, and bowl after bowl of *kajaik*, a delicious fish stew. Victoria ate until she felt her stomach would burst.

The village was small, but with plenty of food, water and livestock, surprisingly prosperous. Chickens clucked around their feet while fat, horned cattle milled about in an enclosure that kept them safely out of the rich green fields of corn at the edge of the community.

They soon had food as well as fresh clothes, their tattered remnants replaced by shorts, skirts and trousers — used, but clean and functional. Homemade sandals made from leather, old rubber and a host of other materials were given, and almost all the children received new footwear.

Victoria and Mary lazed under the shade of a date palm, sheltered from the afternoon sun. "I wish we could stay here forever," Mary said. "What do you think, Victoria?"

It was an understandable sentiment. Compared to the harsh arid landscape they had trekked through, the place was a green Eden.

But it wasn't Rumbek. It wasn't their bustling, dusty town, nor was it their house, with the blue-tiled kitchen and ancient wooden floor in the living room, scratched and worn by four generations of Deng feet. And it wasn't their mother or father. One dead. The other? The uncertainty, the not knowing what happened to her mother, consumed Victoria. "What do I think?" Tears fell from Victoria's eyes, sleep now impossible. "I wish I could go home."

It was fully dark when the children left. The women of the village hugged them each goodbye, and admonished William and Jacob to take good care of them. It took an hour to ferry all of them across the

Nile. The canoes were homemade vessels, carved ages ago from the trunks of single trees, and Mary and Victoria were crammed into the middle of one, their small bodies pressed against each other.

"Be still," the man paddling said as he pushed out into the water, stained red with light from the setting sun. "Crocodiles live in the middle of the river. *Röth* — hippos too. Neither like people much." Victoria and Mary heeded the warnings of the paddlers, and sat like statues, jumping only slightly when distant splashes echoed across the blackening water.

The children wouldn't need to find food or water for some time, loaded down as they were with *kissra* and dried dates. They had water, too, either in gourds or recycled plastic soda bottles, and when the last canoe departed back across the Nile, William wasted no time.

"We're more than halfway there," he announced. "Another three weeks, maybe four, and we'll cross the Baro River into Ethiopia — those that last that long. Then I'll have done my duty and I can get back to fighting. We travel quickly; those who can't keep up will be left behind. Do you understand? I'm as sick of this pointless mission as I am of you."

10

LIEUTENANT COLONEL MOHAMMED Suleiman stood ramrod straight beside the Walid armoured vehicle as he listened to Captain Soulu's report. "They crossed the Nile three days ago, Sir, still heading almost due east."

It hadn't been as easy as Suleiman thought, obtaining the intelligence from the villagers. At first, they'd been obdurate, lying through their teeth that they'd even seen the children, but Soulu and his men were very proficient in their task. After exerting the appropriate amount of force, they always found someone willing to talk. After that, the rest was easy.

Even with the information, finding these damned children was taking far too long and the general was most displeased with the lack of results. The brats had evaded him for the better part of a month now, and Suleiman felt the pressure. Time to end this game.

If only that useless air force pilot had finished the job, none of what was about to happen would have been necessary, Suleiman thought, eyeing the villagers, cowering and whimpering behind a decrepit old man he assumed was their chief.

The children had become a political target. Top priority. It was important from a purely military perspective to eradicate any future SPLA rebels, but there were other reasons as well.

Despite the government's control of the media, it was well known in the country that thousands of these brats were making a mockery of the army and its attempts to stop them. Making a mockery of Suleiman. This was something the lieutenant colonel and those he reported to — from the general to the president himself — would not tolerate.

Suleiman's men formed a semicircle around the villagers as he listened to their crying. What else could they expect, he thought with disgust. Aiding the escapees was a crime, one to be punished harshly.

The lieutenant colonel's eyes scanned the cowering villagers until they landed on a tall woman, a striking figure with piercing black eyes framed by a red shawl, the ends of her long hair cascading down behind it. Unlike the others, with their bowed heads and pitiful pleas for mercy, this woman kept her gaze steady, defiantly on him.

A pity, Suleiman thought, unclasping the Desert Eagle's holster. She was pretty, beautiful for a Dinka, even with those barbaric scars on her forehead and the screaming brat in her arms.

Suleiman's finger slipped off the gun's safety switch and he fired. The bullet thudded into the woman's head, leaving a small red hole almost exactly between her eyes. She fell, her child hitting the ground with a shriek.

The damage to the back of her head was catastrophic. The bullet mushroomed as it flew, taking with it most of her brains and the bulk of the back of her skull. The woman's eyes rolled back in their sockets.

"Kill them all," Suleiman ordered, aiming at the screaming baby, pulling the trigger. "Then burn this place to the ground. Do it quickly; the nearest ferry across the river is one hundred kilometres to the south, and we can't afford to waste any more time."

11

A SOUND ROSE on the morning air. Jacob and William ordered the children down, their faces and thin bodies pressed hard into the dirt while their guides investigated the noise, guns pointing forward as they walked slowly toward a vehicle lying on its side a hundred metres ahead, horn sounding.

A week had passed since they crossed the Nile, pushing ever east. A week of thirst and hunger. More died, more than Victoria cared to count. That day in the village when her belly was full, and her body washed and clean? Nothing more than a distant memory, a wraith just like her family, her home.

Jacob beckoned. Victoria and the others approached to see that the vehicle belonged to the Sudanese Army. Its front end was crumpled, the windscreen smashed. The body of a soldier, a young man not much older than their minders, was inside, his bloodied head pressed against the steering wheel.

He'd not been dead more than a few hours, but blowflies already swarmed about his face. Vultures circled in long lazy arcs above the wreck as well, but the other scavengers that patrolled the scrub, the jackals, hyenas and lions had not yet found this prize, else little would remain save a few handfuls of his tattered uniform.

Jacob took the soldier's head in his hands and lifted it from the steering wheel. Instantly the wailing horn silenced save for the echo that bounced off the distant stone hills until silence returned. Jacob and William conversed, trying to figure out just what had happened here.

Victoria listened as William and Jacob discussed all the possibilities, discounting each one in turn. It was puzzling, this accident. There were no trees to crash into here, nor was there any evidence of a land mine or rocket attack, and the fate of the vehicle and its dead driver remained a mystery until a slight sound came from the tall grass some distance away.

Jacob and William whirled around and crept slowly toward the noise. When they did, two mysteries were solved: the source of the sound, as well as the reason for the destruction of the vehicle and the demise of its unfortunate driver.

An elephant, a young bull, lay gravely wounded on his side in the thick grass. His front right leg hung awkwardly at an impossible angle, broken from the impact with the vehicle. His grey flesh was matted with blood, his breath shallow and laboured.

The elephant looked up. Its eyes deep brown, almost human, were buried in its wrinkled face. The skin under its eye was wet and Victoria's heart broke as she stared at what she knew were tears streaking down its face. Three quick shots rang out. Smoke curled from the barrel of Jacob's rifle. The grey mass twitched once, twice, then lay still.

The bush was silent for a while until another argument broke out between Jacob and William, once again about the children. William wanted to press on, to continue, but Jacob said no, that they needed to rest and to eat. William was infuriated. "Are you mad? This man was a scout, sent to look for us, no doubt. How far away can the army be? We must go now."

Jacob disagreed. "We're only two hundred kilometres from Ethiopia. This man was no scout. He was on routine patrol, nothing more. We will stay here until dusk, so we can rest and eat. The children need to gather their strength if our mission is to be successful. That is my decision."

William knew there was nothing more to say. He cursed in English, Arabic and Dinka then stomped away, leaving the children with Jacob.

Their shepherd.

"Gather wood," Jacob ordered. He pulled out his knife, knelt by the side of elephant, and butchered it into large chunks. "We can afford a small fire. Besides, elephant doesn't taste very good raw."

Victoria ate a piece of half-cooked meat, and though her bowels would pay the price for it later, ate more. Afterward she slept, gaining strength for the final push to Ethiopia, to sanctuary.

"Two hundred kilometres to go," she heard Jacob say before her eyes closed. "Ten days at most until we reach Ethiopia."

Victoria slept in the shade of a thorn tree when a hand clamped down so hard upon her mouth she bit her lip. "Maybe you're not so bony after all," William hissed, his mouth just inches from Victoria's ear. His right hand grabbed a breast, squeezing hard.

Victoria tried to wriggle free, to scream, but William's weight pinned her down, and he pressed his left hand into her face with such force she felt as if her teeth would give. Then William's right hand loosened. For just a second, Victoria thought he would release her, but when his fingers crawled under her ragged dress, she was hit with a terror greater than when the army killed her father and the lion took the sick girl. Victoria kicked and struggled and arched her back in protest, trying to fight her way free, but William was too strong.

"Stop struggling. It will hurt less if you do," William panted, his spit flecking against her cheek, his tongue, his lips almost touching her. Victoria relented and lay rigid underneath him, her eyes squeezed tightly shut.

William shifted his weight and Victoria felt him fumble with his trousers. Then he threw his body hard back onto her, into her, ripping, tearing. Though she could hardly breathe, Victoria screamed, her voice choked by the force of his hand. She was about to die, she knew, but then suddenly William was no longer there, his weight gone.

Victoria opened her eyes to see William lying on the ground beside her. Mary stood over him, a branch in her hand. She was positioned between William and Victoria, brandishing her makeshift weapon, ready to strike again.

"*Ajok*! Bastard! Leave her alone!"

But William would not. "You fucking bitch!"

William sprang back to his feet and his hand, the one just a moment ago that had been between Victoria's legs, shot to his waist for the long knife hanging from his unbuckled belt, next to his half-hard penis dangling from his open fly.

Mary reacted, but not quickly enough. William's blade sliced through the air in a wide swath, the tip of the blade biting deep into her cheek and lay open the skin. Mary howled in pain, but even then, with her face cut open like the belly of a fish, she stayed between William and her sister, holding tight to the stick.

"Enough!" A gun bolt slid behind Victoria.

William seethed, a thin rivulet of blood from where Mary hit him rolling down his face. "You'd kill me? A brother-in-arms over this skinny cow?"

Jacob was resolute. "Put the knife down so I won't have to."

From the ground, Victoria watched in a trance as Jacob slowly inched his finger toward the trigger. She was still, unable even to pull down the ragged dress still hiked up around her waist. Something warm and sticky trickled uncomfortably down the inside of Victoria's thighs, but still she didn't move, as if she were not part of these events at all but rather a distant spectator, observing with detached interest the events around her.

William stared coldly as Mary put her makeshift weapon down and tore off a scrap of her skirt she then pressed to her face to stem the flow of blood. Then he laughed, spit on the ground, and put the knife back in its sheath.

"Well then, shepherd," he said to Jacob, doing up his trousers, "tend to your flock. I'm out of cigarettes and we're not going to get to Ethiopia by just standing around."

12

CAPTAIN SOULU STUCK his finger deep into the remnants of the cooking fire and held it to his nose. "Three, maybe four days old, Sir. Footprints head off to the east, though not as many as there once were."

"Did they kill him?" Shreds of a Sudanese Army uniform and a skeletal leg, boot still attached to the end of it, were all that was left of the soldier inside the Land Rover.

"It's possible, but I don't think so, Sir. There's no evidence of gunfire or explosives on the vehicle, and the damage to the front end is consistent with hitting something large, something like what's left of that elephant in the bushes over there. I also found three shell casings by the carcass. If you ask me, the rebels chanced upon the accident scene, ate some of the elephant and then carried on."

"The trail leads up a small rise," Soulu continued. "It's hard to follow. The ground is rocky, but I'm sure they're going due east. Where exactly is anyone's guess. They've got at least sixty, maybe eighty kilometres on us by now. This country's hard on vehicles; it could take three days for us to find their path again."

Suleiman reached down to the glovebox of the Land Rover for his map. He hated the British almost as much as the Jews and the Dinka, but like all enemies, there was much to learn from them, and nobody surpassed the English in their cartography.

The map was an old Ordnance Survey map of Sudan, made for the British Armed Forces during the Second World War. Precious little had changed in southeastern Sudan over the past forty years, and the map was as valuable to Suleiman as his Desert Eagle pistol. It was far more accurate than the useless charts his own government issued. Without it, the men would have been turned around in the bush more times than Suleiman cared to count.

After a few minutes of study, Suleiman lit a Cohiba, his second to last. The final one he would save for the day he caught up to the runaways, but he was close now, closer than he'd been since Rumbek, and felt more than justified in enjoying the cigar.

"It isn't where they are now that interests me, Captain," said Suleiman, breathing out the smoke, pointing at a spot on the Baro River, his country's border with Ethiopia. "It's where they are going to be that matters. Get the men; it's time we ended this."

13

THE BARO RIVER was narrower than the Nile. Muddier too, Victoria saw, as she emerged from the scrub and stood on its banks at the outskirts of a small rundown village. Jacob was wrong; instead of ten days to reach the border from the Nile, it had taken them the better part of two weeks, and Victoria nearly wept when she saw the dark line of the river cutting a lazy swath through the scrub, marking the boundary between Sudan and Ethiopia.

For a lifetime it seemed they had travelled, these few surviving children, to reach the Baro River and the border with Ethiopia, across a solitude of bones, through a wasteland of tears.

Victoria's body no longer ached from William's assault, but though the physical pain subsided, her mind was racked with anger, shame and a host of other emotions she could not explain to her sister. Or even to herself.

Mary's wounds were more visible than Victoria's. Jacob had done a remarkable job patching her cheek, sewing up the cut with an ordinary needle and thread he'd rummaged up from his backpack. Mary had done her best to keep it clean, but even with Jacob's ministrations, the gash on her face was red and angry. The sight of it prevented Victoria from even trying to pretend what William did to her was only a nightmare.

For his part, William carried on as if nothing had happened. He was no more or less taciturn than he'd been for the entire journey, and, except for the occasional glare that chilled Victoria's bones, he had made no attempt to touch her again.

William's relationship with Jacob also seemed unaffected. The two hardly spoke to each other at the best of times, with William leading the group and Jacob bringing up the rear of the ragtag brigade, but when a lion roared in the distance or when they approached a small settlement, the two quickly slipped back into the role of soldiers, communicating with signs and whispers, working in tandem to protect their mission — a mission now almost complete.

Naked children played in the mud and among the reeds of the riverbank, oblivious to the newcomers. Victoria and the others were just the latest in a steady stream of refugees who have emerged from the bush at this place. The villagers offered no food nor assistance. They even pretended the children were not there. Jacob bore them no ill will for their lack of hospitality; the community was small, dirty and poor and lacked the resources to look after its own people, let alone wave after wave of travellers. That and they no doubt knew the repercussions they would earn from the army for helping.

"There are two canoes pulled up onto the bank," Jacob said. "They can hold six, maybe seven people each. These people won't help us, but neither will they stop us from using the boats. William and I will each paddle one. It's a short trip, no more than ten minutes there and back. We'll go in shifts, youngest to oldest in that order. Three crossings will be enough. Half an hour and we'll be out of Sudan and safe in Ethiopia."

The Sudanese villagers weren't the only ones on the river. On the Ethiopian side was a small military outpost, protected by machine guns, observation towers, sandbagged parapets and barbed wire. A three-striped green, yellow and red flag fluttered in the light evening breeze above the post as soldiers in light khaki patrolled the banks of the river, watching the newcomers intently.

Jacob and William quickly organized the children. Within a minute of arriving at the river, the first two canoe loads set off into the murky water; they paddled strongly, children pressed tightly together.

A few moments later, the first canoe loads landed safely on the other side. They were met by Ethiopian soldiers, who bustled the children into the fort while Jacob and William shoved the boats back into the water and set off to collect those who remained in Sudan.

William and Jacob were almost back on the Sudanese bank when a warning cry from the Ethiopian side broke the silence. At almost the same time, the air behind Victoria erupted with the sound of shouts, the squealing of brakes and slamming of doors, the same awful sounds Victoria had heard at her school. Machine gun fire rang out. Bullets slammed into the ground at their feet and into the river, shooting spray up into the sky.

"Jump in and swim!" Jacob's order shattered the paralysis that had seized Victoria. Not looking, not caring if the others joined them or not, Mary and Victoria held hands and leapt into the water, swimming wildly toward Jacob and his dugout canoe.

Soon, the river was full of splashing and screaming children. Two boys caught up and reached Jacob's canoe at the same time the sisters did. Jacob stopped firing, set his gun down and hauled all four of them into the boat. "Lie down and don't move!"

There was little need for the command. Before she pulled herself into the boat, she had witnessed the fate of the others. Some had died on the shore, falling in a hail of bullets, while others went past their depth in the river and, too exhausted or scared to swim, slipped beneath the muddy surface and didn't reappear. Looking up, Victoria saw the agony on Jacob's face. He could do nothing to help them. His eyes fixed on the distant bank, he paddled toward the Ethiopian shore as quickly as he could.

The Ethiopians aimed their weapons at the Sudanese soldiers but did not fire. If the children remained on the river, the massacre was an internal Sudanese affair. High levels of animosity existed between the governments in Addis Abba and Khartoum, and neither side would risk a possible war over Sudanese refugees.

If Victoria and the others made it across they would be protected. If not? They would die of gunfire or of drowning. Their corpses eaten by the crocodiles. Either way, this episode would end soon enough.

"Stay down!" Jacob ordered, paddling furiously. Bullets whirred past his head, thudding into the thick wooden flanks of the canoe and splashed violently into the water.

Peaking above the gunwale, Victoria watched as Jacob kept his attention fixed on the rapidly approaching shore. Twenty metres away, now fifteen, now ten. Back on the western bank of the Baro, she heard a barked order. The shooting suddenly stopped. Victoria heard the man, their commanding officer no doubt, swear in Arabic, rage etched in his voice, but the children had crossed into Ethiopia and had left Sudan behind.

The bow of the canoe slid into the thick mud of the eastern shore. Victoria slipped and stumbled out of the canoe, into the water, to land. The sisters were both alive. Miraculously, they weren't alone.

Another half dozen or so children had swum across safely as well, surviving the current, the bullets and the crocodiles that made this stretch of the Baro infamous. Counting the ones already ferried across about twenty had crossed the river. Twenty children, when more than three hundred had set out from Rumbek. Not one in ten still alive.

Victoria looked up to see that William had made it to Ethiopia as well. She was not surprised. When the firing started, William gave up any attempt to rescue the children and paddled quickly back to Ethiopia where he stood watching from the safety of the shore.

Jacob stepped out of the canoe into the river. He did not see the cold look on William's face, nor did he see his comrade in arms raise his rifle, aim and pull the trigger. It was all too surreal, too fast for Victoria to register what was happening. When comprehension dawned, it came too late.

A single shot.

Jacob froze in mid-stride as the back of his shirt, in a spot almost exactly between his shoulder blades, was suddenly stained crimson. He gasped something, gargled and unintelligible, then he fell to his knees and rolled down the bank into the river, quickly disappearing under the water.

On the bank, William lowered his gun. "Mission successful, shepherd," he said. "I was wrong. You got your flock to Ethiopia after all."

14

AZANA REFUGEE CAMP, ETHIOPIA
SEPTEMBER 1990

THREE WOMEN HUDDLED outside the entrance of a hut, a make-shift thing of sticks and thatch with a tall pointed roof and a tattered grey sheet that hung over the entryway in place of a door. The oldest had a wrinkled face and wiry grey hair under a black hijab. She wore a flowing floral dress over her large frame, and she grunted in protest as she squatted down in front of a metal pot, stirring a yellowish mush that bubbled over a small fire. The second woman was twenty-one years old, with light brown skin and a round moon face emblazoned with a deep white scar on her left cheek.

And then there was Victoria Deng. She was taller than the others, with high cheekbones and a slightly hooked nose. Her two-year-old son Peter sat at her feet, contentedly drawing lines in the dirt with a stick.

The sheet that covered the doorway pulled open. A young woman in a half-buttoned-up dress stepped out of the hut. When she saw the women by the fire she lowered her head, hurriedly covering up her exposed breasts.

William Chol, shirtless, and with his trousers still undone emerged. He threw a crumpled orange five-birr note onto the ground and scowled at Victoria and the others, ignoring the girl who picked up the money before scuttling away into the crowded depths of the camp.

Mary shot a cold glance at William but said nothing, her hand travelling to the scar on her face. Victoria, for her part, refused to even acknowledge the father of her child. She turned her back to William, picked up Peter and cooed quietly in his ear.

"Pig."

The old woman cooking the food had endured many dreadful things in her life. Her name was Safa, a Muslim from Juba who, in her sixty-eight years, had faced independence, two wars, revolutions, coups, half a dozen famines and a host of other horrors. In that time Safa had buried two husbands, four children and all her siblings, and was well past fearing the likes of Victoria's husband. Muslim or not, Safa had been swept up in this current war just like Victoria and Mary, arriving at Azana barely a month after they did, quickly taking the girls under her motherly wing.

"Pig," she said again, glaring at William. "You disrespect your wife and son with that whore — and in your own house as well." William's eyes flashed. His fists clenched, and Victoria hurriedly stepped between Safa and her husband, not about to let the old woman bear the weight of his well-documented wrath.

"*Jadda*, grandmother, please don't."

In their own way, Victoria's years at Azana had been as bad as the Walk. With no Jacob to stop him, William raped Victoria once more on their first night in Ethiopia then claimed her as his wife the following day.

Since then, he had his way with her body a thousand times. Consent on Victoria's part was not required. The series of assaults both physical and sexual she endured were not seen as crimes, just the routine business between a husband and wife. Nobody in the camp — Sudanese, Ethiopian or aid workers from the Western countries alike — had done anything about it.

William raped Mary as well, beating her so badly afterward she lost two teeth and broke a rib, sending her to the Red Cross hospital for a week. He had not done it since, the assault both retribution for the injury she caused him back in Sudan and to show what he would do if she interfered in his business again.

But there had been some unexpected blessings. Despite his father and the nature of his conception, Victoria loved her son. He bore the name of his grandfather and had given her strength to carry on, to endure the horrors of the refugee camp, the death of her father and the unknown fate of her mother back in Rumbek.

"Are you deaf?" William's voice snapped Victoria back to attention. Her mind had drifted. She'd not heard him talk to her, nor had she seen him approach. Now he stood just inches away, a familiar scowl on his face. Instinctively, Victoria pulled her son tight to her chest.

"I'm sorry," Victoria said, "I didn't hear you."

"I said hurry up," William repeated. "We're late."

A large crowd gathered at Azana's administrative building, among them a number of United Nations and other aid workers. Most were white, wearing the standard khaki shirts and trousers that marked the UNHCR, Médecins Sans Frontières, Red Cross and many of the other Western organizations. Victoria and the others had been selected by the United Nations and camp officials to attend this event, this spectacle, and when they arrived, they were hurriedly directed to the front.

There were a host of other logos as well, prominently displayed on caps, flags and the sides of the Land Rovers and Toyota pickups parked in a semicircle around a satellite news truck. Beside the satellite truck was a camera crew and a reporter, a young woman from an American network dressed in tan.

"Here at Azana Refugee Camp in Gambela Province, Ethiopia," the reporter said, camera rolling, "Sudanese refugees wait anxiously to greet a delegation from the United States who've travelled seven thousand miles on this wonderful humanitarian mission."

William leaned toward Victoria and whispered, "Just remember what I told you. Say nothing else."

"Here it comes!" the journalist exclaimed, as the camera swung once again, this time toward an approaching bus, kicking up a plume of dust in its wake. The bus stopped with a hiss and a spurt of air.

A fat white man in his late fifties stepped off the bus, squinting in the bright sunlight. He put on a pair of sunglasses, stretched and took in the scene, adjusting his shorts that had bunched up on his pasty thighs. Along with his khaki shorts, he wore long white socks, tennis shoes and an Iowa State University hat. He'd not been out of the bus for more than five seconds when a sheen of sweat broke out on his forehead. Dark stains of perspiration radiated down from his armpits, soaking the T-shirt stretched taut across his ample belly.

"Whew! Lord in Heaven, Gladys!" he said to the woman following him off the bus, in a shrill, nasally accent that Victoria could barely understand. "It's hotter'n you-know-what out here without the air con."

The woman walked up to his side. The two were dressed almost identically, as were the rest of the people who dismounted from the bus. Most were old and fat, their skin the colour of paper.

The one called Gladys wrinkled her nose in distaste as she surveyed the camp. "Lord in Heaven! What's that smell, Norman?"

Norman took her hand protectively. "Jus' Africa, hon. They don't have the same standards like back home. Remember? We talked 'bout that."

Norman was now thoroughly drenched with perspiration, but the printing on his shirt — on all the white and blue shirts the visitors wore — was easily read: *Cavalry Baptist Church of Ames: Angels of Mercy Mission Tour 1990, Bringing Jesus to the Desert.* The words were superimposed over an outline of Africa, a cross fitting neatly within the map of the continent. Victoria couldn't help but wonder what the old priest in Rumbek would have thought of this particular group of Christians.

With the camera chronicling the event, the visitors unloaded several boxes and stacked them on the ground. Norman popped one open, grabbed a handful of the contents in his hammy fist and, beaming, walked over to Victoria and the others.

"Here ya go," he said, passing her a purple hand-knit scarf. "The ladies auxiliary's been knitting these all year just for you. God bless."

The temperature at Azana that afternoon was somewhere around forty-five degrees centigrade, a fact perhaps lost on the Americans as they distributed box loads of scarves, woollen hats and handmade mittens. A few Western aid workers grinned in embarrassment, but most maintained their composure, as did Victoria. After all, the God-fearing citizens of Ames, Iowa, had also brought with them twenty thousand dollars in cash and an equivalent amount in medical supplies, enough to keep several hundred sick children alive, and so Victoria and the others were here to bear witness to that generosity.

"Thank you," said William awkwardly in English, taking a hat and putting it on his head. He had been selected as their spokesman and shot Victoria a look, the meaning of which was unmistakable. Mary and Victoria quickly wrapped the scarves around their necks and smiled at the Americans as sincerely as they could.

But neither William nor these American visitors held power over *Jadda* Safa. The old woman donned a set of mittens, glanced up into the bright blue sky and pretended to shiver. "*Inshallah*, do you think it may snow soon?" she asked in a mix of Arabic and Dinka. Despite William's threats, Victoria broke out in laughter.

"They don't seem very 'preciative," said Gladys, shuffling uncomfortably, acutely aware she was somehow the butt of a joke. "Not even Christian, by the sounds of 'em."

Norman turned to William. "Jeepers! What's wrong with you people? We're trying to do you a good turn. We paid our own way here! You need to show some simple courtesy, that's all."

The show ended. Gladys, Norman and the rest were given a short tour of the camp and then whisked away back to their air-conditioned hotel in Gambela for lunch. The refugees were dismissed and trundled home. Victoria entered her hut and had just put Peter down when William's fist slammed into her right ear. After *Jadda* Safa's joke, she'd been expecting repercussions, but the suddenness, the violence of the punch staggered her, knocking her heavily to the hard-packed dirt floor.

Victoria's eyes teared and her ears rang so loudly she could barely hear her son scream. She tucked herself into a fetal position, covered her head with her forearms and waited for the next blow. She had much practice in this.

But it never came. Instead, William rolled her onto her back then sat on top of her, his expression dark. "You embarrassed me today." William leaned down, his mouth inches from Victoria's ear. "What would your shepherd have thought about all this? Surviving that journey, coming all this way here to be nothing more than an animal in a zoo, put on display for fat Americans?"

Victoria said nothing, but her eyes betrayed the pain that surfaced at the mention of Jacob Bok. William leered. "Do you wish I'd shot you that day, instead of him?"

Peter, his body shaking as he cried, toddled over and threw his arms around Victoria's neck. Casually, William reached out and slapped the boy hard on his face, knocking him backward. He smiled with satisfaction as his son screamed in pain.

"You'll thank me for that when you're a man and a soldier for southern Sudan."

Then he turned his attention back to Victoria, running his hands over her breasts and belly. He unzipped his fly, hiked up her skirt and pulled her legs apart. "Perhaps you have room in there to make another soldier for the cause."

William pushed down onto her, Victoria grunting as he did. She lay still, grateful that this would be the last time she would have to endure him for quite some time.

Borders meant nothing to William and the hundreds of other SPLA soldiers in Azana. The camp was little more than a place where they recruited and trained under the eyes of the Ethiopians, who let them slip back into Sudan to carry on their war with Khartoum, a war waged for years now, with no end in sight.

Finished, William stood and zipped up. "I have business back in Sudan for a few months," he said. "I'll find out when I come back."

15

ON A HOT MAY afternoon, Mary, *Jadda* Safa, Victoria and the others lined up for their allotment of food, plastic buckets in hand, ready to collect their rations like dogs, like beggars. Peter waited impatiently at his mother's feet as they shuffled along, feet that ached from the strain her swollen belly put on them.

Overhead the sky was black. A storm built. Victoria was not looking forward to it, but she had more pressing concerns. She was far from the front of the line, her back and feet throbbing. She wished she had a chair. "Go lie down." *Jadda* Safa clucked like a mother hen when she saw Victoria's discomfort. "Mary and I will collect your ration for you."

Victoria shook her head. "That's not how it works, and you know it. No waiting in line, no food."

Safa laughed. "Don't worry. That German fellow's working today — the one with the long yellow hair. He likes me. I'll get your food for you. Go home. Rest."

Victoria handed over her the bucket and took Peter by his hand. Home, she thought bitterly. How did this place ever become home?

They returned to their shack, Victoria and Peter, just as the rain started falling. She was exhausted, and as they curled up together on the floor, she absently ran her hands over her protruding belly. The child would be here soon enough. With mixed emotions Victoria awaited its arrival. She felt guilty that she would bring another life into this camp, but she hoped it would be a girl. If it were, she knew exactly what she would call her, finally able to fulfill a promise she made to herself many years ago.

They were soon asleep. Neither one heard William enter the hut. "Get up," he said, tapping Victoria in the side with his boot.

After months away, her husband was back from Sudan. "You were gone longer than I'd thought."

William pulled up his shirt and showed Victoria a new wound, a bullet hole just below his ribcage. "It took longer to heal than I'd have liked. I was not able to travel."

Then William eyed Victoria's belly in the same way a herder looked at a prize cow. "Good," he said approvingly, walking toward the entryway of the hut. "Make food. I'll be back later." But William didn't return for dinner, or even for the night — not that Victoria complained.

"Too bad he wasn't shot in the head," said Mary as she passed Victoria a bowl of porridge. Rain spat down from the darkened sky. They moved inside the hut to eat.

"Or someplace more important to him!" said *Jadda* Safa, grabbing her crotch. "He's with one of his whores, isn't he? Drinking too?"

What did Victoria care if he were? "Let his prostitutes make soldiers for the glorious SPLA." She was angry, and her words spilled like a hateful stream. "At least William has a cause. Who fights for us? No one gives a damn about ordinary refugees. The world ignores us."

Jadda Safa disagreed. "You might be an ordinary person, Victoria, but sometimes ordinary people are called upon to do extraordinary things. I'll die here, but, *Inshallah*, this place won't be your grave."

Victoria scoffed. "What extraordinary things will I do, *Jadda*?

Become president of the United States of America?" Lightning crackled through the sky. Peter whimpered as thunder echoed through the camp.

"You?" she said, putting a comforting hand on Victoria's round belly. "You will keep these children alive — and get them out of here."

After dinner, Victoria bid her friend and sister good night then took Peter to bed. She shut her eyes and drifted off but sleep tonight would not bring her rest. Instead, the rain resurrected an old familiar ghost.

Ahead in the distance, an old wooden bridge crosses a wadi. Victoria scrambles down the bank to the dry riverbed, ignoring Mary and the lightning that flashes across the black sky overhead.

"Victoria! Don't! We aren't allowed to go past the bridge! It isn't safe! Don't you remember? There's been lion sightings. And hyenas. We're not allowed to come here by ourselves."

"And hippos and dinosaurs too," Victoria laughs. "Come on, Mary. It's the middle of the day. It's perfectly safe."

Before Mary can respond, a little voice pipes up. "Wait for me, Victoria!" Her little sister Alexandra is just a few months past her sixth birthday.

Without another word, Alexandra climbs clumsily over the rocks, making her way down to Victoria. Mary yells for them to stop, but Victoria ignores her, takes her little sister by the hand and walks down the wadi toward the bridge.

Overhead the sky blackens and large raindrops kick up small plumes of red dust. Thunder rolls, nearer now than before. Alexandra looks nervously up. "It's awfully close," she says, as the rain falls harder.

Victoria opened her eyes, her body covered in sweat, her heart racing. Outside the rain bounced off the tin roof of the house, but there was another sound as well. Peter was awake and scared, and he wrapped his arms around Victoria's neck and whimpered as she went outside investigate.

Jadda Safa and Mary shared the hut next to Victoria and they were both awake, standing nervously in front of their home. Victoria joined them as the headlights of an approaching truck cut through the rain. It stopped, and a soldier climbed out, rifle in hand, though this one did not wear any government patches on his uniform.

Jadda Safa moved to stand protectively in front of Victoria. "What do you want?" she demanded, not one to be cowed by any man, armed or not. "We are under the protection of the UN and the Ethiopian government."

The soldier was unimpressed. "Mengistu's been overthrown and the Democratic Front is now in charge of this place. You Sudanese are no longer welcome in Ethiopia. Get your things and leave. This camp is closed down."

Jadda Safa was indignant. "We won't leave! We were promised we could stay!"

Without warning, the soldier lifted his gun and fired a burst into *Jadda* Safa's chest. Wordlessly she fell, her face splashing into a puddle. "Stay then." He aimed his rifle at Victoria and Peter. "Who else wants to stay?"

They ran.

Dozens of soldiers descended upon the camp. Victoria couldn't move quickly — not with Peter and the unborn child inside her — so Mary took Peter in her arms and guided them away from the shooting, just as she did on that day seven years ago when Victoria and Mary were children at school in Rumbek, the day their father had died. The day of smoke and of fire and of blood.

They raced west toward the river, gunfire and screams all around them. Victoria saw a girl a year or two older than Peter. The child was alone and crying, naked and in terror, but she didn't stop to help. She couldn't. She passed by, looking away.

They reached the bank of the river.

"What now?" Victoria asked as she took her wailing son back from her sister.

"I don't know," Mary said, "but there must be . . ."

She didn't complete the sentence. William stepped out of the darkness, rifle in one hand, the rope of a small canoe in the other.

"It won't carry us all," he said to Mary. "You stay."

Victoria screamed. "No! I won't lose another sister! I won't!" She put Peter down and flailed her arms, hitting William as hard as she could. He struck her back, hard across her face, knocking Victoria to her knees.

William aimed his gun. Not at Victoria, but at Mary. "Get in the canoe or I'll shoot her."

Mary stepped past William, pulled Victoria to her feet and held her sister tightly. "Stay alive," she said. "I will find you."

Victoria was inconsolable. "I can't leave you! I won't!" The night air filled with the sound of soldiers approaching from the camp, gunfire erupting in short bursts.

"I'll be fine," Mary said. "I promise. I'll see you soon."

Mary hugged Peter and then delicately deposited him into the canoe. She embraced Victoria one last time and then let go, just as shots rang out behind her. Victoria collapsed into the canoe holding tight to her son as William shoved the vessel out into the black water.

Victoria sat in silence, watching her sister on the riverbank until she vanished into the darkness and the rain. Then she shut her eyes as William paddled out further into the black water until they too disappeared.

II

1

VANCOUVER, B.C.
NOVEMBER 2004

"SO, WHEN YOU compare the increase in economic activity of little Uruguay to its much larger neighbour to the south, it's tremendously exciting to think of the possibilities that this small South American country holds for the future."

Abena Walker listened as the prof lectured with a degree of enthusiasm unshared by most of the students in the Buchanan building. The classroom was normally full for Econ 234. Wealth and Poverty of Nations was a popular course and there should have been close to three hundred students in the auditorium, but most had decided to stay at home today.

The November weather was atrocious, even by Vancouver standards, the rain falling in sheets, the temperature hovering just a few degrees above freezing. He spoke now, the prof, about Chile's growing GDP, his monotone voice echoing through the speakers across the nearly empty theatre, but Abena had officially given up paying attention. Instead, she read the article from the magazine she'd purchased earlier that week for perhaps the hundredth time.

It was the photo on the cover that had caught her attention. It was stark, awful, like nothing she had ever seen before, and Abena had spent her last five dollars on the magazine instead of buying a piece of pizza for lunch at Pie R Squared.

The picture was of a child, perhaps two or three years old. *Years ago, this photo of a little Sudanese girl,* the caption read, *thin and starving, one of thousands trying to make their way to a UN feeding centre, captured the attention of the world.*

She was squatting on the ground, the girl in the picture, bent at the waist, head resting on the dirt, ribs poking through her skin. But what made the picture truly horrific was the vulture standing on the hard ground a short distance behind her, staring with dark eyes, waiting for the child to die.

"Sudan's Forgotten Crisis," the article was called, and although she knew every sentence, every word of the story by heart, Abena read it again and again, her fingers absentmindedly playing with the silver pendant in the shape of Africa that dangled from a thin gold chain around her neck.

With the eyes of the world now firmly placed on the unfolding genocide in Darfur, the victims of Sudan's other humanitarian disaster, the great exodus from the south that began with the Second Sudanese Civil War two decades ago, have good reason to believe that the world has indeed abandoned them.

But Vancouver's own Westshore Education Trust, with a tradition of helping Africa going back thirty years, has never forgotten about the hundreds of thousands of Sudanese men, women and children languishing for years in refugee camps in Kenya, and maintains several schools for these children, providing them with an education — and hope.

"That's it for today," the professor said, snapping Abena's attention away from the magazine. "Don't forget your final is next Tuesday at two. I hope more of you will show up than today."

Class dismissed, Abena shut the dog-eared magazine and joined the students who trickled out of the theatre. She left Buchanan through the large doors in the lobby. She was no longer as awed as she was the first time she came here, but every now and then Abena still found herself comparing the University of British Columbia campus to the tired jumble of bricks that was East Vancouver's John A. Macdonald High School. It was hard to believe that two such different educational institutions could exist so close to each other.

She walked down East Mall toward the bus loop then joined the long line of students who crowded onto the 99. The bus clattered east along 10th Avenue. Abena stood but she didn't mind. It was no more than a half-an-hour ride plus a five-minute walk home to the old stucco three-storey walk up at the corner of East 7th and Main, deep in the heart of Mount Pleasant, her little corner of East Vancouver.

At Main, the bus squeaked to a stop. Abena got off and walked quickly through the rain to her apartment building. She unlocked the front door of the building and walked to the stairs, nearly tripping on the loose carpet the landlord had promised months ago to replace. Soaking wet, Abena reached her apartment on the third floor and unlocked the door, desperate for a hot shower and a cup of tea.

"How was school today?" her mother asked when she entered.

Abena slid the deadbolt back in place, hung her wet coat on the hook and slumped down onto the couch. "All right, I suppose."

"I've seen that look before," said her mother. "I'll put the kettle on, then we'll talk."

The apartment was immaculate, tastefully decorated with African art hanging on the walls and sitting on shelves throughout the small suite. On the top of a bookshelf was a photo of a man in his mid-forties with tightly curled black hair, tinged with grey at the sideburns.

Beside the picture was a vase. Silk roses and two small paper flags rested in it: one the familiar red and white maple leaf, the other three broad stripes of red, yellow and green, with a black five-pointed star in the middle. Her mother returned, cups in hand. Abena took the tea gratefully and sighed again. "Do you ever regret coming here? To Vancouver, to Canada, Mama? Was it all worth it?"

Her mother put her arm around Abena's shoulder. "That bad, was it?"

"School, exams, the economy of Uruguay, it all just seems a little pointless to me right now."

Her mother raised her eyebrow. "Pointless? One of the highest GPAs in your class and a scholarship to UBC? That hardly seems pointless to me."

Abena shrugged as she sipped her tea. "A half-scholarship, Mama, and even with student loans, a bursary and two shifts a week at McDonald's, I'm going to be broke until I'm forty. For what? A degree in economics? There's not a great call for economists in East Van." She looked back up at the photograph. "Do you miss him?"

"Every minute of every day." Abena loved the sound of her mother's voice. Even after more than twenty years in Canada, it still carried the sing-song lilt of her native Ghana.

"I wish I could remember him."

"You were barely two months old when it happened. Sometimes I forget that."

Theirs was a sad history. Effie and Kwasi Walker had left Ghana on a student visa two years before Abena was born. Kwasi had worked for the local Red Cross in Accra. He had so impressed the Canadian in charge of the chapter that he sponsored Kwasi and his wife to travel to British Columbia to earn a degree in Public Administration at Simon Fraser University, with the goal of sending him back home to Ghana to take a key position with the organization.

Competent and compassionate African men like Kwasi Walker were wanted for leadership roles in organizations like the Red Cross, but it never happened. Two years into his degree, on a bright and sunny spring morning, Kwasi Walker was killed, mowed down at a marked crosswalk by a drunk driver.

In Ghana, her mother had been a teacher. Here she had taken a job cleaning office buildings. With a limited income, they had ended up in East Vancouver, in Mount Pleasant, in the same apartment they shared today.

"I don't know why you don't hate him, the man who killed Daddy."

"Hate begets hate. It destroys everything, so I choose forgiveness. And life."

"But you'd only been here a short time and then Daddy died. How could you not be bitter?"

"These things happen in Africa," her mother said. "He could have been killed by a driver in Accra as well, or by a host of other things."

"Did you ever want to go home, back to Africa afterward? Maybe carry on Daddy's work?"

She took Abena's hand. "What's really going on, Abena?"

Abena had been struggling with the answer to that question for months, her feelings of unease intensifying as the term came to an end. She knew she was lucky to be at UBC, but there was something missing, something she had only recently recognized, something she had been working up the courage to tell her mother.

"I just feel as if I've been floating for the last year. I want to finish school but not right now."

"You know what your father would say about this, don't you?" After the accident, her mother had made certain Abena knew her late father, if only through photographs and stories.

Despite herself, Abena laughed. "I'm not sure how 'don't embarrass the snake and it won't embarrass you' fits into this conversation, Mama."

Her mother clapped her hands in delight. "You remember! I don't think I've said that one for years!"

"I remember all Daddy's sayings, although I'm not sure I ever understood half of them. 'The day the monkey is destined to die . . .'"

Her mother laughed. "'All the trees get slippery.' I never understood that one either. To be honest I'm not sure your father did either. Utter nonsense if you ask me."

Outside, the wind picked up and the rain hammered hard against the window. "You know what he'd say about the rain, don't you?"

Abena nodded sadly. "That one was my favourite." She put down the cup and hugged her mother tightly. "I love you, Mama."

Her mother returned the embrace. "Do you remember what your name means?"

Abena grimaced. "They're not very original in Ghana, are they? I hated my name as a girl. I wanted to be called something normal, like Vanessa or Katie."

"Abena, there is nothing ordinary about you! You're meant for great things, and if right now UBC isn't one of them, do you know what is?"

Abena looked to her backpack by the front door, the magazine tucked within. "I may be crazy, Mama," she said, "but I think I do."

The Westshore Education Trust was housed on the third floor of an old, six-storey white-stone building on Davie Street, next to a Vietnamese restaurant in the heart of downtown Vancouver. Abena took a deep breath, walked through the doors to the elevator and pressed the call button.

No turning back now.

The door slid open. Westshore's head office was smaller than Abena would have expected for a charity that ran dozens of schools in refugee camps around the world. A receptionist sat at her desk inside the front door and directed Abena past several offices toward a couch. "Ms. Walker? Mr. Houghton is expecting you. He'll just be a moment."

Abena sat down. Across from her was a wall mostly covered with Christmas decorations and pictures of smiling African children attending school, their hands raised, smiles on their faces. A few minutes later, the door to an adjacent office opened and a slight man in a tweed jacket and close-cropped grey hair walked toward her. Abena stood to greet him.

"Welcome, Ms. Walker," he said, taking her outstretched hand. "I hear you want to join Westshore."

"Yes, Sir," Abena replied.

"Very well. Please come into my office and have a seat. I am curious to know why exactly you want to put aside your course of study at UBC when the fall term ends to join our little organization?"

Charles Houghton, Director of the Westshore Education Trust, listened intently as Abena spoke, answering the same question she had been asked by a slightly surprised university employee at the registrar's office when she withdrew from her spring term courses.

Houghton opened a thin manila folder on his desk. In it was Abena's application form, her letters of reference and the passport-size photograph she'd had taken at London Drugs, stapled to the inside of the cover. She looked at herself, a twenty-one-year-old woman of average looks, height and weight, with medium-length hair she'd paid a week's salary to straighten.

Houghton leaned back in his chair, chin resting on his thumb and forefinger. "Your references are glowing, your grades excellent and your experience as a tutor at UBC definitely helps as well. On paper, you are an ideal candidate for Westshore, but I need to look in your eyes, to hear you speak, to know if you're certain about this. I mean, really certain."

"More than anything," Abena said. "I'm working on a degree in economics and I will complete it, but I really feel the need to do something important with my life now."

"Important." Houghton rolled the word around in his mouth then leaned forward, eyes focused intently on Abena. "I understand that your family is from Ghana, but what do you *really* know about Africa and the *important* things that need to be done there?"

Suddenly Abena felt as if she didn't know much at all. Her face flushed as she struggled to articulate the thoughts that had been swirling in her head for weeks. "There are problems: wars, refugee camps, drought, poverty. It's bad, I know, but I really feel that I can help, that I can make a difference."

Houghton listened intently. Abena's emotions welled up as she spoke with a conviction that surprised her. "I know that I need to go, and I want to teach for Westshore."

Houghton smiled broadly. "In that case, welcome aboard. We don't pay well, I'm afraid. We don't pay at all!" he said, laughing at his own joke. "You'd be a volunteer, of course. Flight and vaccinations are covered. Tools of the trade and a very small honorarium are included as well, but that's it. Conditions are rudimentary at best and, Abena, if I could add one thing about Africa?"

Houghton's grin disappeared. "A lot of people go there full of idealism and then falter. You must be realistic about what you can accomplish. Africa's a tough place. It eats people up."

Abena met his gaze. "I'm from East Van, Sir. I can handle tough places."

Houghton's smile returned. "We shall see, Ms. Walker, we shall see. We do have several opportunities available right now, but I believe I have just the place in mind for you. Come back and see me tomorrow while I confirm it."

The following day, an anxious Abena returned to the Westshore Office as directed. "You're going to Kenya, to Ukiwa Refugee Camp to be exact," said Houghton when she stepped into his office. "We run several schools there and are looking to add one more, with a sizable donation from a most generous benefactor." Houghton handed Abena a large manila envelope.

"Your contract, departure details and all the other information you'll need are in here. Have a quick read and let me know if you are still interested. If so, sign the documents and we'll talk next steps. Your flight is booked for the fifteenth of January. In the meantime, enjoy Christmas with family and friends. It will be the last holiday you'll have for quite some time."

Abena looked through the folder with fascination. Houghton had included a brief history of Ukiwa Refugee Camp. She read that until 1983, Ukiwa was a small, flyspeck of a town in the northwestern corner of Kenya, in close proximity to Ethiopia, Sudan and Uganda. But now, with chaos engulfing four of the neighbouring countries, refugees by the tens of thousands were flooding over the border into Kenya, swelling the population to many times its original number.

The Kenyan government, incapable of handling such staggering numbers alone, turned to the international community for help. The UN, the Red Cross and others, including Westshore, had responded. With the wars in Sudan and Ethiopia dragging on, and with chaos and genocide descending on Rwanda and Somalia, Ukiwa had grown exponentially, now housing tens of thousands of refugees.

The place sounded awful. Awful. Terrible. Perfect. Abena quickly signed the contract.

"Excellent," Houghton said, passing her another piece of paper. "This is a letter you're to take to the travel medical clinic in Pacific Centre Mall. You'll need a shot or two if you want to make it back from Africa unscathed."

2

THREE HOURS BEFORE her flight was scheduled to depart, Abena and Effie Walker drank coffee at the Starbucks in the international departure hall of Vancouver International Airport. "How are you feeling?" her mother asked.

"Hepatitis A and B, yellow fever, rabies, mumps, rubella booster, meningitis, tetanus and diphtheria. I didn't think I'd be able to use my arm for weeks after all those shots."

"I mean about leaving home."

"Nervous, scared, excited all at the same time." Abena had followed Westshore's advice and packed lightly: clothing for use at the camp was provided by the Trust and would be available at Ukiwa. She had just one small case that she'd already checked and carried on nothing more than a laptop bag stuffed with her computer, several books on African history, culture and politics and a Kiswahili phrase book. It was a very long trip; she intended to use the time wisely.

"It's almost ten hours to Amsterdam, Mama. I get there in the morning, wait ninety minutes for my connecting flight then leave for Nairobi. I should be there in just under twenty-four hours. Can you believe it? In not even a day, I'll be in Africa! What a way to start the new year!"

Her mother's cheeks glistened. "I'm so proud of you. Your father is, too, I just know it. You are completing the work he had planned on doing. You are going home."

Abena glanced at the departure board. It was time to make her way to the gate. They walked slowly toward the checkpoint. Abena checked her passport, ticket and visa for what must have been the hundredth time since arriving at the airport.

"I must be crazy to do this."

"No," her mother said vehemently. "You're not crazy at all. This is what you were meant to do — I can see it in your eyes."

They hugged tightly. "I just want to make you proud, Mama."

Effie Walker reluctantly broke the embrace. "You don't need to do anything to make me proud, Abena. You do that every day. Just remember what your father would say: 'if you see any snakes . . .'"

"I won't embarrass them. Or you either. I promise." Abena picked up her bag then showed her passport and boarding card to the CBSA agent who herded her into the long line of travellers waiting impatiently to get through security.

"I love you," her mother said as Abena was slowly carried away in the crowd. "Don't forget that there will be insects there. Big ones. You know how much you hate them, you shriek like a baby when you see a ladybug!"

Abena laughed through her tears. "I know! I won't let them get to me."

"You're going to make me proud," her mother said. "I just know you will."

After passing through the checkpoint, Abena made her way to the gate and then, when her flight was called, walked down the ramp and took her seat on KLM Flight 682.

She'd booked herself into a window seat and was sitting and buckled in before her row mates arrived: a retired woman from Rotterdam returning home from a holiday in Whistler and an American businessman who did little but nod as he sat down and pressed his nose into his computer.

The flight attendant went through the pre-flight ritual. She spoke in English as well as Dutch for the benefit of the Netherlanders on board, though no doubt their English was as good as Abena's, if the chatty old woman beside her was any indication.

Finished, the flight attendant took her seat. With a slight jar, the plane moved backwards as it was pushed out of the gate. The whine of the engines increased as the jet taxied to the runway then took off, the force of the acceleration pushing Abena back in her seat. Abena had never flown before and her emotions ran somewhere between exhilaration and terror.

The plane climbed quickly. It winged eastward, and though the day was overcast, there was no fog. Through the small window, Abena could see the high-rises of downtown, the Strait of Georgia, the snow-bathed North Shore Mountains and Vancouver Island to the west. They crossed Burrard Inlet, flying north. Out her window, Abena saw the green and grey expanse of Vancouver spreading out below. She recognized the city, finding familiar landmarks like BC Place and the cruise ship terminal.

As the plane climbed higher, Abena followed the track of East Broadway, and though she couldn't see it from this altitude, she knew exactly where a small, nondescript apartment building on East 7th Ave. would be: her home, far below and getting smaller. The plane banked and entered the clouds. By the time Abena saw the ground once more, her home, Mount Pleasant and Vancouver itself were gone.

3

KENYA

JANUARY 2005

THE ARRIVALS LOUNGE at Jomo Kenyatta International Airport was uncomfortably warm, a chaotic, colourful, congested jumble of people and smells and strange accents, a microcosm no doubt of the city it served. Not that Abena knew Nairobi at all, or any place in Africa for that matter, despite her Ghanaian heritage. She'd not left Canada at all save for a few trips to Seattle.

After several missteps, and now quite damp from perspiration, Abena found her way to Immigration where — through luck more than anything else — she ended up in the proper line. Her visa was inspected, her passport stamped and then she was waved through with little more than a cursory look from the bored immigration official.

Clear of customs, Abena was not quite sure what to do next. West-shore Education Trust staff in Vancouver had told her she would be met at the airport by a local employee, but they were less than specific in the details.

Abena stood at the airport exit, a crush of people flowing past. Feeling suddenly very alone, she fought off the panic that started to climb in her chest until she noticed a bank of men and women standing by the exit doors holding up placards. One had her name on it.

Relieved, Abena made her way quickly over to the sign and the person who held it, a short, cheerful-looking, slender man in his mid-twenties, wearing dark slacks and a crisp white golf shirt with the Westshore logo prominently displayed on his chest.

"You must be Miss Abena Walker. Welcome to Kenya." The man put down the sign and extended his hand. "Please, let me take your bags. You must be very tired; it's a long flight from Canada."

Instead of taking his hand, she froze. It was no more than a few seconds, but he noticed Abena's reluctance. He laughed. "I see that Charles warned you about thieves in Kenya, didn't he? Told you to be wary of strangers and keep your possessions close?"

His laugh was kind and warm-hearted and Abena blushed. Charles Houghton had said that very thing the day before she left. "I'm sorry. You must think I'm terribly rude," she said, quickly shaking his hand.

"Not at all. To be honest, I was expecting a white woman, else I would have picked you out sooner. Most of our new teachers tend to have, how do you say, a 'deer in the headlights' look when they arrive in Nairobi. My name is David Ndereba, yours is Abena Walker. Now we are no longer strangers but co-workers, and hopefully soon friends. May I take your luggage for you now? I promise not to steal it."

Abena handed him her bag. "What do you do for Westshore?" she asked, as Ndereba escorted her through the crowd and through the exit doors.

"That's a harder question to answer than it should be," he said as they walked into the brilliant sunlight of a scorching Nairobi day. "Officially? I handle logistics and transportation matters. I also liaise with local bureaucracies. Unofficially? I help Westshore negotiate the various challenges that invariably pop up in Kenya for Western NGOs. In short? I fix problems."

A throng of ragged children in T-shirts, shorts and sandals immediately surrounded them as they entered the parking lot. "Now is when you keep your eyes on your things, Abena. As much as I hate to admit it, Charles was right; the best pickpockets in Africa live in Nairobi, and the finest of them are younger than ten."

Ndereba threw the children a handful of coins and stepped quickly aside as a mob dove onto the pavement, grasping for the small shiny coins. "Fifty Kenyan shillings," he said as they reached a white, snub-nosed Toyota van. "About fifty American cents; well worth it to keep them too busy to reach for our wallets. And change sides with me unless you want to drive," he added as Abena reached for what she thought was the passenger door. "Kenya's right-hand drive, remember? One of the many traditions left to us by the British."

The air inside the vehicle was hot, stale and dry. Instinctively, Abena reached for the switch to roll down the window. "Best not, Miss Walker. We've air conditioning in the van. Doors locked, windows closed is the safest way to travel until we leave the city. Nairobi has some very good carjackers as well as pickpockets; we don't want to give them an opportunity."

Ndereba flicked a switch on the dash and cool air instantly flooded the inside of the van. "Thanks," Abena said. "Even in the middle of summer I can't remember Vancouver ever being this hot. It must be more than thirty degrees outside."

David Ndereba smiled. "Thirty-four degrees centigrade today to be exact. Quite a nice temperature. Up north in Ukiwa, it's pushing forty-five today. Very unpleasant, I can tell you, that sort of heat." Ndereba turned up the fan. "It's winter for you as well, isn't it? I sometimes forget how cold the West Coast can be in January, snow or not."

"You've been to Vancouver?" Abena realized instantly how rude the comment sounded. Great, she thought. I've been in Kenya for only thirty minutes and I've insulted my host twice. But if her response offended Ndereba he didn't show it.

"I have. Westshore doesn't just send Canadians to work in the refugee camps. The board of directors likes to bring us Africans to headquarters from time to time as well, sort of like an exchange. Makes them feel good, I suppose. I interned for Charles Houghton a few years ago. Six months in Vancouver from October to March. I never thought I'd get the chill out of my bones. Still, there are some things I miss. Tony's up on Hastings, for example. Best pepperoni pizza I ever had. Nothing like it in Nairobi."

Ndereba stopped, signalled right and merged onto a busy multi-lane road, weaving his way expertly through a throng of cars, buses and motorcycles. He drove toward a city skyline that wouldn't have looked out of place in North America save the slums alongside the road, the piles of garbage and the countless lines of laundry that fluttered in the sun.

Suddenly Abena's head swam. After twenty hours on a plane, stopping briefly in Amsterdam to change flights, she was tired and jet-lagged to be sure, but it was more than that. Two months ago, she was a third-year economics student at the University of British Columbia, living with her mother in a small apartment on East Vancouver, working part-time at the Granville McDonald's downtown.

Now? She was driving on the wrong side of an African road, through a landscape of both obvious wealth and immense poverty, casually talking about a familiar restaurant in Vancouver where she'd once gone on a bad date with an econ major back in her first year at UBC. The experience was disconcerting. Abena suddenly felt nauseous, afraid she would throw up or pass out, or both.

"Are you all right, Abena? Shall I stop?" Ndereba looked alarmed. Abena caught a glimpse of herself in the side mirror and could see why he would be concerned. She was flushed, her eyes dilated, a sheen of sweat glistening on her forehead, despite the air conditioning.

"No. Keep driving. I don't know what happened, I just felt sort of funny suddenly."

Ndereba reached to a small cooler that sat between the seats. He gave Abena a cold bottle of water. "Have this. Most likely you're a bit dehydrated. You need to be mindful of that here."

The water was cold and delicious and Abena greedily drank it down in a matter of seconds, feeling almost instantly better. "Thank you," she said. "I can't remember the last time I had a drink."

Ndereba gave her a second bottle, its cold plastic surface covered in condensation. "You'll need to drink much more water than you would at home. But only purified water; it's quite easy to get very sick in Africa."

With her head and stomach settled, Abena was able to focus on both the passing landscape as well as her new companion. David Ndereba was a very interesting man, she learned as they talked. The son of an illiterate Mombasa fisherman, Ndereba had been identified by his primary teacher as a young man of promise. The teacher convinced his father that David would be better served attending the Aga Khan High School on a scholarship than going to sea.

It was a wise choice. Ndereba excelled, he told Abena reluctantly, earning himself another scholarship, this time to the Technical University of Mombasa, where he distinguished himself by graduating at the top of his class with a bachelor's degree in community development. The Westshore Education Trust recognized his potential as well and hired him before he'd even completed his final exams.

As they drove northwest through the seemingly endless Nairobi sprawl, the conversation lessened. Abena's eyelids grew heavier by the moment, finally closing somewhere in the middle of a slum on the western edge of the city. She slept solidly for two hours, jarring reluctantly awake only when they stopped for fuel in Nakuru, a town of several hundred thousand people 150 kilometres northwest of Nairobi, she learned when she awoke.

North of Nakuru, a long string of low, brown mountains dominated a harsh landscape of scrub and trees, the road little more than a thin sliver of civilization through the savannah. To their left, a massive lake sparkled in the late afternoon sun, flocks of countless birds wheeling in the blue sky over the water.

Suddenly, on the other side of the road, giraffes appeared. The animals seemed oblivious to the van, focusing instead on eating the leaves of a tall acacia tree. "Oh my God," Abena said, staring at the giraffes. "They're beautiful."

"This is how Westerners see Africa isn't it?" said Ndereba. "Animals, white *bwanas* and black porters out on the hunt. That and our ability to kill each other and die like flies in famine, drought and war?"

Abena sensed no bitterness in his words, just an underlying sadness at entrenched Western stereotypes. "Yes, I suppose it is." Abena could hardly disagree and felt ashamed because of it.

"If you don't mind my asking, you are Canadian, but your name is African. West African, if I'm not mistaken," said Ndereba a short while later.

"My parents were from Ghana. They moved to Canada before I was born." Her own heritage aside, most of what Abena knew of the continent had come from academic coursework, Discovery and CNN.

"Hopefully in your time here, you'll see there is more to your ancestral homeland than safaris and civil war."

"When will we reach Ukiwa?" They had been driving for almost six hours. Abena was anxious to get to the camp and, in her own small way, provide the hope that Ndereba spoke about.

"Not until tomorrow. We've got only an hour or so of daylight left, and it's best we aren't on the roads after dark. We'll spend the night in a little town called Sigor. It's just a little way up the road. We'll have dinner, stay in the hotel then carry on in the morning. From Sigor it's only about three hundred kilometres to Ukiwa."

"Only three hundred? Why not just push through tonight?"

"Two reasons. North of Sigor the road gets rough. It may be only three hundred kilometres, but it will take us the better part of seven hours to get to the camp. Besides, I don't know about you, but I've spent enough time in the van for one day."

"And the second? Are you worried about hitting an animal in the dark?"

"Wildlife, I can handle. Bandits own these roads at night, and it's just not safe to drive on them. Two weeks ago, an aid convoy was ambushed not more than one hundred kilometres from here. Only one man survived. He'd been shot a dozen times by a masked man with an AK-47. He survived three days alone in the bush before anyone found him. It was a miracle he only lost a leg."

"Don't the police patrol the roads?" Abena had read that Kenya had problems to be sure, but it was also one of the more developed countries in the region.

The van entered a small village. David Ndereba slowed down and turned into the parking lot of a small hotel. "Indeed, they do," he said, "but in this part of the country, very often it's the police who *are* the bandits. Hopefully, you don't find that out first-hand."

4

THE POLITICS OF water consumed Ukiwa. Ten litres per day per, person. Never more and sometimes less. Ten litres for drinking, washing, cooking. Victoria was in line now for her family's share. Forty litres drawn and measured from a standpipe, access limited to two hours a day.

It was a long snaking thing of women and children, the line. On their heads and in their hands, they bore all manner of containers to take back their precious allotment. Victoria carried two white plastic jugs emblazoned with the blue logo of the UNHCR.

She waited her turn patiently. Not so for the young woman who tried to cut into the line some ten metres ahead of her. Those who waited, who followed the rules, had no patience for such people, and she was set upon with words, harsh and discordant in English, Dinka and Kiswahili. To accentuate the point, the empty plastic buckets were turned into clubs and swung at the woman who cheated the line. The interloper got the message and scurried to the back, thoroughly chastised.

Ten litres per day. No more. Ten litres a day for which people would lie, cheat and steal. Ten litres for which some would give their bodies, would pay others to collect, would sell afterward. Ten litres a day and not a drop more, yet somehow *chang'aa* was sold and drunk across the camp, made with the UN's precious water.

It was things like this Victoria lamented. To line up like cows, like animals for water, for food, for help. Victoria resented it all. She resented the process, the people, the system. The system, after all, had failed her.

The politics of grief and of waiting also consumed Ukiwa. Victoria knew this as well as anyone. Before Azana there was the loss of her home and her parents. And after the Walk? For fourteen years she had been here.

Fourteen years since she left Azana and her sister behind. For most of that time she had been here, in Ukiwa, lining up to see this UN worker or that UN worker, asking about Mary and her mother, begging the UNHCR to help her find her lost family. Fourteen years of forms, of interviews, of questions. Of lines.

Fourteen years of nothing.

But today Victoria felt better, felt almost good, in fact. William had forbidden her children to attend any of the schools offered in the camp. William hated the Westerners almost as much as the government in Khartoum. They had done little to support the south in its war with the north save for words. Some had even declared his beloved movement an insurgency, no better than terrorists. No, William would do nothing for them.

Besides, William had met many Westerners in his life, she knew. Aid workers, missionaries, journalists — Americans who had come to the camps to stare at the people there like animals in a zoo. They came for their own purposes, not to help, and William had vowed that no child of his would ever go to a school run by a Westerner. Grudgingly, Victoria had complied.

Until today.

A chance meeting with an aid worker earlier that morning. A new school freshly built next to the Catholic church in the Sudanese section of Ukiwa, not ten minutes from her home. A school looking for students.

And William was away in Sudan.

Despite the risk, Victoria registered her children with the agency running the school, a Canadian charity she had never heard of before. An unsurprising fact. There were many charities here and Victoria could only guess what they did. Things had not changed for her because of them. William could not know. Peter and Alexandra understood that. They knew that they could never speak of it to their father, the rare times he was home.

The school was nothing much: benches and tables under a canvas tarp, nothing like St. Matthew's, the old brick school of Victoria's youth, another life, another world away, but it was a school nevertheless. It was time for such risks. Victoria had done all she could to teach her children in secrecy. When William was off fighting his interminable war, she had taught them to read, to write, to do their sums.

Victoria was almost embarrassed by her lack of skill in this regard. What would their grandfather, the last headmaster of St. Matthew's, have thought of her efforts? But still. Peter and his sister spoke and read Dinka of course, had learned Kiswahili — the language of their reluctant hosts — and English as well, along with a smattering of Arabic. She had done her best and that was something. Ahead of her, the line shuffled forward. Victoria moved slowly along with it, but for the first time in an age, she did so with a smile.

5

"I'M IN ROOM number two," said Ndereba, handing Abena a key. "You're next door. Freshen up; when you're ready, we'll go out for dinner."

"I'm starving. Any chance there's a McDonald's around here? Or maybe a Kenyan branch of Tony's Pizza?"

"Unfortunately, no, but my cousin's restaurant is just down the street and it's quite decent."

"Is it safe? The food, I mean?"

Ndereba laughed. "I see that Charles warned you about Kenyan food as well as Kenyan pickpockets!"

Abena blushed again. "I'm sorry, David. It's just that I have a bit of a weak stomach."

"Don't worry," he assured her. "The most exotic thing on the menu is lamb curry. The food's fine, believe me. Many Westerners pass through here on their way to Ukiwa; my uncle caters to them as much as the locals. Wash up and when you're ready we can go. Sigor's a small town; places close down early here."

The hotel room wasn't much to look at: a small bed, night table and ceiling fan that squeaked gently as it spun, but the linens were clean, and the room had its own bathroom with a working toilet. Several bottles of water sat next to the sink, with a sign saying that tap water should not be used for drinking or brushing teeth.

It was wise advice. Abena remembered the needles and the pills she received back in Vancouver. A thousand dollars of medicine courtesy of the Westshore Education Trust, an investment in keeping their new teacher healthy.

Shots or not, Abena was decidedly not prepared to take any chances. She brushed her teeth with bottled water then changed clothes. Feeling slightly refreshed, she locked the room behind her and knocked on Ndereba's door.

The sun had set faster than Abena had ever seen, and so they walked the short distance to the restaurant in near darkness, the only light coming from a lone street lamp. The place was almost empty save for a handful of middle-aged Kenyan men who sat at a table in the corner, smoking cigarettes, drinking large bottles of Tusker beer. David Ndereba said something in Kiswahili to the men. They nodded brusquely in acknowledgement before turning back to their beer and their own conversation.

The waiter, who was the owner of the place, the head cook and David Ndereba's cousin, apparently, greeted them amiably, two bottles of Tusker in his hand as he sat them at a table, cheerfully ignoring Abena's protestations that she didn't want it.

Not bothering with menus, he disappeared into the kitchen, returning a few minutes later with two large plates of fried chicken and sweet potatoes in his hands. The chicken was cooked with a spice Abena didn't recognize but, just as Ndereba promised, the meal was delicious. She wolfed it down quickly.

Abena had never been a drinker, but to her own surprise, she finished the beer almost as quickly as she did her meal. A short time later she stood up, stumbling slightly on her feet. The excitement of finally arriving in Kenya was gone, replaced by the effects of exhaustion and alcohol.

Abena fumbled in her pocket for cash. She'd picked up some Kenyan shillings back home and was about to pay for the meal when Ndereba stopped her. "Westshore has an account here. Since you're working for them, let Mr. Houghton pay."

Too tired to disagree, Abena followed Ndereba from the restaurant and walked the hundred metres or so back to the hotel. "Good night Ms. Abena. It's just past eight," said Ndereba. "I'll wake you at four and we'll get on the road early. With luck, we'll reach Ukiwa by ten thirty or so, before the heat of the day sets in. Have a good sleep; if your first day at Ukiwa is anything like that of most Westerners, you're most definitely going to need it."

Abena moaned when she heard the knock on the door, opened her eyes and checked her watch. Five minutes past four. Even though she had the better part of eight hours of sleep, she was still groggy, and it took her a few disorienting seconds to remember just where she was.

She dressed, packed her small bag and joined Ndereba outside. It was still dark, impossibly so, with stars brighter than Abena had ever seen, stars not obscured by the ever-present layers of the light pollution back home. The night sky looked different for another reason. It was full of new constellations, and though Abena saw the Big Dipper and several other formations she recognized, they hung in the wrong places, their familiar shapes strangely disconcerting because of it.

They drove through the darkness, the van's headlights reflecting off dozens of pairs of eyes that glittered yellow and red on the edge of the road before vanishing away into the night.

"Jackals and hyenas mostly," said Ndereba, as a large black shape darted away from the van. "Nasty creatures, hyenas. You wouldn't want to be out here alone with them."

The drive felt surreal to Abena. Unfamiliar stars, yellow eyes glinting in the bush, eyes that vanished when night faded quickly away, replaced by the large red sun that rose over rugged treeless mountains.

The road wove its way through the brown scrub speckled with umbrella-shaped trees and long, tawny grass. Abena drifted in and out of sleep and would remember little else but these half-dreamt snapshots during the final push to Ukiwa, until she was awakened by a gentle nudge from Ndereba.

"Almost there," he said, pointing to a faded, wooden WELCOME TO UKIWA sign. Houses and other buildings appeared, as if out of nowhere. Land Rovers, Toyota utility vehicles and large trucks were everywhere. Rows of them were lined up on the side of the road, United Nations logos prominently displayed, drivers standing or squatting beside them, smoking and drinking water.

The place crawled with armed men, dressed in khaki uniforms, driving dust-coloured four-wheel drives, personnel carriers and things that look like six-wheeled small tanks. "Why are there so many soldiers at the camp?"

"Actually, we're not at the camp yet. This is Ukiwa town. The camp's still about fifteen kilometres to the north. They're not all soldiers, by the way. The men with the red berets are soldiers from the Kenya Defence Force. The ones wearing blue are Kenya National Police, Turkana West division."

"Police, army: it still seems like an awful lot of guns, no matter who's carrying them."

"There's a large police station in Ukiwa as well as a military barracks," said Ndereba. "The bush around here crawls with bandits, poachers, undocumented refugees and guerillas. The security forces maintain a large presence in response."

Ndereba slowed to a crawl as they approached a checkpoint, manned by half a dozen officers. "Also, there are ten times as many refugees at the camp as citizens in the town. It would be an understatement to say that tensions exist between them. This is one of the poorest places in the country; many here feel that the government ignores its own people while feeding foreigners. There's tremendous resentment against the refugees, resentment often expressed violently."

Ndereba rolled down the window and passed their passports and Westshore IDs to a heavily armed policeman. Unlike the bored officer who waved Abena through the airport with little more than a glance at her passport, this one studied the documents carefully. The officer beside him said nothing as he stood stone-faced, his finger never leaving the trigger guard of his assault rifle.

Several more police checked the inside of the van while another stuck a long pole with a mirror attached to the end of it underneath the vehicle, looking for bombs. Satisfied they were here on legitimate business, the officer waved them through.

"Random security check," Ndereba explained, driving slowly away. "Somalia is in shambles and its people leak across our border for god-knows-what reasons, though none are good. Then there's the Sudan People's Liberation Army, *genocidaires* from Rwanda, the Lord's Resistance Army from Uganda: all of them and more find ways to seep across the border, bringing their wars with them. If it looks like a war zone here, that's because it is, Abena, a war fought against enemies from within our borders as well as outside. A war I sometimes fear we are losing."

They reached Ukiwa Refugee Camp thirty minutes after clearing the police blockade. Ndereba drove steadily along a dirt track lined with blue and white markers, following a thick fence made from branches stuck into the ground.

The road branched. To the right it was blocked with a traffic gate manned by an armed police officer sitting in a small wooden shed, like the kind you'd see in a parkade back in any Western city. Ndereba took the left fork.

"The road to the right goes into Ukiwa Camp proper, about three kilometres past that check post," explained Ndereba, "but for now, we're going to the camp's administrative compound." After another kilometre or so of driving, they arrived at a much larger gate made of sheet metal, painted in United Nations colours. A small sign next to it read simply UKIWA REFUGEE CAMP.

Two pale and tattered flags fluttered in the light breeze above the gate: the crossed spears and shield of Kenya and the blue-and-white banner of the United Nations High Commissioner for Refugees. A second pole stood next to the flagpole, this one housing a security camera aimed directly at their van.

A small peephole slid open in the gate and then quickly shut again. A few seconds later, a heavily armed police officer pulled the gate open and Ndereba drove in.

They passed the gatehouse and entered a clearing full of buildings, surrounded by a thick fence twelve feet tall, made of what looked to be thorny branches tightly interwoven with razor wire.

"The administrative compound is reserved for NGOs, United Nations personnel and Kenyan government staff. Refugees aren't allowed in unless they have specific business," explained Ndereba. "The *boma*, the thorn-tree fence that surrounds us, along with the gate and the armed police, aren't here to keep the camp residents safe by the way — they protect you. There are more than a few people in this part of the country who dislike Westerners more than they do refugees."

Ndereba showed Abena a solid-looking two-storey brick building, unique among the temporary buildings and trailers. "That's the central administration office of the Kenyan government. The police station is over there and UNHCR headquarters is behind it. Médecins Sans Frontières, International Rescue Committee, World Vision, Red Cross, Red Crescent are all here as well."

The van stopped outside a collection of white trailers, the Westshore logo and maple leaf embossed on the sides of all of them. Ndereba turned off the engine. "Here we are. 'Home sweet home,' I believe they say?"

Abena opened the van door, heat hitting her like a fist to the face. She could hardly breathe and felt as if she'd stepped into a furnace. "I told you it gets hot up here. Thirty-nine degrees and the sun's just warming up. By three it will reach forty-seven, maybe even fifty."

Ndereba took her case and walked toward a trailer. "The dormitories are here. The main office and dining room are in that larger building. Toilets and the shower block are to your left. You won't bathe much at Ukiwa, though," he said. "Water's rationed, so you get only three showers per week. But don't worry, you'll get used to being dirty in a month or so."

They walked down a hallway in the trailer past a series of doors. Ndereba opened one and showed Abena into a small room that wouldn't have looked out of place in any one of UBC's student dorms. The place was perhaps ten feet by eight feet in size, deathly hot inside and sparsely furnished with a single steel-frame bed and a small metal desk and chair. It had an open closet with several bare-wire hangers within and sitting on top of the small bed was a pile of linens and neatly folded sets of shirts and trousers. A Westshore ball cap was beside the clothes, while a pair of sturdy-looking thick-soled boots sat on the floor beside a cheaply made, three-drawer wooden dresser.

Ndereba put down Abena's case, reached up to the ceiling, opened a vent and, within a few seconds, cool air flooded into the room. "That's better. I'll leave you to unpack and freshen up before Mr. Hughes arrives to greet you. He likes to meet all the new teachers personally."

Abena Walker knew that name, had learned it back in Vancouver. Roger Hughes oversaw all of Westshore's operations in the camp. "Mr. Hughes will probably drop by when he gets back from his meeting," Ndereba continued. "The UNHCR, camp administration and security, as well as the heads of the various NGOs meet weekly in Mr. Angara's office. It's a 'state of the camp' sort of thing: information sharing, problem solving and the like. After all, there's always problems to solve here in Ukiwa."

Abena had not heard the other name. "Who is Mr. Angara?"

"Richard Angara. He's the camp director from the Kenyan Department of Refugee Affairs. Nominally, the camp's run by the UNHCR but this is Africa; Mr. Angara's the real power here. Nothing gets done without his say-so."

The bare light bulb on the ceiling flickered off for a second or two then came back to life. "Listen, do you hear it?" Abena concentrated, picking up a faint sound in the background. "Our own generator. It's fairly reliable but it surges occasionally, breaks down from time to time and sometimes we run out of diesel. To conserve fuel, we shut it down at night. There are also strict curfews in place for everyone who works for the NGOs at Ukiwa. By six in the evening you must be out of the camp, and if you're in town on errands, you must be back in the compound by nine or you won't be let in. By nine-thirty, you are to be back in your room. Lights go out at ten."

"I haven't had a curfew since I was seventeen."

"There's good reason for it. Ukiwa Camp's hardly safe in the middle of the day. At night? Even with the *boma* and armed guards, you wouldn't want to be walking alone, even in the compound. The toilets are the only place you're allowed to be after ten."

"Not quite the Hilton, is it?"

"Believe me, Abena, the camp residents can only dream of the luxuries we have in the compound. Clean latrines, showers, hot food, and air conditioning are luxuries. We even have wireless internet — on a good day."

Ndereba gave her a small card. "The password for our network; we change it monthly. Internet access is like gold here, so please don't share it with other NGOs. We barely have enough bandwidth for our own purposes; we'd never get online if the others logged into our server. Power's turned off at ten, but there's bottled water in the desk drawer for drinking and brushing your teeth, as well as a flashlight for trips to the toilet."

"What comes next?" asked Abena.

"You can rest for a while. The place is pretty much deserted right now since the others are out at their schools, but Frank will be here soon as well. Like Roger, he always likes to meet the new people for himself, though that is where the similarities between them end."

"Frank?" Here was another name Abena was not familiar with.

Ndereba's grin grew wider. "There's no one in all of Ukiwa quite like Frank McClune! Everyone knows him here: refugees, NGOs, Kenyans. Frank's second-in-command to Mr. Hughes, in charge of the schools and the education program, sort of like a headmaster. He also works with the refugee community to select new school sites and organize their construction. There's no mistaking Frank — you'll know him when you meet him.

"And Abena," Ndereba added, choosing his words carefully before closing the door behind him, "many Westerners — Americans, Canadians, British — come here and become somewhat discouraged. They leave before they've given Ukiwa — and themselves — a chance. I like you. I hope you stay."

Alone, Abena took a deep breath then unpacked her belongings. She put her clothes away in the closet, set up her books and placed a photograph of her mother on the desk. Then she took her laptop from its bag and turned it on.

Once the computer was powered up, she typed in the network password, only to discover that while the computer was connected to the Westshore network, the network today wasn't connected to anything outside the camp. "So much for the World Wide Web."

Abena started unbuttoning her blouse, about to try on the Westshore shirt when she was interrupted by a gentle knock on the door. She opened it to see a man, angular and tall, in a tan suit standing in the hallway. "Ms. Walker? I'm Roger Hughes, Director of Operations for the Westshore Education Trust. Welcome to Ukiwa."

He spoke in a patrician British accent, his tone oiled and sibilant. Abena shook his hand. Unlike Ndereba's strong and confident grasp, Hughes' hand was soft. She watched as his eyes roamed over her then remembered that the top two buttons of her blouse were undone.

She suddenly felt uncomfortable, a memory flashing back of an old high school gym teacher, a lecherous man not afraid to let the girls know what he thought of their breasts by the way his eyes rolled over them. Abena took back her hand and folded her arms protectively across her chest. "Thank you, Sir. I'm glad to be here."

"I won't take up much of your time," Hughes said. "I'm just coming back from a meeting and I wanted to pop in and see how you're settling in."

"Your meeting with the camp director? David told me."

"Did he indeed? The locals are quite well informed, aren't they? Always seem to know what's going on. Bush telegrams and jungle drums as they used to say back in the colonial days.

"I'm joking of course," Hughes said, after a few seconds of uncomfortable silence. "Our Kenyan friends are fiercely protective of their sovereignty, and our weekly meetings are hardly state secrets. Welcome aboard. We eat at six-thirty in the main building. I'll see you then. Don't be late. This isn't a holiday resort or a cruise ship; we have only one sitting for dinner."

6

A FEW MINUTES after Hughes left, Abena felt a sharp spasm tele-graph itself up the length of her torso and into her belly. She sat down on the edge of her small cot, her mouth dry. She waited for the sensa-tion to pass then cautiously stood up, a little unsteady on her feet as she walked to her desk to get a bottle of water.

She drank deeply then lay back down on the bed, trying to fight the nausea that swept over her, seemingly from nowhere. Her stom-ach cramped again. She breathed sharply, focusing on a black spot in the corner of the ceiling she'd not noticed before, willing herself to feel better.

The spot moved. It was an insect, a cockroach, the largest one she'd ever seen, with long antennae and six scuttling legs. Despite herself, Abena squealed as the bug scurried across the ceiling and disappeared in a small gap in the wall.

Stomach heaving, Abena launched herself off the bed and through the door, staggering down the hallway, clutching her belly as she ran toward the exit, searching frantically for the latrines.

"You don't look so good." Through watering eyes, Abena saw a man leaning against the side of a dust-coloured Land Rover. He was white, of average height and build, with short-cropped black hair and three days' worth of salt and pepper stubble on his face. The man was pulling on one of the ubiquitous khaki vests, an old Pink Floyd *Dark Side of the Moon* T-shirt underneath.

"Where's the bathroom?" Abena doubled over in pain, wishing she could remember where David Ndereba had told her the latrines were.

The man tilted his head to the left. "I'd hurry. You don't have much time to waste, by the looks of things. Don't forget to check under the lid for spiders and scorpions, though. I don't think you want to get bitten on the ass your first day in Ukiwa."

"Spiders?" Abena stopped in mid-stride.

"Big fucking spiders. But hell, this is Africa; big spiders happen in Africa." Spiders or not, Abena lurched forward again toward the latrine.

"Seriously, are you OK?" the man repeated. "You look like shit."

"I don't feel well," she said weakly.

The man grinned, lit a cigarette and leaned casually against the side of the Land Rover. "No shit. Belly acting up, eh? Everyone gets a good case of the trots at Ukiwa. Frank McClune. You're Walker, right? The new girl? You work for me, so hurry up and finish your business; we've got things to do."

Without answering, Abena entered the latrine and slammed the thin wooden door behind her. A few seconds later she howled in pain as her guts exploded. "Jesus, don't tell me David took you to that restaurant in Sigor on the way up?" she heard McClune say through the thin door. "I keep telling him the food's shit there, but he won't listen, loves to take the newbies to his fucking cousin's place."

A painful moan was all Abena had in response.

"Didn't have the chicken, did you?" McClune seemed oblivious to any embarrassment or discomfort he was causing as he waited outside tears

the toilets. "The chicken, definitely the chicken. Those fucking chilies will kill the uninitiated. You're gonna be in there for a while. It's probably nothing serious, but if I were you I'd avoid eating meat for a while. It takes time for your system to adjust."

Abena's stomach twisted in response, although this time she retched, nearly gagging on the vomit that had come out of nowhere.

"Jesus. Both ends. That's not good. Best to avoid fish too. You think you're feeling bad now? Just wait until you eat a bad Nile perch. You'll feel like you're shitting out your intestines. Some unlucky bastards actually do."

Ten minutes later with nothing left inside her belly, Abena left the latrine to see the man named Frank McClune still waiting there, now sitting behind the wheel of his Land Rover. "Come to think of it, I'd avoid food altogether for a day or two; the local cuisine doesn't seem to agree with you. Now get in, there's something I need to show you."

Mortified and furious, Abena climbed into the passenger seat without saying a word. McClune drove to the main gate of the compound where they were waved through. They drove in silence until they reached the fork.

McClune turned left, stopping briefly at the security gate guarding access to the main camp. The post was manned by a young police officer, still in his teens by the looks of him. He raised the wooden gate then waved as McClune drove through, up the road toward Ukiwa Camp.

"The gatehouse is new. Kenyans built it last year and then they ditched the road on either side," McClune said, once the bar lifted. "'Enhanced security to control the flow of traffic,' the Kenya Police said, though it does neither. With all the Jihadist crazies floating around the bush, the compound's the place that needs protection. Besides, you can't really secure this place. No fences guard Ukiwa. A thousand dirt tracks lead away from the camp into the scrub. People can come and go as they choose, though where the fuck they gonna go?"

Several hundred metres past the checkpoint, McClune turned the

Land Rover sharply to the right and bounced off the main road onto a trail that led steeply up a small rise. McClune reached into the glovebox and pulled out a package of pills.

"These will settle your stomach. Take two every couple of hours and drink as much as you can. There's water in that cooler behind you; drink half a dozen bottles at least today. It's fucking hot and you'll need it. Don't guzzle, though; taking small, regular sips is the best way to stay hydrated. If your head starts to hurt, you feel dizzy or your piss gets dark and stinky, that's dehydration. We have Gatorade as well, so have a couple of those when we get back."

Still angry at the man, Abena refused the medication McClune offered. "Take the fucking pills," he said, not amused with her reticence. "A bad case of the shits is pretty common in Africa. Hell, if I had a dollar for every time I crapped my pants, I'd have enough money to buy a place in Saint Tropez. Get over it. You don't have the luxury of either pride or privacy out here, so quit your pouting."

Abena reluctantly accepted the medicine. "Point taken."

"Good choice. Now here's some perspective for you, Walker," McClune's tone softened. "You're gonna get sick once a month here at least. It may put you in bed for a day or two if it's really bad, but that's it. The refugees? A bad case of diarrhea can put them in the ground. Couple dozen a week die at Ukiwa because of it. You bury a few hundred toddlers who died because they didn't have eight ounces of water or some electrolytes? You learn to stop worrying about a lot of the things that used to bother you back home."

"So where exactly are we going?" When they had left the administrative compound, McClune hadn't mentioned their destination, had just said there was something he needed to show her.

The Land Rover turned tightly around a corner and slid to a sudden stop at the top of a small hill. "Here, Walker. We're going *here*."

McClune leading, the pair walked to the edge of the hill. "Oh my God," said Abena as McClune lit a cigarette and watched her take in the view. Ukiwa Refugee Camp lay below, spreading everywhere, disappearing in the distance, into the waves of heat that radiated from the ground.

People, little more than dots, moved about, tens of thousands of them, crawling around like ants on a mound. Black smoke from countless little fires curled up in the air, mixing in with the russet dust kicked up by the wheels of trucks and the movement of the people themselves.

At the far edges of the camp, hundreds, thousands of what appeared to be little white pillows sat in stark contrast to the earth-coloured houses that surrounded them. "What are those?" Abena asked.

"Tents for the newcomers. Refugees arrive, are processed and placed in group dorms for a week or so. Then they're given a little plot of land, one of those tents and instructions on how to make a mud house. Once the walls are up, they're provided with corrugated metal for a roof and door. The camp is like the rings of a tree: outer ones are the newest homes, inner are the oldest."

"They come from all over." McClune pointed to the east. "Somalia's that way. Famines, warlords, murder; it makes this place look good. There's ten thousand Somalis here now, and more coming every day. Now it's your turn. Pop quiz time, Walker. What's to the north?"

"Ethiopia?" she replied uncertainly.

"Correct. A world-class shithole. This I know from personal experience. Famine, plus a war with Eritrea that killed half a million people over where to draw a line in the fucking desert." McClune indicated northwest. "And that way?"

"Sudan." That much Abena knew at least.

"Two for two, Walker, and to the southwest is the Congo. Rwanda as well, millions dead, murdered over nothing but religion, tribal identity and diamonds. Question three," he said, "and the most important one of all: tell me what you see down there?"

"Excuse me?" Abena was not quite sure she understood what he meant.

McClune swept his arm toward the camp. "You go to university, right? Down as opposed to up? It ain't a hard question."

"Ukiwa Refugee Camp, obviously," she said, not appreciating the sarcasm.

McClune made a sound like a buzzer. "Wrong at last, Walker.

First, Ukiwa isn't one camp; it's really a bunch of camps, ethnically divided, each made up of denizens of the lovely countries we just talked about. We keep them separated as best we can, or else they'd be killing each other faster than you could say 'boo.' It's like *Lord of the Flies* down there."

Abena knew that, though she disliked the reference. Back in Vancouver, when she had first signed up to spend a year in Ukiwa, Mr. Houghton had fully explained the camp's demographics. He'd also informed her that she would be placed in the Sudanese sector, part of a group of teachers working with the children of the largest ethnic group at Ukiwa.

"With the possible exception of Afghanistan, we're in the middle of the most dangerous, dysfunctional, screwed-up place on earth and Ukiwa's the epicentre. Heart of darkness, Walker. Heart of fucking darkness."

"Does that make you Marlow or Kurtz?" McClune wasn't the only one who could throw a literary reference into the conversation.

McClune lit another cigarette, took a long drag and, when he spoke again, his voice was soft, almost philosophic. "That is the question, isn't it? And speaking of questions, now that you know *where* you are, can you tell me *why* you're here?"

"You're the expert; why don't you tell me?" Abena's reply was sharp. Her head and belly ached and was in no mood for his games.

"You must be in law school or something with that smartass answer, but you won't get off that easy. Come on, you're a clever girl; why did you come here? Why did any of us come here?"

"To help these people? To make a difference?" Her response was simple but true.

McClune made another buzzing sound. "Wrong again. You started strong on this little quiz, but you're fading quickly. We're not here to help those poor bastards down there."

Abena was rapidly growing frustrated with this maddening conversation. "Like I said, Frank. You're the expert, you tell me."

"We are here as part of a great scam," McClune replied blithely.

"You, me and everyone else here is in on it." McClune looked right through her, his hazel eyes focusing on the sprawling mess below.

Abena studied him closely for the first time and realized she didn't have a clue how old McClune was. If someone were to say her new boss was in his fifties she would have believed it — but she would also have believed McClune to be only in his late thirties, his face worn down by the African sun, strong Kenyan cigarettes and years of hard living. "What are you talking about?"

McClune's voice carried no sarcasm as he spoke this time, just a mixture of sadness and anger. "All those people — Sudanese, Somali — arrive for a chance at a better life, while people like you and me come thinking we're gonna make a difference for them, change the world. You came here because you wanted to make a difference, wanted to save those poor fuckers, right?"

"Yes, of course, but I don't see —"

McClune cut her off. "The real tragedy of Africa is that neither side gets what they came for. We've been 'helping' Africa for more than two hundred years. Slaving, colonizing, exploring, stealing and proselytizing. Most of these countries are worse now than they've ever been because of us. It isn't help we bring. It never has been."

"That's a little cynical, don't you think?"

"Study your history and your economics before you lecture me about cynicism, Walker. Western aid's a fucking sham, no different than the Victorian missionaries who went out to tame the savages in the 1800s. We don't help. All we do is keep up the illusion that, some-how, things will get better. It's a joke. That's the con we've been pull-ing on these people for decades."

"There must be some good we are doing here." Abena refused to accept McClune's position. Perpetuating a fraud is not what she had signed up to do.

"There is no saving people here. This isn't some feel good story where we parachute in and fix things. There is no fucking fix. Look at the facts, Walker. There are about one hundred and fifty, maybe two hundred thousand people at Ukiwa. Nobody knows for sure, especially not the UN, no matter what they tell you. More refugees come into Kenya by the hundreds every day, over a porous border the army could never hope to seal off. They get warehoused in that mess down there and then wait. Some have been here for years, decades, hoping that some Western country will accept them."

"But they do get accepted. The USA, Canada. We all take refugees," Abena argued. "A few went to my high school in Vancouver."

"Grains of sand on a very large beach. Makes politicians look good, but that's about it. The United States took in about 50,000 refugees last year and the rest of the West accepted another 20,000. That's not even a quarter the population of Ukiwa. There are hundreds of camps and thirteen million refugees worldwide. Hell, Kenya has more refugees at any given time than all of the Western countries combined. At best, one in two hundred gets relocated. The rest of them wait, stay, hope and eventually die, while people like you show up for a few months then go home, patting themselves on the back for the great job we did. Do you know what 'Ukiwa' means, by the way?"

"No." Abena had assumed it was nothing more than a name on a map.

"The most common Kiswahili definitions are 'isolation,' 'desolation,' and 'loneliness.' They all fit because this shitty little corner of Kenya is all that and more, but there's another meaning as well. 'Abandonment.' That seems to me to be the most appropriate word. This is what this place is, after all: a place of abandonment for the most desperate people on Earth."

Listening to McClune speak, Abena felt deflated, crushed like the half-finished cigarette McClune ground into the dirt with his heel as they walked back to the Land Rover. "So why do you work for an NGO whose mission is to help? Why do you even . . ."

"Bother?" McClune finished the sentence for her. "That is the question isn't it, Walker. Promise me that if you ever figure it out, you'll let me know. I can't remember anymore."

7

FRANK MCCLUNE'S OFFICE was a small, cluttered space in the main Westshore administrative building. It was full of papers and books, the walls adorned with photos and pieces of African art. Walking into it for the first time, Abena didn't see any pictures of family, friends or loved ones important enough to McClune to occupy either wall space or a frame.

"We run a bunch of open-air classrooms in the camp," he said, sitting behind his desk, feet up on its top. "Yours is grandly called Westshore Five. Brand new and shiny. You've got forty students age twelve to seventeen waiting to start tomorrow. I drive you and the other teachers out to your schools first thing, then you get to work. You finish teaching at one, give the kiddies a little snack, then you wait for me to pick you up."

Abena held out her arms as McClune loaded her down with binders and books. "English and rudimentary math: ABC, 123. Not much else. Here are your lesson guides. Have you done any teaching before?"

"I was a volunteer tutor three hours a week back at UBC," she said.

That got McClune's attention. "Holy shit! The world-famous University of British Fucking Columbia! We have a scholar among us. How lucky can our little Sudanese kiddies be?"

"Mr. McClune," she said testily. "I'm in third-year economics; I'm sure I can handle . . ."

McClune interrupted. "At UBC, they taught you how to *handle* kids illiterate in their own language, hungry and suffering from post-traumatic stress, did they?"

She flushed. "No, but I'm sure that I . . ."

"And you also learned how to *handle* students willing to slit some-one's throat if it would get them an extra bag of beans? All of these kids have seen people die, and a good number of them have killed, so tell me, Miss Abena Walker, from the sainted campus of the University of British Columbia: have you *handled* children like that before?"

McClune ushered Abena out the door. "Of course you haven't, so go back to your room, read the fucking binders and be in the dining room for six-fifteen. But if they serve the chicken tonight, don't eat it. It doesn't seem to agree with you."

Dinner was a blur of names and faces. Roger Hughes introduced Abena to the other teachers and Westshore workers, and she spent the next hour picking at her rice, drinking water and listening to conversations about everyone's day in the camp.

At 7 o'clock, tired and still feeling sick, Abena excused herself, going to the latrine for the seventh time that day at least. Afterward she returned to her room, stretched out on the bed, and opened up one of the binders, reading until her light flickered off and the room fell dark.

10 o'clock.

Cool air stopped flowing through the vent as the rumble of the generator died. Abena looked out the window into darkness, the compound black, silent and still. Then she felt a gentle pressure in her bowels and was surprised she had anything left inside her guts at all.

She stood up, fumbled her way across the dark room to the desk, found the flashlight and made her way outside, hoping it would be her last trip to the toilets.

An animal — Abena didn't know what kind — yelped faintly in the distance. She stared up into the star-splashed night sky. The air was cool, surprisingly so. She almost wished she had a long-sleeve shirt instead of her T-shirt and shorts.

"Beautiful, aren't they? I could stare at the stars for hours." Abena had finished her business in the latrines and was returning to the dorms when she heard the voice. She turned quickly and shone the flashlight onto a young woman with long, black curly hair, sipping a beer, sitting in a plastic chair beside the building. Abena had seen her at dinner, had been introduced, but couldn't remember her name.

"Denise Martinez. Don't worry, you had twenty names to memorize and I had only one. You're Abena Walker. I hope I didn't startle you. Want a beer? Compound's supposed to be dry, but a girl's gotta do what she has to do, right? Besides, the rule isn't enforced. This place would fall apart without black market booze and the Kenyans know it."

"No, thanks." Although the cramping in her guts had subsided, Abena's system was fragile enough. God knows what alcohol would do to it.

"Your tummy, right? You hardly ate a thing at dinner."

"Food hasn't been agreeing with me much."

Martinez laughed. "I hear you. First week I got to Ukiwa, I was running to the bathroom every five minutes. Finally lost the ten extra pounds I'd been carrying around since college, though I wouldn't recommend the diet."

"'Better off not eating or drinking for a while.' That's what that jerk said. He's probably right, though I hate to admit it."

Martinez drained her beer and popped the lid on another. "Frank. Got the 'this whole thing is a scam' speech, did you?"

"This afternoon."

"Don't worry about it — part of a test, I think. Lets Frank see what kind of a person you are. He does it to everyone. Frank's OK."

"I find that a bit hard to believe."

"Don't mind Frank. You'll like him once you get past his bluff and bullshit. He's been in Africa for years, knows everyone in the camp, developed the entire program we use. Frank was some sort of genius back in Canada, I heard. Despite what he says, he does care about these people — at least he did once. He's seen a lot of bad shit. It leaves a mark on you, this place. Roger? That guy gives me the creeps. I'll take Frank over him any day."

Abena remembered Hughes' lingering gaze on her chest, and on that part could at least agree. "How long have you been here?"

"Six months. I've a teaching degree from NYU. I taught math in Harlem for two years — that was all I could handle. Sad to think that working in a refugee camp is preferable to public education in New York. You?"

"Third-year UBC. Economics. I'm taking a year off, trying to figure some things out."

"Well, you don't have to figure everything out tonight. It's gonna be a very long day tomorrow — first days always are. I'll see you at breakfast. Even if you're not hungry, try to eat something. Toast, even. That should be safe enough."

They left a little after seven the next morning, five teachers, all squeezed together in the Land Rover. The metal doors of the compound rolled open and Frank hit the gas, red plumes of dust flying up into the morning sky as they travelled down the road.

Frank turned left at the fork then stopped at the checkpoint, waiting for the young police officer on duty to take their names and raise the heavy iron gate blocking access to Ukiwa. Five minutes later they reached the edge of the camp.

As McClune said, there was no fence around Ukiwa itself, no clear border that delineated the start of Ukiwa or its end. Just a sprawling mess of tents, wood shacks and mud houses with tin roofs sprung up on the dry plain.

"This is the Sudanese sector," McClune said. "Official name's Ukiwa One. The Somalis are to the west in Ukiwa Two, the Ethiopians are east in Ukiwa Three. The sub-camps are separated by wadis — dry riverbeds and nothing else. In the rainy season when they're impassable, we don't get any problems between the groups. When they're dry? Angara and his police have some work to do. Some of our guests don't much care for each other."

There were no paved streets in Ukiwa Refugee Camp, no sidewalks or signs, but McClune seemed to know exactly where he was going as he dodged ramshackle buildings and the growing number of men and women and children who went about their business in Ukiwa — whatever that may have been. Many knew Frank by the looks of things, waved at him, calling out his name as they passed.

"Quite the fan club you have," said Abena.

McClune ignored the comment. "There's pressure on the UN to establish Ukiwa Four for the Congolese and the other nationalities who've started showing up, but Angara's not given his approval yet. Probably waiting for a little *rushwa*, a cash incentive from the international community to grease his chubby little palm. For now, the newcomers find space where they can."

McClune stopped in a clearing. Ahead was a simple wood frame with a large tarp providing shelter from the sun, already intolerably hot. Underneath the tarp were several rows of crude wooden tables. At the front stood an ancient chalkboard that would have looked right at home in a nineteenth-century, one-room schoolhouse. Above it all, Westshore and Canadian flags hung limply on a crude flagpole.

"This is me, Westshore One," said a slight, ginger-haired woman. Gillian Probin, a thirty-something Brit from Luton, on the southern outskirts of London, climbed out and waved goodbye. Frank sped off. Denise Martinez was next to go at Westshore Two.

"Good luck, Abena," she said, gathering up her binders. "You're going to do just fine. Tell me all about it when you get back."

The pattern repeated itself two more times until just Frank and Abena were left in the Land Rover. "I'll drop you off then go back and deliver the teachers who work in the Somali and Ethiopian zones. Five schools in each zone with staggered start times since I'm the only taxi driver on the Westshore payroll. Ninety minutes to take you all to the schools, ninety to pick you up. I requested another driver to help with the trips, but Hughes said no. Something about tightening budgets. I was surprised he had the money to hire you and open a new school in the first place, but it looks good to the board of directors, I guess. Houghton is probably hoping he'll get some media out of it. Fucking reporters like to come here and do happy stories."

"Fifteen schools in a camp of two hundred thousand people doesn't seem like a lot."

"True, but we're not the only game in town, Walker. IRC, Norwegian Refugee Council, the Kenyan government and a few other NGOs either build schools or staff them. Maybe twenty percent of the kids in Ukiwa attend one school or the other. It isn't much but it's a start."

McClune pulled to a stop. "Well? What do you think? I finished construction two days ago. Newest of the lot. A special school for our scholar from UBC."

Westshore Five. The covering over the newly built tables and benches was fresh and white, unlike the tattered and weatherworn tarps of the older schools. Above it, the maple leaf and the Westshore flags, both new and crisp, dangled on a new-cut pole.

New sawdust sat on top of the dust, not yet mixed in by the boys and girls who stood expectantly next to a brick-walled church with a large white cross on the metal roof thirty metres away, their eyes fixed on the Land Rover.

On Abena.

"Your adoring public," said Frank, giving her a box full of pencils, notebooks, binders and granola bars. "Lunch. Don't feed them until school ends or half will disappear. Don't kid yourself: they're here for the food, not the high-quality teaching we provide. This might be the only meal some of them get today."

Abena's stomach was tied in knots, from nerves, the after-effects of the chicken dinner in Sigor, or a combination of both. She climbed out of the Land Rover, arms full of notebooks and pencils. McClune noticed her discomfort. Pills and a large bottle of water appeared from under the driver's seat. "Take these. With a bit of luck, they'll bung you up and you won't have to use the camp latrines."

McClune pointed to a metal-walled, square construction. "Those are the camp latrines if you're desperate, but between the heat and the flies and the smell, you don't want to go anywhere near those things. Take it from me; wait to go potty until you get back."

McClune slipped the Land Rover into gear and spun away. "Teach 'em good," he said. "I'll be back around 1:30 or so. Heart of darkness, Walker, remember that. Don't go wandering off. Stay at the school until I get you. Some of the locals ain't very friendly."

Abena walked to the front of the open-air classroom, one hand in the other to prevent them from shaking. Despite McClune's pills, her stomach twisted as she watched the students, in twos and threes, cautiously approach, silently taking their seats on the new benches.

A dozen, fifteen, twenty-five and more appeared out of the bustle of the camp. Within ten minutes, the outdoor classroom was crammed with serious-looking boys and girls, dressed in an astonishing assortment of clothing.

Most were barefoot. Some of the older girls wore skirts, their heads covered with colourful scarves, but the bulk of the children were in T-shirts with the names of small-town Little League teams, American elementary schools and professional sports logos from cities in Europe and North America printed across the chests.

With the mercury rising steadily north of forty degrees, Abena stared at a young boy wearing a Vancouver Canucks shirt. It was very strange for Abena to see a boy in northern Kenya wear such a familiar thing, a boy who'd never seen ice, and most likely didn't have a clue what hockey, a Canuck or even Vancouver was. She mustered her confidence and began, trying to control the shaking in her voice. "Boys and girls, welcome. My name is Miss Walker. I'm very excited to be your teacher. How are you doing today?"

Silence greeted the question. Abena fought a growing dread that none of the students spoke English. She had assumed they did. Abena suddenly felt afraid, but running away was her only other option, so she took a brand-new piece of chalk from the supplies McClune gave her and squared up to the chalkboard.

She began to print the alphabet in neat, upper case letters, the chalk squeaking on the surface of the board. Abena's stomach cramped as she spoke, her throat dry, her voice cracking.

"Let's start with the basics then." On the bottom bubble of the letter B the chalk snapped, a piece clattering off the board, landing in the dirt. Flushing, Abena quickly picked it up, carrying on until she reached J. She faced the students. "Who'd like to tell me what these letters are?"

More silence. Wide eyes. Closed mouths. This was not going at all as she had planned. "This is A," she said pleadingly. "Can anyone tell me what the next letter is?"

"OK. What about . . ." she belched, her stomach yielding to the pressure. It was unexpected and loud and Abena covered her mouth abruptly, even more humiliated than she'd been after her first encounter with McClune when he had waited for her outside the toilets in the compound.

For a few seconds, the silence continued, until a little boy in a blue tank top sitting in the second row burped as well. "*Mbweu!*"

The dam of silence burst, and the entire class erupted in laughter. Though the girls refrained, most of the boys were now burping as well, volunteering the names of other bodily functions in more than passable English, and in other languages she assumed were Dinka, as well as Kiswahili.

Abena laughed too. Seizing the opportunity, she quickly wrote "burp" on the board then handed out notebooks and pencils to eager hands. Soon, forty brand-new pencils scratched away eagerly onto crisp white paper.

"A, Miss." A tall boy with sharp, angular features and a long, slightly hooked nose spoke shyly as he raised a tentative hand into the air. "The first letter of the alphabet is A. Everybody knows that."

By the time Abena reached F, the entire class was reciting the letters in unison, copying them down in their notebooks, pencils held in awkward grips. It was a magical moment, but then the class finished the alphabet and quiet returned. The students looked at Abena with increased interest, curious what their brand-new teacher was about to do next.

She'd read McClune's binders, had created what she thought was a brilliant lesson plan, but everything Abena had prepared seemed to have left her brain. Not sure exactly what possessed her to do it, Abena took the chalk and drew a simple picture of a laptop computer on the blackboard. "Does anyone know what this is?"

Judging by the stillness, nobody did, until a young round-faced girl with skin noticeably lighter than the other students sitting next to the boy who knew the letter A raised her hand. "A television, Miss?"

"No. It is a computer." The girl was corrected by the boy next to her.

"Yes," Abena said. "It is a computer. What is your name, young man? How old are you?"

"Peter. Peter Chol. I am seventeen."

The girl turned angrily to him and spit a few words in Dinka. The boy glared back. "*Deng*, Miss. My name is Peter Chol *Deng*."

Peter Chol Deng stood and addressed his classmates. "*Kompyuta* in Kiswahili." The other students murmured in understanding. "They know what it is, but your picture . . ."

The girl hissed at Peter again. "I'm sorry," he said, "I did not mean to cause insult."

"No need to apologize. Your English is very good. And you're right, I was never the best artist."

The boy looked over at the girl, a slightly victorious look on his face. "Our mother taught us how to read English."

Abena held out the chalk. "Peter, why don't you draw some things on the board the class knows?"

Engage students. Build on what they have experienced. Having them participate in the lessons is one of the hallmarks of good teaching. At least according to McClune. He'd written down those words, somewhere in one of the binders he'd given her. With a studious look on his face, and with his classmates cheering him on, Peter Deng slowly stepped forward and took the offered chalk.

His first few lines were tentative, uncertain things, but as he drew, the boy increased his strokes in both speed and confidence. The stick of chalk streaked quickly across the board, a small cloud of white dust falling to the ground. A moment later he stepped back to survey his work. "What is this?" he asked the class.

"AK-47." Thirty-nine voices responded as one.

"And this?" A few more quick chalk strokes and a devastatingly familiar object appeared.

"Grenade."

Peter drew one horrible thing after the other. On the board, a chalk plane dropped bombs onto small chalk people drawn crudely on the ground, some whole, but most in pieces.

It went on, one horror after the other, the children listing the names as casually as if they were reciting their multiplication tables.

Another half-dozen chalk abominations soon came to life on the board. When he was done, Peter handed the chalk back to Abena. "You said to draw things they know. These are things they know."

Abena dismissed the class shortly before one, drained physically and emotionally from the heat and the lesson. She'd taken McClune's pills, but desperate to avoid a trip to the camp latrine, she'd not drunk nearly as much water as she should, and her head pounded from dehydration.

The students said their goodbyes, took the offered snacks then drifted away into the camp, back to whatever it was they did until the sky fell dark on another day in Ukiwa. Soon, only two children remained, standing patiently before Abena.

"Thank you, Miss," said Peter.

"You are a good teacher," said the girl. "My name is Alexandra Deng. I am thirteen years old. Will we see you tomorrow?"

"Yes, of course, Alexandra. Tomorrow."

Nodding, Alexandra took her brother's hand. They left together, walking past the church until they disappeared into the sprawl.

Abena watched them go, not hearing the Land Rover approach. "Just the ABCs eh, Walker?" McClune stood staring at the chalkboard.

"He just started drawing, Frank. The things these kids have seen . . . I just couldn't imagine . . ."

McClune wiped the board clean then picked up her box of supplies and deposited it on the back seat. "These things happen in Africa," he said with a gentleness Abena hadn't heard before. "It's been a long day, Walker. Let's get you home."

8

WILLIAM WAS DRUNK again. William drank often, more so now than ever. He used drugs as well: *bangi, kaht* and any number of other things that could be smoked or chewed. Victoria preferred him on the drugs; they calmed him, and he didn't hit her then. But today he was drinking the strong homemade *chang'aa* found everywhere in this place, brewed in buckets from the water, millet and maize provided by the UN.

"I'll teach you to respect me!" William bellowed, shoving her hard against the metal door of their mud hovel. At first, Victoria thought it was because William had found out about the school. He hadn't, though. No, today Victoria was guilty of another affront, imagined or otherwise, and would be punished for it. Twenty years of broken bones, knocked-out teeth and bruises bore witness to that.

In that time? Lost parents, dead friends in the wastelands, Azana Refugee Camp, and Mary, vanished in the darkness of the riverbank. And for the past fourteen years? Ukiwa.

A neither-here-nor-there place. That's how the camp was described to her by a Congolese man she met years ago when she had first arrived. He was educated, that man, a college student forced to flee his homeland because he opposed their president. He was a person with the qualities the UN looked for in resettlement. He was a man who deserved better than life in a refugee camp, they thought. He was chosen and left Africa years ago for Belgium, to a new life far from here.

But Victoria?

When she first arrived, Victoria had held out hope the Westerners would help, but after all this time she had come to learn that it was not hope they offered, not at all. Instead of leaving? Victoria remained.

William punched her in the face again. She stumbled through the open door and fell out onto the street, landing hard in the dust. People watched but quickly turned away, pretending not to see. Her husband was well known here. Nobody trifled with him.

Almost nobody.

"Mama!" Victoria's daughter cried out. Peter and Alexandra were home to witness her sprawled on the ground, bleeding from her nose, clutching her stomach, with their father standing over her, his fists clenched.

Alexandra ran to Victoria, pushing past William. She was rash and impetuous like Victoria in her own youth. Alexandra ignored her father's threats, falling on top of Victoria as if her little body could stop him through sheer force of will. William laughed then stepped back to take in the scene. From out of his trousers, he drew his pistol. He pointed it at Victoria. Alexandra screamed as Victoria covered her head with her hands. But he did not shoot.

Peter hung back. His father would call that cowardice but, despite what William believed, Peter was no weakling, Victoria knew. Instead, he was cautious and sensitive with a strength about him he hadn't yet discovered.

"Will you not help your mother?" William looked at his son, daring him to move with his cold eyes, pistol pointed at Victoria.

Peter had been reading a book he'd picked up from one NGO or the other. He put it down and moved slowly toward her, but Victoria knew all too well what would happen if he intervened, if he took the offered bait.

"Stay where you are." Most likely, William wouldn't hurt his daughter, but Peter was another story, and Victoria would not be responsible for that. And so, Peter remained still. William waved the gun lazily in his hand then shoved it down the back of his trousers.

"Coward," he spat with contempt. "When I was your age, I was a soldier, a warrior, and you read fairy tales?"

Peter's face flushed with anger. His hands clenched tightly on the paperback, but Victoria held up her hand, warning Peter again to stay away. After all, the offence, imagined or otherwise, was Victoria's. And she would bear the consequences for them all.

9

AS THE WEEKS passed, Abena settled into the rhythm of Ukiwa and started to feel almost at home. Students came and went from her class, but most remained and she learned their names, their personalities, their desires. At the end of each day, she was tired, but deeply happy with the choice she'd made to come to Kenya, despite missing her mother desperately, a feeling not mitigated by the occasional phone call or email home when the sporadic Westshore network chose to cooperate.

Denise and several other teachers were soon her good friends. Even Frank McClune, with his obnoxious cigarettes, stubble, and cynical affectations, became tolerable. Abena had to grudgingly admit McClune knew what he was doing: taking care of repairs at the schools, ensuring the teachers had enough supplies and providing remarkably helpful advice — solicited or otherwise. For the first time in her life, Abena felt truly connected to something great, something important.

"OK, everyone, listen closely as I tell you your homework." The chalk scratched over the board as the children groaned good naturedly at the thought of the assignment. "If you were an animal, what kind would you be, and why? Due tomorrow, full sentences and proper grammar. We've been working on both for weeks. You can do it."

Abena dismissed the class. The students evaporated into the camp as she tidied up and waited for Frank. Then she saw the notebook sitting on the tabletop. She knew whose it was before even reading *Peter Deng* carefully printed across the cover. She picked it up and quickly scanned the camp, hoping Peter and his sister hadn't gone too far.

There was no sign of them in the warren of wood and dirt shacks near the school. Abena was about to tuck the book into her bag and return it to the boy in the morning when she paused.

Peter Deng was her best student, extremely diligent about his work. He never failed to complete any assignment and frequently helped the others with their own work. To not have his own book, to not write the short paragraph down in his neat, methodical printing, would be devastating for him.

Abena looked at her watch: 1:03 p.m. McClune would be at least twenty minutes. Abena didn't have a clue where Peter and Alexandra lived, but she knew they arrived each morning from somewhere behind the church.

They'd only been gone five minutes at most. How far could they travel in that time? Abena paused for another few seconds, drew a breath then hurried off into the camp.

Thirty seconds later, the wooden cross on the church's rooftop, her beacon back to familiar ground, disappeared. Not one hundred metres from the school, she felt lost in the maze of shacks that pressed closely together, their sheet metal roofs searing in the early afternoon sun.

There was no wind. The clothes on the washing lines strung between the huts dangled limply in the stifling air. Uncertain of where to go, Abena stopped to find some semblance of bearings. As she did, a feeling of unease grew in her stomach.

Abena was acutely aware of the glances and glares from the knots of men who lounged in the entranceways of nearby houses or stood huddled together on the street. *Heart of darkness, Walker. Heart of fucking darkness. Some of the natives ain't so friendly.*

Most women in the camp, Muslim, Christian or otherwise, wore dresses and covered their heads with scarves or hijabs. Abena's exposed hair and khaki Westshore outfit were hardly scandalous by North American standards, but certainly something no female resident of Ukiwa would dare to wear.

She approached an old woman in a ragged dress and dusty black headscarf. "Peter Deng? Do you know where Peter and Alexandra Deng live?"

The woman grunted quizzically then grinned, the few teeth in her mouth black and rotting. She said something Abena didn't understand then shuffled away.

1:10.

McClune had insisted above all else that Abena not wander off, but she had done just that. She had maybe fifteen minutes to find Peter, return the book and get back to school before he found out, but she saw no sign of the children, and she had almost run out of time.

About to give up and return to the school, Abena finally saw the Dengs, fifty metres down the dirt street, a tall gangly figure walking side by side with a young girl.

1:12. Just enough time.

"Peter!" she shouted, setting off in a jog. "Wait!"

10

FRANK MCCLUNE FLIPPED the two small boys a ten-shilling coin each then asked again, this time in more than passable Dinka instead of Kiswahili, "The teacher? Do you remember now?"

McClune had spotted the boys — impish-looking things maybe eight years old, and not among the lucky few attending school — playing soccer by the church, kicking a makeshift ball made of rags and twine.

They had been less than helpful until McClune produced the money and spoke to them in their own language. McClune understood. People here learned from a very early age that it took the right sort of persuasion to get things done.

Their minds now properly motivated, the boys answered the question. The taller one grinned, tucked the coin into his pocket and pointed past the church into the depths of the camp. "That way."

"When?" McClune gave them both another ten-shilling coin.

"Not long," said the other. No doubt they were as unfamiliar with time as they were with reading. *Not long* could well have meant one minute or one hour, but it was as good an answer as McClune was likely to get. He slammed the Land Rover into gear then sped off in the direction indicated.

McClune was early for the pickup and had waited in the Land Rover for a while, unconcerned. He had first assumed that, despite his advice against it, Walker's stomach had forced her to make use of the camp's latrines. He had a smoke and waited, but by the time he threw the butt on the ground McClune realized that his rookie teacher was not in the toilets after all, but somewhere else entirely.

It was hard for McClune to figure out if he was angry, worried, scared or a stew of all three. Aid workers were generally left alone by the residents, but robbery, rape, kidnapping and even murder were common occurrences in Ukiwa.

Walker wasn't hard on the eyes, he had to admit, despite her princess attitude, and it was far too easy for him to picture some of the men in the camp taking a liking to her.

That would be very bad. People, especially women and children, vanished here on a regular basis, disappearing into the dust and the sand, gone forever. But so far not one of them had been a Westerner — or anybody of any nationality under McClune's care. He was determined to keep it that way.

McClune shifted hard into third gear then reached into the glovebox. It was an old semi-automatic pistol, a 9mm Browning he'd managed to get from a friend in the Kenya Defence Forces years ago.

The police in charge of Ukiwa strictly forbade civilians to carry guns in the camp, especially foreigners, and Westshore itself had strict rules against arms as well, but McClune had learned from personal experience that some rules were meant to be broken — if you wanted to stay alive.

11

A WOMAN TUMBLED out of the shack, landing hard on the dusty ground in front of her. A man followed her, kicking and shouting. As he did, Abena's surprise gave way to anger. "Hey! Leave her alone!" she cried without thinking.

Abena watched as Alexandra hurled herself protectively on top of the woman. She realized she must be her mother, just as she grasped the identity of the man assaulting her. Peter and Alexandra's father. It had to be, or at least the man their mother was with now.

The man looked up at the sound of Abena's voice. He left the mom curled up on the ground then stormed over to Abena. "This is not your business!" he screamed in English, waving a pistol.

"I'm sorry," Abena stammered, quickly realizing the seriousness of her situation. She held the notebook out in front of her like a shield. "I didn't mean anything. Peter left this at school. I was just trying . . ."

The man smacked the book from her hand and pointed the gun in her face.

"You sent them to school?" he spat at the woman lying on the ground. She said nothing in response, although Abena could see the defiance in her eyes. He turned his attention back to Abena. She could hardly breathe, her fear threatening to engulf her.

"This is Sudan business!" Abena picked up the sour stink of alcohol on his breath as his spittle sprayed over her. "Fucking American! This is not your concern!"

"She didn't know. We're leaving." McClune said, standing a metre or so behind Abena, his voice calm and measured. Then he said something to the man in Dinka. Although Abena didn't understand the words, she'd never been more grateful to hear a familiar voice in her entire life.

The man lowered his pistol slightly, the shock of a white man speaking his language taking him off guard, no doubt.

McClune eased over, put his hand gently around Abena's waist and manoeuvred her backward toward the Land Rover. "Like I said, we're leaving."

Before Abena could move, the man's left hand shot toward her neck. She let out a frightened squeal as McClune's own hand slipped behind his back, fingers clutching the gun tucked into his jeans. The man snatched her pendant and pulled, the gold length digging painfully into Abena's skin before it gave way. The man lowered his pistol but still held it tightly in his right hand, ready for use at any second.

He looked at the jewellery contemptuously. "You think because you're black, you know Africa?" His English was thick and halting. "Go home. You are nothing but a slave-boat nigger, no better than a *mzungu*. Go back to America!"

"What's your name?" Abena said, not to the man but to the children's mother. She knew she should be scared, should run away, but instead she stood, watching the woman struggling for breath against the side of the hut, her children standing on either side of her like pillars.

"Jesus Christ, Walker! Shut the fuck up and get in!"

"What can I do to help you?" Abena said, struggling as Frank hauled her roughly into the Land Rover.

The woman lowered her head. "There is nothing you can do for me. There's nothing anyone can do for me."

McClune turned the key and the engine jumped to life.

Suddenly, Peter cried out. "Miss! I would be an eagle!"

"What? What did you say?" Abena strained to hear the boy over the racing engine.

"Our homework!" Peter shouted as they sped off. "I would be an eagle so I could fly my family as far away from here as possible!"

Two minutes later McClune slammed on the brakes and threw the pistol back into the glovebox, removing in its place a small silver flask. "What the hell were you thinking?" he said after taking a long drink. "I tell you not to leave your school, ever, under any circumstances. What do you do? Go for a little walkabout and end up pissing off an SPLA member in his own house!"

"SPLA?" Abena rubbed her neck, still burning where the chain snapped against her skin.

"Sudan People's Liberation Army. Guerrillas, freedom fighters, terrorists, saints, murderers, heroes. Who they are depends on who you ask. That asshole? He's probably killed more people than you and I have ever met. You're lucky you weren't one of them."

"Guerrilla? How can the UN let him into Ukiwa? And how can he have a gun?" The memory of the pistol pointed at her face was something Abena would live with for a very long time.

"Walker, haven't you learned a goddamn thing since you got here? That guy and ten thousand like him come to Ukiwa for some R & R, then round up new recruits and sneak back across the border to carry on their war in Sudan." McClune took another long pull from the flask. "*Let him* into Ukiwa? We're twenty miles from the Sudanese border. Pricks like him come and go as they please. And you risk getting shot because of some stupid notebook?"

"He hit her, Frank, I saw it. He hit her then he kicked her and nobody did anything about it." Tears welled in Abena's eyes. She'd been threatened with a weapon, robbed and had watched a man physically abuse his wife in front of her children, children she cared about.

Abena was upset and the reprimand from McClune, although deserved, didn't sit well. "Then he called me a . . ." The word was too ugly for her to spit out.

"Nigger. He called you a nigger. Sticks and stones, Walker. Get over it. You could have been raped, shot, buried in a hole in the desert. Instead, you lost a necklace and had your feelings hurt. You got off lucky."

"And the other thing he called me?"

"*Mzungu?* Means white person in Kiswahili." McClune was calming down, breathing easier, looking as if he could talk without feeling the urge to strangle Abena himself.

"To guys like him, you're no different than me, and he couldn't give a fuck about Canadian or American either. Of course nobody did anything about it," McClune added, as if she were stupid. "Why would they? Women here are like cattle, a commodity to be bought, sold and traded. Nobody did anything to help her because it's perfectly acceptable for a man to treat his wife like that here."

"But in front of her children? I know those kids, Frank. They're sensitive, kind. What sort of damage is he inflicting on them? There are police in the camp, government administrators, the UN. Surely the camp director, somebody, should do something?"

McClune laughed bitterly. "The camp director? The police? Are you fucking kidding me? Short of an armed insurrection or riot, those assholes consider most things that happen to the people in the camp 'domestic matters.' Not their worry. The UN and the Kenyans certainly know what's going on with the guerrillas. They won't, or can't, do much to stop it. This entire continent runs on money and guns. The SPLA has plenty of both and some of it makes its way into the camp director's pocket."

"So that's it then? That's just how it is?" Abena put her face in her hands. The last person she wanted to see her cry was Frank McClune.

"Yes," he said with finality. "That's exactly how it is. The big con, remember? What you saw? It happens every day. We don't get involved and we don't interfere. That's how we get to stay and do our jobs."

12

NOT TWO HOURS after returning to Westshore's headquarters, Abena was summoned to Roger Hughes' office. "Come in please, Ms. Walker," he said. "We've been expecting you."

The "we" referred to the Westshore director, Frank McClune and two other men Abena had never seen before. Hughes sat ramrod straight in a chair beside his desk, his normal spot taken up by a Kenyan in a black suit. In the back of the room, McClune stood stone-faced next to a monstrously large man in a crisp khaki uniform, polished black boots and a blue beret over his bald head. The Kenya National Police wore blue berets, Abena remembered, one of the many things David Ndereba had told her on the long drive from Nairobi.

The man at the desk was in his sixties, short-cropped hair tinged grey, face framed by thick black eyeglasses. Several gold rings filled up the thick fingers on his hands. A red handkerchief was tucked and folded precisely into his left breast pocket, matching the silk tie knotted around the collar of his starched white shirt.

"Mr. Angara here wanted to talk to you, Abena," said Hughes tersely, as Richard Angara, Director of Ukiwa Camp Operations, Kenyan Department for Refugee Affairs stood up and directed her to an empty chair beside his.

"Ms. Walker." His voice was deep and measured. "I heard that you had a little encounter with one of the camp residents today. Is that correct?"

Word certainly had travelled quickly. "Yes, Sir. One of my students forgot his notebook. I was just returning it to him."

"I was just apologizing to Mr. Angara about that," said Hughes. "You were under strict orders to stay at your school and wait for Frank to pick you up, were you not? Or was Mr. McClune not clear enough with you on that point?" If the comment bothered McClune, it was hard to tell from the blank look on his face.

"Let's not get too upset about it, Roger. Diligent, commendable even, returning a schoolboy his lost book, don't you think? You must be a good teacher, are you not, Ms. Walker?"

"I suppose I try to be." Expecting to be chastised, Angara's response caught Abena off guard.

"Indeed. And you go to work every day and teach our little Sudanese guests their sums and their letters?"

"Yes, Sir."

Angara beamed. "And when you're done for the day you head back to your safe little compound, have a nice glass of lemonade with your fellow teachers and feel good about the difference you have made in the lives of your students, do you not?" The director's smile vanished. "But what you don't do is interfere and create unrest and unhappiness in my camp. With all our guests, you can understand how difficult it can be to keep the peace at Ukiwa, let alone when people meddle in things that don't concern them, can you not?"

"Yes, Sir," she stammered. "I didn't mean to do anything, but he pulled a gun and . . ."

"You have to understand the reality of this place," said Angara. "We house more than one hundred and fifty thousand refugees from half a dozen conflict zones. It's unfortunate, but sometimes weapons find their way into this camp. We are aware that the SPLA has a presence, but as long as they don't cause discord, we give them a little space."

Angara looked to the back of the room, to the large police officer standing beside McClune. "But when they, or any other group, get a little too ... exuberant, Chief Inspector Obanda here reminds them they are guests of the Kenyan government, and that they need to follow our rules."

Angara leaned over Abena, his large body nearly enveloping her. "And you must also follow our rules, Ms. Walker. After all, the NGOs are guests here, too, and should you forget that again, I'm afraid that the chief inspector will have to remind you, and his tone will be far less civil than mine. Then, when he's finished what will be a most uncomfortable conversation for you, you'll be removed from Ukiwa and sent out of Africa."

Angara laughed at his own remark. "*Out of Africa*. Very funny. A film about a *mzungu* woman in Kenya, correct, Roger?"

Hughes chuckled weakly. "Yes, indeed. Quite funny. Ms. Walker? Do you understand?"

Abena certainly did. "Yes, Sir. I'm sorry. It won't happen again."

Angara walked toward the door. "Excellent! Thank you for this little chat. Now please feel free to go about your marking or whatever else it is you fine young teachers do in your free time."

"Frank," Hughes said, "escort Ms. Walker back to her room and keep a better eye on her in the future; I will not tolerate any further incidents. The only contact your teacher is to have with the residents of the camp is in her capacity as teacher — at her school."

Dismissed, Frank turned to leave, but Chief Inspector Obanda blocked his way, refusing to move, standing as still as if he'd been carved from marble. McClune squeezed past his large frame, dragging his feet over the police officer's highly shined toes, leaving long scuff marks in the polished leather.

"Looks like your footwear needs some attention, Chief," McClune said innocently, following Abena out the door. "Guess I'm not the only one who needs to keep a better eye on things."

Obanda glared, the vein in his neck ticking. "I'll not forget that, McClune," he said coldly. "You'd best be more careful where you tread in the future."

McClune hurried to catch up to Abena. She felt as if she were about to throw up and wanted nothing more than to get back to her room without talking to anyone, especially McClune, but he closed the gap between them quickly and grabbed her by the shoulder. "Wait. We need to talk."

She spun around angrily. "Why? So you can say I told you so?"

"So I can say sorry. I never gave you credit for what you did. Standing up to that asshole? That took guts. I don't think I'd have had the balls."

Despite herself, Abena managed a weak smile. "What would you have done?"

"Not gone into the camp and got in the face of an SPLA guerrilla for starters."

"But didn't you do just that when you came looking for me?"

McClune shrugged. "Moment of weakness. Plus, it's a pain in the ass to recruit new teachers. Protecting my investments, that's all."

"Why do you have a gun, Frank? Weapons are forbidden in Ukiwa Camp, remember?"

"Protection. Hyenas, snakes, sometimes lions. It's a jungle out there."

"And for saving stupid girls. Thank you. I'm sorry for not listening to you." Both gratitude and an apology were overdue, Abena knew. McClune had had a gun stuck in his face because of her, after all.

"Apology accepted, Walker," said McClune before he walked away. "Just stay away from that family. You got off lucky this time; it won't work out so well again, I promise you that."

Going into town was Denise Martinez's idea, but the thought of some drinks and a few hours out of the camp seemed a very good one to Abena as well. There was only one bar that catered to Westerners in Ukiwa town, and it was packed. A handful of locals were there, but mostly the crowd was made up of young aid workers cutting loose.

Old rock music pumped out of the jukebox. Smoke from countless cigarettes curled to the ceiling, a thick haze filling the bar, people appearing and disappearing like ghosts. Abena and Denise drank Tusker at a small table not far from a long stool-lined counter full of customers.

Two Swedes in their late twenties joined Abena and Denise. Medical students doing an internship with a Catholic agency that distributed TB vaccinations in the camp, they said. Lars and Henrik. They spoke English, but with the music and the noise, Abena could easily have misheard their names. What they wanted, however, was obvious.

Both were very drunk and very friendly. Denise, who'd had more to drink than Abena thought wise, had somehow ended up on Henrik's lap, giggling at something he said. Lars brushed up uncomfortably close to Abena, his hand stroking her arm.

"The guys aren't going back to camp tonight. They've booked a couple of hotel rooms in town," said Denise excitedly when the Swedes excused themselves to go to the bathroom. "They want us to party with them. They promised they'd get us back in time for work tomorrow. Do you want to go?"

"No, not really." Abena knew what *party* meant and wanted no part of it. Despite the day, all she had managed to drink was two beers. She was exhausted, wanting nothing more than to go home and sleep.

The Swedes returned from the toilet and stood expectantly by the table. "You girls ready?"

"Abena?" From the look on her face and the way she threw her arm around Henrik, it was clear that Denise wanted to carry on the party very much.

"No. You go, have fun."

"You sure?" said Lars. He was a good-looking guy, Abena had to admit; they both were, with white teeth, corn-blond hair and skin toasted brown by the equatorial sun. Handsome or not, Abena wasn't interested.

Denise stumbled to her feet, arm tightly wrapped around her new friend's waist. "I'll see you tomorrow then?"

Abena gave her a hug. "First thing. And Denise; be careful."

"Don't worry, I'll look after her," said Henrik, a promise that made Denise giggle again as she kissed him, obviously looking forward to being taken care of. Denise shouted one last farewell and blew a kiss to Abena as she and her new friend vanished in the smoke toward the exit door.

Lars quickly got over his disappointment and hurried off to a table full of Australian nurses, looking for someone else to party with. Abena didn't know whether to laugh or feel disgusted. In any event, it was time to go.

If she left now, a five-dollar ride on a *boda boda* motorcycle taxi would get her back to the compound just in time for curfew, but before she could leave, a man at the bar stood up, walked unsteadily over and sat down uninvited in the chair recently evacuated by Denise. "Good call not leaving with those guys, Walker."

Frank McClune took a deep sip from a glass full of honey-coloured liquid. "They may work for a Catholic charity," he said, his words slurred, "but believe me, those two ain't altar boys."

"And you would know?" Between the crowd, the noise and the smoke, Abena hadn't recognized McClune, his back to her at the bar. She wasn't sure if she was happy to see him or not.

"You do this job long enough, you get to know people."

"And how long is that?"

McClune held the glass in front of his eyes for a second or so then shot the contents down his throat. "Honestly? I can't remember anymore."

A waiter appeared with another glass and a bottle of Hunter's Choice, the closest thing to whisky the Kenyans made. He looked at Abena then spoke to McClune in rapid-fire Kiswahili.

McClune laughed, shook his head then said something in return. The waiter seemed to find the comment quite hilarious, judging by the response. He winked at Abena, put the empty glass down, slapped McClune heartily on the back then went about his business.

"Thomas is a friend. He wanted to know how an over-the-hill old dog like myself managed to find such an attractive young girlfriend — and one the right colour, as well. I told him you were a co-worker, not a girlfriend, said you don't have a boyfriend because you don't do as you're told and you talk too damn much."

"Did you? I see that you're as charming drunk as you are sober. Have you always been such a jerk?"

McClune filled the empty glass and held it out. "If you're going to insult me then you must have at least one drink, Walker."

"Fair enough. I supposed I do owe you for today." She took a small sip and grimaced — the stuff that McClune tossed back so easily tasted like diesel.

McClune filled his glass again. "In answer to your question? My ex-wife would say I was always an asshole, but that Africa really brought it out in me."

"Your ex-wife?" Abena felt triumphant to have wheedled something so personal out of McClune. In the entire time she'd been at Ukiwa, she'd not learned a single thing about him.

"More of a memory than anything else. I've been in this shithole for twenty years." His words were slurred. Abena could tell McClune had been drinking for a while now.

"If you're so cynical, why stay?" Instead of answering, McClune reached into his shirt pocket and pulled out a folded piece of paper. He slowly opened it and placed it carefully, almost reverently, on the tabletop.

It was a page cut from a magazine, a very familiar picture of a small child huddled on the ground, a large vulture standing expectantly, patiently behind her. McClune saw the recognition on Abena's face.

"You know this picture." It wasn't a question.

Her voice was barely a whisper. "That photo's why I'm here."

"What do you *really* know about it, Walker?"

"A journalist saw the child making her way to a refugee camp. The bird was standing behind her when he took the picture. He won a Pulitzer Prize, I think."

"He did at that." McClune took another drink, a larger one this time before he spoke again. "Photographer's name was Kevin Carter, nice kid, South African. Met him a few times, had drinks with him in this very place. This same fucking table, I think."

McClune's eyes were locked onto the old, creased page. "Carter took the photo in 1993, outside Ayod, in southern Sudan. If you think things are bad here, you should have seen that fucking place. 'Famine Triangle' they called it, that part of the world. NGOs were there, helping the UN run feeding centres. The kid in the picture was exhausted, running from famine. God knows what happened to her family."

"But he helped the child, right? Carter? I tried to find out what happened to her, but I couldn't."

McClune played with his glass, the golden liquid swirling slowly. "No, Ms. Walker, he did not. Kevin Carter took the picture, chased the vulture away and then left. Nobody knows just what happened to that kid, except maybe Carter, and he's not about to say. A couple of months after he took the photo, Carter put one end of a hose onto the exhaust pipe of his car and the other into the window. He was thirty-three. Officially, his death was ruled a suicide, but it was really Africa that killed him." McClune picked up the photo, his eyes distant. "We all have them, those of us who've spent enough time here."

"Have what?"

"Our own Kevin Carter moments."

McClune folded the paper carefully and slipped it back into his pocket. He drained his glass and poured another. "In 1994, Westshore sent me from Ukiwa to Kigali. Houghton had the brilliant idea of educating kids before they ended up in a refugee camp, but within a couple of months things went fucking crazy there. Guys on state radio were coordinating the massacres of the Tutsis, gangs of kids walked the streets with machetes, chopping up anyone they saw. Everyone was trying to get the fuck out. Almost nobody was doing a thing to stop it."

"You were in Rwanda?" Abena wasn't yet a teenager when the genocide occurred, but she knew very well the significance of the name and the date.

"Westerners were fucking useless except for Dallaire and a couple hundred troops. He begged for backup, to stop what he knew was about happen, but the world just ignored him." McClune spoke so softly Abena strained to hear him. "I was on this bus heading to the airport, me and a bunch of other aid workers. The road was full of debris and bodies. We were crawling along when I saw this woman in the ditch. Her baby, maybe six months old or so, was dead beside her, all hacked up."

McClune stopped talking, lost for a moment in the past. It was a long time until he spoke again. "She wasn't much more than a kid herself really. She was lying on the side of the road being raped and she turned her head when our bus pulled up and she stared at me, tears running down her face. She begged for help. *Aidez moi*, she said. The window was open. I heard every word. *Aidez fucking moi.*"

McClune finished his drink and in the same motion poured another. "But the rapist wasn't alone, you see. No, there was a line of others waiting their turn. None of them could have been more than sixteen. These kids, they just smiled at us and waved their fucking machetes, just fucking waved as they stood there, dicks in hand waiting their turn."

"What did you do?" The horror of the scene McClune described was overwhelming.

"What did I do? We had guns — weren't supposed to but its Africa, for fuck's sake, everyone has a gun. What did I do? There was a dozen of us. We could have gotten off the bus, scared those assholes away, shot them. Could have saved her life. What did I do? Not a goddamn thing, Walker. I just turned my head and we drove off. That's what I did. That's what we all did. We say we're here to help these people, but when it really counts, all we do is turn away. *Aidez fucking moi.*"

McClune's voice was raw as he drained what was left of the bottle into his glass. "You asked me why I'm still here? I've spent the better part of ten years trying to answer that question. Best I can figure that since I didn't do a damn thing to save that woman in Kigali, maybe I should stick around Kenya until I find that kid and help her get to safety."

McClune finished the whisky and stood up, legs wobbling under his own weight. "That day on the hill. Marlow or Kurtz, do you remember? You asked which one I was."

Abena did. "What about it?"

"I started off one then became the other. Now? Who knows." McClune fumbled in his pocket for his keys and passed them to Abena. "You better drive fast, Walker. Curfew's in fifteen minutes and we've pissed off Angara enough for one day, don't you think?"

Peter and Alexandra weren't at school the next day. The other students professed ignorance of their whereabouts, but the nervous silence that greeted Abena when she was dropped off by McClune — remarkably unaffected by all the alcohol he'd drunk the night before — indicated they knew more than they were willing to say. All, no doubt, had heard about her visit to the Deng household.

Abena's mind was far from her lesson on pronouns, but she managed to make it through the day, and the ones after that, each without any sign of Peter and Alexandra, their spots on the hard, wooden bench at the front of the class remaining empty.

Their father must have forbidden them to return, no doubt punishment for her visit. Abena rubbed the back of her neck, feeling the phantom sting of the broken chain. A few slurs and a lost piece of jewellery — no matter how precious — were all she endured. Nothing compared to what those children and their mother had to survive every day.

There is nothing you can do for me.

The woman's words, her bowed head and downcast eyes haunted Abena, as did the sight of her lying on the ground, Alexandra on top of her, fending off her father's blows and kicks. But that family and whatever happened to them was not her business. Not anymore. Mc-Clune had said as much. And Hughes and Angara as well, with his less than veiled threat of setting Chief Inspector Obanda on her if Abena interfered with the Dengs again.

McClune and the woman were right. There wasn't anything Abena, or anyone else, could do to help.

13

WILLIAM HAD RETURNED to southern Sudan with the SPLA once again. Victoria's bruises faded, and her cuts healed, but she had not allowed Peter and Alexandra to return to school. William would find out about that, regardless of where he was. Victoria knew well enough what would happen to her and her children should she try.

"Your teacher, was she good?" Victoria had been thinking of the woman of late. She was, at first, angered by the teacher's arrival. It was because of her they were found out and punished accordingly. But now, Victoria's anger had diminished. The woman couldn't have known William would react the way he did, and she had come with the best of intentions.

"Very good," Peter said with certainty. "I miss her." Alexandra was not there while they spoke. That was by design. Victoria had sent her out of the hut on an errand because what she wanted to talk about was for Peter's ears only. He did not let his emotions cloud his judgement as much as his sister. "She was brave to come."

On that point, Victoria agreed with her son. To wander into the camp, to face William, to offer assistance as a gun was waved in her face? All these things showed a great deal of courage. Something had been on Victoria's mind, something she hadn't thought about for ages. An idea, crazy no doubt, destined to fail like so many others. "Would you like to see her again?"

The question surprised Peter. "Go back to school?"

Peter's attention was focused completely on his mother. Victoria knew that Peter wanted to be a doctor. Without William's knowledge, she had told her children the story of the Walk and of Jacob Bok a thousand times, although Victoria had never told them who fired the shot that killed her friend. Her shepherd. To be like Jacob, to be like the man who saved Victoria, was all Peter had wanted since he first heard the tale.

"For now, no." That much was certain. That was far too dangerous for them all.

"Oh," Peter said dejectedly. "So why would I see her?"

It was a very good question — one Victoria would answer as she swore her son to secrecy. "Because I need you to ask her a favour."

14

AFTER THREE MONTHS of dry, scorching heat, the rains returned to northern Kenya. The wadis, the riverbeds that separated Ukiwa Camp into its ethnic enclaves, were full again, and travel anywhere in the camp became difficult. On the day of a particularly heavy downpour, three weeks after Abena last saw the Dengs, McClune was late for the pickup and she waited for him under the tarp that covered the student benches, taking shelter from the early April storm.

When she'd arrived, the covering was new and crisp and white. Now it was faded and weathered in the sun and wind. Rainwater pooled on top of the sagging tarp. Abena watched as it dripped through the rips and tears in the canvas and onto the tables below, the rest falling in torrents off the side of the tarp, creating rivulets that ran into large muddy puddles.

"Miss." The voice was as familiar as it was unexpected, and Abena wasn't sure if she could trust her eyes when she saw Peter Deng standing in the rain several metres away.

"Peter?" It wasn't an illusion. The boy was real, right there in front of her.

"My father has forbidden us to attend school." Peter looked as if he were about to cry.

Abena had been right to think it was her fault. Peter's words ripped into her soul. "I'm so sorry," she said, walking toward Peter, out into the rain.

The boy's eyes were panicked. "I'm not supposed to be here, Miss. My father has men everywhere in Ukiwa. I don't want people to see us, for you to have more trouble because of me."

"Because of you? What are you talking about?"

"If I hadn't forgotten my book, none of this would have happened."

"Oh, Peter. It's not your fault." That the boy blamed himself for her foolishness was heartbreaking.

"When you asked if you could help my mother, did you mean it?" Peter's eyes darted everywhere as he spoke, like an antelope searching for lions.

"Yes, why?" Abena stood motionless, oblivious to the rain pounding down on her.

"My mother's name is Victoria Deng," he began. "She is from Rumbek, in southern Sudan. She is thirty-seven. I was born in Azana Refugee Camp, in Ethiopia. My father is William Chol, one of the troops who brought my mother and aunt out of Sudan. He married her when they reached Ethiopia. We lived at Azana with my aunt until I was just a little boy, then we came to Ukiwa."

Peter quickly got to the heart of his visit. "My mother has a favour to ask of you."

"Anything," Abena replied. Anything she could do to assuage the guilt she carried would be a blessing.

"My aunt didn't come to Ukiwa. She stayed behind. My mother's not heard from her since. Do you think you could find her? Her name is Mary, Mary Deng. Could you find out what happened to her, if she's still alive, at least? She is a year younger than my mother. And perhaps you could find my grandmother as well?" he asked. "Her name is Alek Bol. She was last seen in Rumbek in 1984. Please, if you can help, Miss, it would mean so much to my mother."

"I don't know where I'd even begin to look, but, yes I'll try, Peter, I really will."

"And books?" Peter added shyly. "I can't come to school, but I can still read if I get some new books."

"And books. I promise."

A crowd of young men, speaking noisily in Dinka, walked past them. "I have to go," Peter whispered, "before someone sees us together and tells my father."

Peter agreed to meet Abena again in two weeks' time to see what she had learned. He would find a way to sneak away from his house and come back to the school. Then, without another word, he turned, loping off into the deluge.

And you must follow the rules as well.

When Abena realized the ramifications of her promise, she felt dizzy. Richard Angara was clear; she was ordered to stay away from the Deng family, to have nothing to do with them whatsoever, and she had promised as much.

Instead? She had met with Peter, talked to him, offered to help his mother find her lost family — though she had no idea how — and then to see him again. Any one of these actions was an obvious violation of Angara's directive. And what would Peter's father, William Chol, do if he caught her with his family again? Abena pictured the gun pointed at her face and shuddered.

But Abena had said yes, and it was too late to change her mind now. She walked quickly through the rain toward her school. McClune would be here soon and the last thing Abena needed was for him to see her anywhere but waiting obediently for her ride. "Two weeks. What on earth was I thinking?"

The internet was hit or miss at Ukiwa, and mostly miss, but today was a good day, at least in terms of the unpredictable Westshore computer network. Abena powered up her laptop and was nearly giddy with excitement when she saw four bars on the bottom of the screen. She opened Google, took a breath and typed.

Mary Deng

One million hits. Abena scrolled through the pages, one after the other, digging slowly through the electronic haystack. An hour passed with no luck. She tried searching for Mary Deng in all manner of combinations:

Victoria Deng

Azana

Rumbek

Refugee

Sudan

Alek Bol

Frustrated and needing a break, Abena stood and stretched, her back creaking in protest as she did. Abena had been hunched over the keyboard longer than she had been for months, and she wasn't used to sustained sitting anymore. Back at UBC, she would attach herself to her computer for hours in Koerner Library, lost in a world of economics, politics, of the GDP of Turkmenistan and the per capita income of Bolivia. All that seemed a lifetime ago.

Abena was good at research, and she prided herself on her ability to ferret out the most arcane or obscure facts from the web or from journals and books in the vast stacks of the library. That she couldn't find one clue, one small thread that Mary Deng of Rumbek, Sudan, the younger sister of Victoria Deng, had even existed at all was infuriating.

Her back still aching, Abena returned to her computer. Half an hour to go until the compound powered down for the night. She spent twenty fruitless minutes searching for Mary Deng. Then, on a whim, Abena typed something very different into the search engine.

Frank McClune

Not as many hits as for Mary Deng, but the ones that came up were very much about one Mr. Frank McClune of the Westshore Education Trust. Abena read one site in particular, not knowing whether to be impressed or angry with the man. She picked up a pen and was still hurriedly writing when the power clicked off and the internet connection vanished, taking with it the very surprising past of Frank McClune.

15

THE LAND ROVER bounced through the mud toward Westshore Five. There was something Abena needed to ask McClune when they were alone, and though the last teacher had been dropped off five minutes ago, she only worked up the courage to ask the question when he pulled to a stop at her school. "Frank, you said once that this place runs on bribes and favours."

"Did I now? And pray tell which one are you looking for?" Involving McClune was the last thing Abena wanted, but if she was going to help Victoria Deng, she had no choice.

"I need you to help me find somebody. Two people, actually."

He said nothing the entire time she talked, which Abena didn't take as a positive sign. Better to be yelled at, Abena thought, than endure another second of it. "Well?" she asked when she'd finished. "Mary Deng and Alek Bol. Can you find out what happened to them or not?"

"You actually met with that woman? Talked to her?" Frank was incredulous when he finally spoke. "After all that happened?"

"No. Her son came to me. I asked if there was anything I could do to help, that day in the camp. You heard me say it yourself. Victoria's been looking for her sister and mother for years. Nobody will help her, no NGO or the Kenyan government, UNHCR. Nobody. Except maybe me."

"I'm assuming you remember that psycho we had the pleasure of meeting a few weeks back?"

"Yes, of course, but this is important."

"*Important?* You've got to be fucking kidding me." McClune lit another cigarette and puffed furiously. "Have you also forgotten that unpleasant little chat you had with Angara? How do you think he found out so quickly you'd gone into the camp? That asshole husband of hers or one of his flunkies called the director five minutes after we left, most likely."

"Why would he have done that?" Angara was a bureaucrat, a man with links to the UN, to all the NGOs. That he would protect a thug like Victoria's husband made no sense to Abena.

"Jesus, Walker! Of course Angara knows the SPLA operates out of Ukiwa! They pay him for the privilege, no doubt. Guns, money, drugs; they have it all to fund their war, and Angara gets his piece of the pie. Do you think he's going to jeopardize that cozy little relationship because some guy beats his wife and you don't like it?"

"Do you seriously expect me to believe what you're telling me, Frank?"

"Use your head, Walker. The reason she can't find any information about her sister is because her husband doesn't want her to. Accept it; there's sweet fuck all you can do to change things. That's the way things work here."

"*That's the way things work here?*" Abena took a piece of paper from her pocket and read aloud what she'd written down last night before the power went out, something she'd thought to do just in case the conversation went this way. "'UBC's own doctoral student and Rhodes

Scholar Frank McClune shocked the academic world when he turned down a tenure-track offer for a position with the Westshore Education Trust, in drought-ridden Ethiopia. When asked why, McClune, a PhD graduate in economics, and his wife, a doctor at Vancouver General, would give up promising careers to go to Africa, his response was that . . .'"

"What the hell?"

Abena ignored him and kept reading. "'Too few people are prepared to help when they see a fellow human being suffer. This is something I need to do, McClune said when pressed.'"

Abena met McClune's gaze. "Your own words back in 1985, a week before you left for Africa. Did you mean those words when you said them, Frank, or was it just more of your typical bullshit?"

"Listen, if you think for one goddamn second I'm just going to sit here while you . . ."

"Me, I'm just a lowly undergrad, but you had a PhD. You could have been a professor if you'd stayed. Hell, you could have taught me. Tell me, Frank — what would you have done if you were in the position I'm in now, back when you believed that '*too few people were prepared to help their fellow man?*'"

The anger completely left McClune's voice. "Christ. I really said all that?"

"And more, but that was all I had time to write before the power went out. I was looking on the internet for Mary Deng and Alek Bol. I couldn't find anything about them, and then I typed in your name. You haven't answered my question, Frank. What would you have done?"

"Not waste my time on the internet for one thing. You're not gonna learn about her family there, for Christ's sake. You could search Google for a hundred years and not find a thing."

"But you could — if you wanted to help." Abena folded the page and passed it to McClune. "Mary Deng. Everything Peter told me is written down here."

McClune took the sheet, looked at it for a moment then tucked it into his vest pocket. "You go fucking around with the SPLA and you'll be lucky if you're still alive to be deported, Walker. You know that, right?"

"You'll help? To keep me safe and sound?"

"No promises, but I'll think about it. Maybe."

Abena could have hugged him. Instead, she climbed out of the Land Rover. Her students had arrived and were now sitting patiently on the benches, waiting.

"Your wife. What happened to her?" Abena wasn't quite sure why she asked the question.

McClune popped the clutch, tires spraying mud behind him as he sped away. "Not a chance," he shouted over his shoulder. "You've unearthed enough of my ancient history for one day."

16

THE UNHCR OFFICE was headquartered in a collection of semi-permanent modular trailers, stacked together fifty metres or so away from the Kenyan government building. Frank McClune parked by the flagpole, the light blue UNHCR banner fluttering in the gentle breeze as he reached into the back seat for a backpack that clinked when he picked it up.

"I don't believe I'm doing this," he muttered, making his way to the front door. Inside, a man sat at the reception desk, eating a roasted chicken leg. A tall stack of files was beside him on the counter, next to his plate of food. The man was in his thirties, African, with wireframe glasses and a large paunch.

"Frank McClune. I can't tell you how thrilled I am to see you." The man spoke in English, his tone indicating McClune's arrival was anything but thrilling.

"Nice to see you too, Eddy," said McClune easily in Kiswahili. "Sorry to disturb your meal."

"It's Edward," the man replied coldly, absently waving away the blowflies that buzzed around his lunch. "What do you want, McClune?"

"Just a small favour, *Edward*."

McClune placed the backpack carefully on the counter. "Mary Deng. Sudanese. She'd be about thirty-six years old. Hasn't been seen since '91 when the rebels cleared out Azana. She may have ended up in another camp somewhere. You've got access to the UN database — I was hoping you'd take a little look for me. And since you're poking around, could you see if a woman named Alek Bol, mid-fifties to mid-sixties, from Rumbek is anywhere in the system as well?"

Edward Mboya looked over his glasses at McClune. "Two lost souls in a sea of millions. Why would I do this for you?"

McClune reached into the backpack again, removed a bottle of Johnnie Walker Red and placed it on the counter. "Because I asked nicely?"

"Alcohol is forbidden in the camp, McClune. I should call the chief inspector and report you. Obanda would love a reason to run you out of Ukiwa." While Edward Mboya spoke, his eyes remained riveted on the bottle. Hunter's Choice was as common as dirt and cost less than purified water in northern Kenya. Real whisky? Now that was a much more precious commodity.

McClune put another bottle in front of Mboya. "True, but then you wouldn't have these — or the other two you'll get once you find the women, would you now, Eddy?"

"Most likely their bones turned to dust years ago."

"Most likely."

"Or drowned in the Baro or the Nile. Eaten by crocodiles. Shot by one army or another."

"All three are distinct possibilities, Eddy."

"Even if they made it to safety, both could have died of disease. After all this time, McClune? There's not one chance in a hundred either are still alive and in a UN camp. This is a waste of your time — and your Scotch."

McClune leaned against the counter, running his fingers gently over a bottle. "Most likely you're right, Eddy, but it's my Scotch and we'll never know unless you look, will we?"

Mboya hesitated for just a moment before taking the bottles and stashing them under the counter. "One week, McClune. Whether I find them or not you'll give me the rest."

"One week. I'll see you then."

"These women, McClune. What's so important about them?"

"I have no idea," McClune said, opening the door to let himself out. "You can add that to the list of things I haven't figured out myself."

17

THE AIR IN the mud hut was thick with smoke from the large, expertly rolled *bangi sigara* William Chol held in his hand. He sat at a small plastic table with two other men, his subordinates in the SPLA. American gangster rap blared from the tinny speakers of a small cassette player. AK-47s and large machetes rested upright in the corner of the hut next to full drab-green metal ammunition cases.

He passed the joint to one of the men. He was maybe twenty, thin and tall, with razor sharp cheekbones and skin the colour of coal. "Good news isn't it, William?" the thin man said, drawing deeply. "Garang has agreed to a peace treaty with the north if our autonomy is guaranteed. We've almost won."

A well-used pistol was on the table next to a bag of green herb. William picked up the weapon, twirling the gun lazily around his index finger. "Won? What have we *almost* won?" Chol's voice was heavy with both *bangi* and scorn. "Our political leaders are nothing but sheep, talking about autonomy when we could have full independence. Khartoum knows they can't beat us, so they try to buy us off with *autonomy*? That's not what I fight for. That's not what my family died for."

The thin man handed the *bangi* to a slightly older, heavily muscled man wearing sunglasses, a dirty black tank top and khaki pants.

"What are you saying?" asked the man in the tank top, once he'd blown out the smoke, now rising lazily to the tin roof of the hut. "Are you suggesting we act against the leadership of the movement?"

William filled his own lungs with pungent smoke, shut his eyes and tilted back his head, savouring the high. The *bangi* he'd picked up from a friend, a lieutenant in the Kenya Police Service, was good, the best he'd had in ages, but he was getting low on the stuff and needed to get more before embarking on his next mission.

"Politicians are cowards. Ours, theirs, everyone's. We haven't fought so long for compromises, for deals, for autonomy. There will be no peace in southern Sudan until the last Arab lies rotting in the sand and the flag of our own nation flies over our cities, our villages and our oil fields. Don't forget that there are men stronger than Colonel Garang willing to carry on the fight."

He took another long drag then ground the remnants of the joint into the dirt floor with his boot. "There are thousands of boys here, soldiers for the final push. All they need is training and guns. My own son is almost ready. He will soon join us in the fight." William stood up, tucking the pistol down the back of his trousers. "We leave for Sudan tomorrow," he announced. "One more successful offensive, and our leaders will see how close we are to real victory. Then there will be no more talk of autonomy.

"You," he said to the man in the tank top. "Stay here, keep an eye on my wife and let me know if she gets up to something. That woman has a habit of finding trouble when I'm not around."

18

MCCLUNE WAS AT his desk in the Westshore offices going through the books, trying to figure out how to spread his ever-diminishing budget. There were other calamitous events that had grabbed the world's attention of late, and this obscure part of Africa had become somewhat passé. Besides, since 9/11, Afghanistan and the war in Iraq, the purses and wallets of donors in Canada and the United States had become increasingly closed.

McClune looked at his watch. It was almost time to pick up the teachers, but as he stood up to leave, Edward Mboya knocked on his door. McClune was surprised to see him. They'd agreed on a week, but barely half that time had passed since he'd asked for his ill-advised favour.

"It seems that God smiles on fools and Americans," said Mboya, walking into McClune's office, a thin manila envelope held in his hand.

"Jesus, Eddy! You found them?" McClune reached for the envelope, but Edward pulled back his hand.

"Edward. You mentioned a price?"

"Two of Scotland's finest, Edward, but I want to know what you dug up first."

"Fair enough," said Mboya. "There's no record of the old woman anywhere, but yes, I found the younger one." Edward Mboya gave McClune the envelope, watching with amusement as he tore it open and read the file within.

"Holy shit." McClune could hardly believe what he'd just read. Mboya had more than earned his precious Scotch.

Mboya allowed himself a thin, satisfied smile. "It wasn't easy without raising the attention of my supervisors or Obanda's spies, but everything you need to know is in the file. Like I said, McClune, God smiles on fools and *mzungus*. I used to think you were both; now, I'm not so sure."

The rains disappeared and the ochre dust that blanketed Ukiwa returned. "Gonna be a hot one today, Walker," said McClune as he dropped her off at the school. "You have water?"

"Three bottles. I should be fine. See you at 1:30."

"She was an ER doctor."

"Excuse me?" said Abena.

"My wife. Six months into our time in Ethiopia, I got home from work to see her waiting for me by the front door, our bags packed. She couldn't stand it anymore. The suffering, the lack of resources, the tragedy. Said she was going home, with or without me."

"What did you do?"

McClune leaned back in his seat, arms folded across his chest. "This fucking place gets in your blood, you know? I stayed in Ethiopia until Mengistu kicked us out in 1991. Been here ever since, except for my time in Rwanda. I hear she's doing well: married a cardiologist, has three kids. Lives somewhere on the North Shore now."

"I'm sorry, Frank."

"Shit happens. We make choices in life and we live with them." He passed Abena a file folder. "I wasn't the only one who left Ethiopia in '91. Mary Deng: do you really want to know what happened to her? Are you prepared to deal with whatever happens if you do? Choices and consequences, Walker. Think carefully."

"Frank? Seriously? You learned something? Finding Victoria's mother and sister is all I've been thinking about for days." McClune gave Abena the folder. Her eyes widened as she read. "Oh my God! How did you ever manage to do it?"

"Favours and bribes. You owe me four bottles of Scotch — the good stuff too."

"And her mother?" Abena looked as if she could hardly dare to believe that Frank had located both women.

Frank shook his head. "God may know where she is but the UNHCR doesn't. But if she was in Rumbek when the army invaded, the odds are good she's still there, Walker. Buried in the sand or burned to ash. What are you going to do with the information?"

Abena knew what McClune was really asking. The last thing he wanted was to run another rescue mission in the camp. Neither Peter's father nor Obanda would be as forgiving, should there be another incident.

"Peter's coming to see me next week at the school," Abena said quickly. "I'm not going back to their place, if that's what you're asking, believe me."

"That's it? That's your plan?" It sounded almost reasonable to McClune. "You promise? No more field trips?"

"Cross my heart." The last thing Abena wanted was to run into William Chol.

"Good. Don't go more than ten feet from your school. I mean it, Walker. There's no telling what will happen if you piss off her husband again."

19

"I CAN'T BELIEVE IT, Denise. It's just amazing! Victoria was just a kid when the army invaded their town. She saw her father die, couldn't go home to her mother, and so these two girls walked across Sudan for weeks until they reached Ethiopia. They were among a handful of survivors who made it, but they were separated in Ethiopia. Victoria came to Ukiwa while Mary ended up in a refugee camp in Uganda. Now she's been selected for resettlement!"

Abena had read the information McClune obtained at least two dozen times, and each time she did Victoria and Mary Deng's story seemed more remarkable than ever. Alek Bol had disappeared, dead for years now no doubt, but Mary was very much alive. She'd walked from Sudan to Ethiopia and then to Uganda, where she married a man not soon after arriving at the refugee camp. He had died not long after her second daughter had been born.

"The UNHCR is sending Mary and her two daughters to Toronto

as part of the Canadian quota. She's scheduled to fly out in six months. They're all going to be relocated to Canada!"

Denise was not convinced. "I still think you're crazy to have anything to do with these people after what happened to you. Roger and Obanda are going to be the least of your problems if that kid's psycho dad finds out you are still talking to his family."

"I know. I promise I'll be careful."

Abena crossed the room to Denise's desk, examining her small pile of paperbacks, a mix of thrillers, murder mysteries and horror books: Baldacci, Kellerman, Koontz and King. "Can I borrow some of these? Peter's asked for some books as well."

"Keep them," she said. "I've read them all at least three times each. God knows what that kid would want with *Cujo*. His real world's scary enough, don't you think?"

Peter would be at the school just after one. Abena was excited to see him and was hardly paying attention to her teaching. Instead, she imagined giving Peter the folder, drinking in the look of joy that would be on his face when he learned his aunt was alive.

The file in her backpack held a copy of Mary Deng's refugee status determination file, completed more than a decade ago at Matumaini Refugee Camp in northern Uganda. The heart of the file was a four-page document chronicling Mary's journey from Rumbek to Azana and then to Uganda, outlining her case for refugee status.

The report was poorly written and full of spelling mistakes, the account no doubt quickly jotted down by the clerk who'd signed and dated each page. But bad grammar aside, the story was incredible.

The journey Mary endured with her sister was just the start of a remarkable passage that took her back and forth across east Africa — a journey about to take a new turn with a resettlement flight to Toronto.

Mary's health records, the Ugandan birth certificates of her daughters, as well as a checklist with the proper boxes carefully ticked off were also there, the proper lines carefully signed confirming her refugee status with every i dotted and t crossed. There were photographs of the family as well, and Abena wondered just what Victoria would feel when she saw the face of Mary and of her daughters: one ten, the other thirteen — the nieces she had no idea existed.

"I'll be late picking you up this afternoon," McClune had said when he dropped Abena off. "I'll get the others, take them back to Westshore then come for you. That should give you some time — just in case you have someone you want to chat with after work, if you know what I mean."

"How will you explain that?" Abena had asked, surprised and grateful that McClune was willing to deviate from the normal routine to give her time with Peter.

"Who knows? Probably with some of my typical bullshit." Mc-Clune left, the students arrived and somehow Abena made it through the interminable day, paying more attention to her watch and the hot yellow sun as it made its slow journey across the Kenyan sky than her lessons.

1:00.

Class dismissed. The students gathered up their things, said their goodbyes and dispersed into the camp. When the last had gone, Abena packed up her supplies, took the precious folder from her bag, drew a deep breath then waited.

But Peter never came. For the first fifteen minutes, Abena was filled with excitement, with anticipation, but as the minutes clicked slowly past with no sign of the boy, her expectation faded, replaced by concern, fear and panic.

1:30.

Something was wrong. Peter and his sister had always been the first students to arrive, the last ones to leave. Abena had never met a more reliable, diligent teenager in her life. For the boy to pull a no-show for something as important as this, something terrible must have happened.

1:35.

McClune would be here in less than forty-five minutes. Abena did the calculations. Ten minutes to get to Peter's house now that she knew the way, ten back and five to hand over the file — twenty-five minutes at most.

It was an insane thought. Not only had Abena promised Roger Hughes and the director of the camp himself that she would never return to the Deng house, she had also repeated that same pledge to Frank McClune that very morning. Too risky. Too reckless. Too much at stake, not just for her and the Dengs, but for the entire Westshore Education Trust.

But still.

Abena's fingers clenched so tightly on the folder that her knuckles whitened. To not let Victoria know. To be so close to giving her the answer she had been seeking for almost fifteen years?

Too few people are prepared to help when they see a fellow human being suffer.

A gust of wind blew across the camp, kicking up a small dust devil that spun down the street and over a clothesline outside a mud hut a few metres from the church. Abena watched a long floral print dress and a dark blue headscarf dance in its slipstream on the rope.

Too few.

Clouds rolled in. Thunder pealed in the distance as Abena approached the clothesline on feet that didn't feel her own.

The dress was large and would easily slip over her body, disguising her Western clothes. And with the scarf wrapped modestly over Abena's head? Nobody would know she was a Westerner — at least from a distance. A large raindrop caromed off the dusty ground. What few people were about hurriedly made their way to shelter, paying no attention to the young Western aid worker staring oddly at a clothesline.

1:37.

The rain fell harder. Abena tucked the folder and a couple of paperbacks into a plastic bag then pulled the scarf and dress off the line. Twenty-three minutes. Almost enough time.

20

PETER WAS SICK. Dengue, breakbone they called it, and for three days now he had been rocked by fever, by aching muscles and by pain. He said he was cold and wanted a sheet, but his skin burned to the touch and sweat rolled down his thin body like monsoon rain.

There was no treatment for breakbone short of rest and water. It was common in Ukiwa and they had all suffered its ravages through the years. Even William, who claimed no bullet, land mine or bomb could kill him, had been struck down by it and had thrashed about on the floor of this very hut, shaking like a child.

He was still in Sudan, William, fighting his war. Each night Victoria prayed that he had been killed in battle, shot by a government soldier, blown up by an artillery round. Victoria used to feel guilty that she would ask God for such an awful thing, but that was before she had children to protect. From him. Besides, she knew nothing would happen because of her words. God hadn't heard her prayers for a very long time.

Victoria shook these thoughts from her head and focused instead on Peter, taking solace that breakbone rarely killed. But still, for a mother to see her child racked with pain? To see him so sick he could not open his eyes or sit up to take a sip of water without assistance? She hated herself for her helplessness to make the dengue go away. What mother, after all, would not trade places with her child in this situation if she could?

Peter hallucinated. In his sickness he spoke incomprehensibly about his aunt, a woman who was little more than a ghost, a shadow to him, kept alive only through Victoria's stories, memories and words, brought on no doubt by recent events.

"Be still," Victoria said. "You need rest."

But Peter tried to get up, to struggle against the fever. He said he must go to the church to meet the teacher, but he hadn't the strength and collapsed back to the ground.

"Hush. Don't bother your mind with all this." Nor could Victoria go to the church, not with Peter in this state. Not that it mattered. There had been so much disappointment over the years, what would one more be? Mary and her mother were dead, no doubt. The teacher would have had no more luck than anyone else. Better to focus on the living.

Victoria lifted her son's head and put a bottle to Peter's thirsty lips. Alexandra wasn't back yet. She'd sent her out ten minutes ago to get more water. Peter had almost finished the last of it and would need more.

Water was all she had. The Belgian nurse at the Médecins Sans Frontières clinic offered no medicine and instead provided extra water and said to keep him hydrated and comfortable as the disease ran its course.

The door to their house opened and Alexandra returned, empty-handed. "Where's the water for your brother?" Victoria snapped. "He's sick, you know that."

She paused when she saw the odd look on Alexandra's face. "What's wrong with you, girl? I haven't time for your nonsense. Why didn't you bring back the water?"

"Because I brought something else back instead." Alexandra entered but she was not alone. A young woman walked in behind her. A stranger, not Sudanese, Victoria could tell, even with her head and face covered in a soaking scarf.

"Who are you?" she demanded in Kiswahili. To walk into someone's house like this uninvited was something one should never do, even in Ukiwa.

"Who are you?" This time Victoria asked the question in English.

"We've met," the woman said. Before Victoria could say another word, her uninvited guest removed the scarf from her head. A frightened gasp of recognition escaped Victoria's lungs.

"You must go!" What could she possibly be thinking, this teacher, to put them all in danger like this?

"Please! I wouldn't have come if it wasn't important," Abena said frantically.

"Why have you come here?" Victoria demanded.

"I'm sorry, but I didn't have a choice. Peter wasn't at the church and there is something important I have to give you."

"Then it's a good thing for the both of us my husband's in Sudan. If he were here . . ." Victoria scanned the street outside for any sign the teacher was followed. But there was no one, she was sure. The rain pounded down. The camp seemed deserted, everyone inside, seeking shelter. She shut the door. "What do you want to give me?"

Victoria maintained a distance between them, but before Abena could respond, a moan from the corner of the room caught Abena's attention. "Peter!" she cried. "Is he all right?"

Victoria relaxed, if only a bit. She realized the woman cared very deeply for her son and had risked a great deal to come here. "Dengue. For three days now, but he'll be fine." Victoria turned to Alexandra, still standing by the doorway. "Water. Get it now."

"Yes, Mama," said Alexandra, smiling broadly as she scurried out of the house.

"I know Peter's not allowed to attend school, but he still wants to read." Abena handed Victoria two paperback books.

"His father's doing." Of all the things William had done over the years, Victoria had never hated him more than for taking school away from her children.

"I know," Abena said, a small file folder now in her hands.

Victoria felt a strange sensation in her belly. "What is that?"

"In 1984, when you were sixteen years old, you and your sister Mary were part of a group of children that left Rumbek and walked to Azana Refugee Camp in Ethiopia. Most didn't make it; they died at the hands of Sudanese troops, famine, illness, but you were two of a handful of survivors. Then, in 1991, when the Ethiopian government fell, you were forced out of Ethiopia and back into Sudan, where you were separated from your sister. You ended up here. She disappeared."

The words shook Victoria. Her knees buckled, and she collapsed to the ground. "How could you know all this?"

Abena crouched down beside her and gave her the file. "Can you read English?"

"Yes." Of course Victoria could, though now was not the time to inform Abena that she had read the collected works of Jane Austin before her thirteenth birthday. Abena watched in silence as Victoria opened the file and read. Great racking sobs shook her frame as she did. "Alive. After all this time, alive."

"Your sister and her family are now in Uganda, but, next September, they're going to Toronto, in Canada, as government-sponsored refugees."

"Daughters." Victoria hardly believed what she read. "Mary would be a very good mother. For a long time she mothered me, even though I was the older one."

"Is Mary your only sister?"

"There was another. But that was a long time ago."

Victoria stood silently, lost in the past. "And my mother?" she asked. "Have you found her?"

"I'm sorry," Abena said. "Nothing."

Silence fell between them once more, broken only by Peter's cough.

Victoria hung her head. "I suppose it was too much to have hoped for."

"Would you consider it too? Resettlement, I mean?" Abena asked, changing the subject.

Victoria knelt by her son, cradling his feverish head protectively. "My husband would not be pleased to hear you say that. He has no time for the United Nations, for Westerners."

"Time! Oh my God, the time! I have to go," Abena said, placing the damp scarf over her head. "I've stayed too long."

Victoria stopped her before she reached the door. "You said that you'd help me, and you did. Keeping your word is a rare thing in my experience. What is your name? You know mine, after all."

"Abena. Abena Walker."

"Abena. An odd name for a Canadian."

She grinned. "It's African, actually. My parents were from Ghana. My father and mother came to Vancouver for school." Now it was Abena's face that clouded at the mention of family. "My father died a long time ago. I don't remember him. I was very young when it happened, but it still hurts."

"Yes, it does." Victoria understood that feeling very well. "A strange world we live in, Abena Walker. An African with an English name and a Canadian with an African one. What does it mean, your name?"

"Born on a Tuesday." Abena seemed embarrassed to say it. "A Ghanaian thing, apparently. Not very original. Tuesday's supposed to be my special day."

"And what day is today?" Victoria asked.

"Tuesday," Abena said with surprise.

"Toronto. Is it a good place?"

"I've never been. I know Toronto gets a lot of snow in the winter, though. Vancouver doesn't. We normally just get rain."

"I don't much care for the rain." For a second, Victoria's heart lurched once more though she quickly regained her composure. "I'd like to think about it."

Abena smiled broadly as she opened the door. "Shall I come back and see you again?"

Victoria's face registered alarm at the thought. "No. It is far too dangerous for you to come here."

"So how will I know if you decide to apply for resettlement?"

"I will find you." With a final farewell Abena left. Outside, the rain came down harder than ever. Victoria watched her run, picking up the hem of her borrowed dress, splashing through the mud and the puddles until she was gone.

21

"ARE YOU SURE you don't want any?" Denise Martinez asked, holding out the wine bottle.

"I'm good, thanks." Finding Mary Deng had pumped up Abena's adrenaline, giving her all the buzz she needed.

Denise poured herself another large glass of cheap South African red. "Well, I need another drink after listening to that. You're *loco*, girl; I should report you to Roger for your own safety! To dress like a refugee and stroll over to their house like you owned the place? Crazy!"

"Denise, you promised you wouldn't!" Abena panicked at the thought of Roger Hughes finding out.

Denise laughed. "Relax. I'm not saying anything; you've got dirt on me too." Denise's voice was heavy from the wine. Not for the first time, Abena thought her friend was drinking more than she should. At any given time, Denise had half a dozen bottles tucked away in her room — any one of which could get her into serious trouble. The camp was supposed to be dry, after all.

The UN and the Kenyan authorities could do little to control the drugs and the rampant production of *chang'aa* by the camp residents. A recent bad batch of the stuff had killed several dozen people in the Somali sector, and something needed to be done — for appearances' sake at least. And so, in response, Chief Inspector Obanda turned his attention to the foreigners in the compound.

Just the other week, several German engineers were sent packing after a raid discovered a case of beer in their dorms. Not twenty-four hours later, Roger Hughes called a staff meeting, reiterating to all Westshore employees that the ban on booze was now serious and there would be consequences for those who ignored it.

"You're not going back, right?" Denise asked. "You gave her the information and now she knows. Good deed done?"

"Victoria's considering applying for resettlement. She'll need someone to get her the paperwork if she does."

"Abena! You can't go back in. Not ever! You know what will happen if you're caught."

"I know, but she's an incredible woman to have endured what she has and survived. I'd like to get to know her better."

"Incredible or not, just promise me you'll be careful, for both your sakes." Denise's concern was justified. Abena's luck getting to the Deng house and back unseen was considerable, managing to get back to the school, soaked from the rain and the mud and sweat, just before McClune arrived.

McClune.

He hadn't asked Abena how it went with Peter when he picked her up, hadn't said anything at all until they had returned safely to the compound. Of course, McClune had assumed the boy was coming to see Abena. He had no idea what really happened.

"Mission successful?" was all he'd asked.

"Mission successful." Abena offered no more information nor did McClune seek it.

"Good. Now you owe me five bottles of Scotch."

"Five? I thought you said four?"

"Consider it payment for my troubles. Favours and bribes, Walker. If they're good enough for the Africans then they're good enough for me."

Obtaining the resettlement registration form was no problem for Abena. The UNHCR had a box of them on the front counter of their office. Abena was taking a liberty with the resettlement form and she knew it; Victoria hadn't expressed any concrete desire to start the process of resettlement, but there was a spark, a fire in her eyes when she'd read her sister was going to Canada. If Victoria was prepared to take the chance, the least Abena could do was have the form handy.

For a moment, Abena considered taking McClune into her confidence but quickly decided against it. She'd pushed her luck with Frank already and didn't want to put him in an awkward position. After all, she'd promised she was done with the Deng family. It wouldn't do Frank — or her — any good if he knew the truth.

For the next week, Abena went about her business, focusing on her job, but always with Victoria and her children in her mind. "Good work everyone," Abena announced to her students at a little past 1 p.m., four days after her trip to the Deng home. "See you tomorrow."

She gave them snacks and within five minutes, the last of her students left school, happily bounding off to play soccer, hide-and-seek or whatever other games occupied their time.

"Miss." Abena lifted her head to see Peter.

"You look a lot better than the last time I saw you," she said, smiling.

"My mother wants to speak to you." Peter did look better. He'd lost some weight, if that was even possible on his thin, lanky frame, but he had clearly recovered from dengue.

"I thought it was too dangerous to go to your house?"

"My mother is inside the church." Abena had seen the sand-coloured brick of St. Josephine's every day since she'd begun teaching but had never made her way inside the building until now.

She followed Peter through the doors. The inside was spartan and bare, with little more than a wooden altar at the front and a few paintings of Christ, Mary and the saints adorning the walls. The dozen or so rough-cut wooden benches were empty save for one.

"It is good to see you again." Victoria stood and hugged Abena. Their embrace was nervous, tentative, but genuine nevertheless. "I would have liked to invite you to my house, but it is probably wiser to meet here, though my father would appreciate the irony of me coming to a church by choice. Attending service was not something I looked forward to as a child."

"I have some things for you in case anyone gets sick again." As well as the resettlement form, Abena had brought other things for Victoria, and had been carrying them with her in her bag in the hopes of seeing the woman again. She gave Victoria several vials of pills: pain killers and anti-diarrheal medicine.

"This too," Abena said tentatively. "I know you said you'd think about it."

Victoria's hand didn't move. "Don't you want it?" Abena asked. "I mean, with your sister alive and going to Canada, I thought . . ."

Victoria's voice trembled. "What I want is for my children to stay alive. If my husband were to find this . . ."

There was no need for her to complete the sentence. Abena flushed. "I'm so sorry. I didn't mean to overstep any boundary. I wasn't trying to cause you problems."

"The papers. May I see them?" Victoria took the envelope as outside, the distant echo of thunder rumbled over the camp.

"My ride will be here any minute," Abena said. "I should be going."

"Are there good schools in Toronto?"

"I would think so. Better than the one I run here, anyway. At least they'll have four walls and a roof."

"Next Tuesday? Is it all right with you if I come back here and talk to you again?"

"Yes, absolutely," said Abena. "That's my day after all."

Victoria smiled shyly. "Perhaps Tuesday is my day as well." They hugged and this time there was no hesitation in the embrace.

"Tuesday. See you then."

Abena slipped out the church door and hurried back to the school. Frank would be pulling up any second. The last thing he needed was to chase her down again.

22

THE SUDANESE GOVERNMENT soldier was little more than a boy. No more than eighteen and looking much younger as he knelt on the ground, hands tied behind his back, the front of his ill-fitting uniform stained dark where he'd pissed himself. The boy was terrified, his face caked with blood, tears and snot. He cried out for his mother and begged for mercy, said he'd not wanted to fight at all but had been pressed into service against his will.

It was probably true, William Chol knew, not that it made a difference. The young soldier was the last survivor of a government patrol William and his men had ambushed near Bor. The ones not killed in the firefight had been interrogated, stripped of their maps, uniforms and boots. Then, when no more information was to be squeezed out of them, they were executed. No prisoners were taken.

Begging was hopeless. In one minute the boy knew he'd be dead, lying still on the rain-sodden ground like the rest of his company. Yet he continued to plead anyway.

"Shut up."

William knew the boy would die as well. After all, he would be the one to kill him. He stepped behind the boy, pistol in hand. William carried a 9mm Marra pistol, an authorized Sudanese knock-off of the Czech CZ 75. He liked the gun very much. He'd taken it from the corpse of a Sudanese lieutenant who'd had the misfortune to step on a land mine several years ago.

William had found the weapon a dozen metres from the man's body. A lucky find. The pistol was undamaged, powerful, reliable, and quite accurate at close range. Ammunition was easily obtained from dead soldiers, and William had put it to good use ever since.

A ringing interrupted the soldier's sobbing. "You've a call," one of his men said, satellite phone in hand. An irritated William took the device, listened for a few moments then hung up, saying little more than a few grunts.

Without warning, he fired a single shot into the back of the kneeling boy's head. The bullet, and a significant amount of brain matter and bone, flew through the air and spattered onto the ground. The boy fell forward, blood and gore spilling out of the large hole that used to be his face.

"Is everything all right, William?" The satellite phone was normally used only for the most important of messages.

The tips of William's fingers played with the Africa-shaped pendant hanging from his neck. "I have to go back to Ukiwa," he said. "It seems I have a domestic situation to deal with."

23

VICTORIA RETURNED FROM the food distribution centre, dragging several kilos of corn flour behind her in a large burlap sack. The food was her family's biweekly allocation, carefully measured and checked against their ration cards. Each refugee got enough to stay alive, to sustain life such as life is in Ukiwa — but not one flake of wheat, not one bean, not one drop of cooking oil more.

Victoria would take the flour and, just as she had for years, would boil it in water to make an unpalatable goo that would give her family just enough energy to carry on for another day.

She reached the house and saw Peter and Alexandra standing, backs pressed fearfully up against the mud wall, their arms wrapped around each other. William Chol sat in a chair beside them. He held up one of Peter's books and waved it accusingly in Victoria's face. "What's this?" he demanded.

"It's only a book," Victoria said.

William stood up. "I said no school ever again."

Victoria spoke slowly and respectfully. "Peter is not going to school. This is just a book he found somewhere in the camp."

"You are a liar." William tossed the book down on the table. Next to it Victoria saw the UN paperwork, William's pistol on top of it. Her heart raced, her breath ragged. "And I suppose this is *just a book* too?"

Victoria had hidden the documents in a small hole she'd dug in the dirt floor of the house until she'd made up her mind what to do about them. She'd thought they were hidden, she thought they were safe.

"You've been talking to that American whore!" William moved fast, scooping up the pistol, hitting her squarely with it on the bridge of her nose. Popping lights burst before Victoria's eyes as a flood of warm blood cascaded down her face onto her clothes. She fell to the ground, barely conscious, and could not see for the pain and the blood that ran into her eyes.

"Leave her alone!" Peter screamed at his father.

Victoria lifted her head, the movement agony, and through a veil of blood she saw her son run toward William, saw his flailing arms connect with William.

William was delighted. "About time my boy shows courage!" He swung his arm, the butt of his pistol connecting hard with Peter's face, just below his right eye. "You are ready," he said to Peter, now writhing on the ground a few feet from his mother. "Ready to take your place defending your homeland."

Alexandra sobbed and rushed over to help her brother, but William ignored her and turned to Victoria instead, the UN papers in his hands. "Do you think that I would just let you go? Let you take these children away? You think they will grow up to clean toilets for some American? They will never leave Africa. Their home is Sudan."

William ripped up the paper, the little pieces falling onto Victoria, sticking in her blood. She rose to her knees and crawled toward her children. William kicked Victoria in the ribs and her breath exploded as something cracked inside her chest.

"You would take them back?" she croaked. "To die for your useless cause?"

"They may well die in Sudan," William said, looming over Victoria, his fist raised, "but you can die here."

He hit her again.

She heard no more.

24

THE RAIN BOUNCED off the tarp covering Abena's class, playing the canvas like a timpani. Abena still had an hour to go, but teaching today was a lost cause in the downpour.

"Go home," she said, distributing the granola bars. "That's it for today. We will catch up tomorrow." Tomorrow was Tuesday. The week had dragged, time passing slowly as Abena wondered how her new friend was doing and whether she'd decided to fill out the resettlement paperwork. Abena was angry at the weather. She'd planned on dismissing early tomorrow, not today. To let her students go early two days in a row would not be proper.

"Miss!"

Abena was not sure she heard the voice at first, a soft sound barely rising above the thunder and rain. But then it came again. She followed it to the church where a tall, familiar figure huddled against the wall. "Peter?" Oblivious to the downpour, Abena ran toward the boy. "Your face! What happened?"

His right eye was swollen shut and his cheek was inflamed. A large gash split the skin and a great bloody scab had started to form on the edges of the cut, creeping over the wound like winter ice on a lake.

"My father. He came back early. He knows about your visit."

"Oh my God! Your mother? Is she OK?"

"Please," said Peter desperately. "She's hurt. You're the only one I know who can help her."

McClune's Land Rover squeaked to a stop in front of Westshore Five. He was fighting a cold, soaking wet and feeling like hell. He was early, but McClune didn't care; all he wanted to do was pick up the teachers, get back to his room, pop a handful of Tylenols then crawl into bed.

Number Five was McClune's first stop in the Sudanese zone. He had ninety more minutes of running around in this awful weather until he could get his wish and wasn't impressed in the slightest that Abena Walker was nowhere in sight. Again.

"I don't fucking believe it."

McClune climbed out of the Land Rover, staring at a set of footprints that led away from the school. They belonged to a large child or a woman, perhaps, by the looks of them. They were sneaker tracks, the ridges clearly visible in the mud. Western donations aside, most of the children in Ukiwa Refugee Camp still went barefoot.

Walker.

It had to be her. McClune followed the tracks toward the Catholic church, its large wooden cross looking more like a lightning rod against the black sky. Here the tracks stopped, next to another set of footprints, these ones barefoot and larger.

From the church, the two sets of prints led away together into the camp, quickly disappearing in a morass of mud and puddles. McClune sprinted back to his Land Rover, illness forgotten. The tracks had vanished, but he had a very good idea where they would lead.

25

"IT'S SAFE. My father isn't at home," Peter explained as they sprinted through the camp. "He went out drinking. He won't be back until tomorrow morning at the earliest."

Abena and Peter reached the house. She threw open the door and entered, a trail of rainwater following behind her. As Abena's eyes adjusted to the gloom, she saw Victoria lying huddled on the floor wrapped up in a thin sheet, tended by her daughter.

Victoria's nose was shattered and twisted awkwardly on her face. Her cheek was deeply gashed, thick crusted blood stuck to her nostrils and lips, and her eyes were swollen and streaked with red.

"You shouldn't be here," she wheezed, seeing Abena. "My husband..."

"It's OK." Abena bent over, took a wet rag from Alexandra and gently dabbed Victoria's fevered, burning face.

"Her sides, too, Miss Abena," said Alexandra. "Look."

Abena gently pulled down the sheet, Victoria wincing in pain as Abena exposed her ribcage. From her small breasts to her waist, Victoria Deng was a mass of red and purple bruises.

"You need to go to the hospital."

Victoria grabbed Abena's wrist with a strength that surprised her, considering her state. "No hospital." She pulled Abena down toward her face, her lips almost brushing up against Abena's ear. "Another paper. For resettlement."

Before Abena could respond, the door swung open. "For Christ's sake, Walker, are you fucking crazy?" Soaking wet and with a pistol in hand, McClune stepped into the house, shutting the door quickly behind him.

"She's hurt, Frank," Abena said as he tucked the gun into his pocket and ran his hand expertly over Victoria's body.

"No shit, she's hurt. Broken nose, broken ribs, probably a fractured cheekbone. Internal bleeding as well, no doubt. She needs a doctor, not a teacher without enough common sense to follow simple fucking instructions."

"No doctor," Victoria repeated.

"Frank? Can you help her?"

McClune was silent for a few uncomfortable seconds. "I'll see what I can do, but she's lucky she isn't dead. You both are. I told you not to mess with these people. Their concept of the value of human life is somewhat different from ours."

McClune stepped outside, quickly returning with a bag much larger than the first aid kit Abena's mother kept in a kitchen drawer back home. It was about the size of a briefcase, jam-packed with bandages and medical supplies. McClune pulled out a cylindrical tube that looked like a large felt pen.

"First we deal with the pain. Morphine auto-injector. It will take the edge off things."

Abena watched McClune remove the red cap and push the device against Victoria's thigh until she heard a loud click. "US Army issue. Meant for battlefield injuries. Civilians aren't supposed to have these, but they beat the hell out of hypodermic needles."

McClune eased Victoria back to a prone position and put his head against her chest. "Breathing sounds OK. I don't think her lungs are punctured, thank Christ."

"You know a lot about medicine for an econ prof."

McClune reached back into the case and took out a roll of thread, a hook-shaped needle and what appeared to be a small set of pliers. "You pick up a few things after being married to a doctor — however briefly."

He rubbed a clear gel onto Victoria's face. "I can fix the cut in her cheek. A little topical anaesthetic, a few turns of the needle and some gauze, but the nose is another matter entirely. It's pretty messed up and is going to need to be set properly."

McClune waited a moment or two for the gel to take effect then threaded the needle and deftly pushed it through Victoria's tattered skin. She didn't flinch. Within a minute, McClune had put five neat stitches into her cheek. He covered the wound with antibiotic cream then pressed an adhesive bandage over it.

"Will my mother be all right?" Alexandra hadn't left Victoria's side while Frank worked, holding her hand tightly the entire time.

"She'll be fine, kid," said McClune, finishing up.

"My husband knows you were here last week. He has eyes throughout the camp," Victoria wheezed.

"You were here? Before today?" McClune had been remarkably cool since arriving at Victoria's house, but that was before Victoria's unwitting revelation. "Shit, Walker. There'll be hell to pay now. You promised me you'd stay away. There could be someone watching us right now. We need to leave."

"No, I'm staying here with Victoria."

Frank was having none of it. "The hell you are! So help me God, if I have to carry you out on my shoulders, I will. You're coming back with me right now."

Victoria agreed. "Your friend is right; it's not safe for you here."

Thunder rattled the zinc roof of the house as the storm outside intensified.

"Rain," Victoria mumbled drowsily, her words slurring as the morphine coursed through her system. "Never liked the rain."

"When I was a little girl, I didn't like storms either," Abena said, holding Victoria's hand. "But my mother taught me one of my father's old sayings. He was born in Accra, but his parents were from a village in the north, the dry part of Ghana. They were farmers, so rain was everything to them. Without it the crops would fail. When the rain finally came, my grandparents would rejoice and say the rain fell from the sky like joyful tears from the eyes of God."

"We don't have time for a walk down memory lane, Walker." McClune paced nervously, his pistol in his hand.

Abena ignored McClune. "His name was Kwasi. He left Ghana on a student visa. My mother came with him to Canada and I was born not long after. He worked for the local Red Cross in Accra. He did a good job, I suppose. He was sponsored to go to university in Canada and then he was supposed to go back."

"What happened?" Victoria asked, her voice slurred.

"He was hit by a car. He died before he could finish his studies."

"Seriously, Walker. We need to leave right now."

Victoria hugged Abena as tightly as she could. "A friend of mine once told me that sometimes, ordinary people do extraordinary things. You've done an extraordinary thing for me. Thank you."

Victoria whispered something into her ear. McClune stood impatiently by the door. "Hurry up and say goodbye to your pal, Walker, and do something extraordinary by actually listening for once and getting into the goddamn Land Rover."

Abena had pushed her luck enough. She stood, hugged Peter and Alexandra and walked to the door alongside McClune. They had barely stepped out of the house when McClune exploded.

"Walker! Was it not made crystal fucking clear that you were to stay away from these people? Please help me understand just what the hell you're doing! Why do you care about them so much and what the hell did she say to you?"

Abena climbed into the Land Rover. "Do you remember telling

me when I first arrived that you didn't have a clue why you — why anyone — still bothered, Frank?"

"No. Maybe. I say a lot of shit. What does that have to do with any of the things you've pulled?"

Abena's voice was calm and measured. "Because I figured it out, Frank. That family? They're why I'm here."

26

INSIDE THE HOUSE Alexandra cooled Victoria's forehead with a wet cloth as Peter covered her shaking body with a sheet. The drugs mixed with her blood, coursing through her veins, pulling her into sleep.

Abena had gone, but Victoria struggled to stay awake. She needed to keep her children close, to keep them safe, but sleep — and the things that came with it — were inevitable, unstoppable, like a sandstorm blowing in from the north, like a charging elephant, and she was helpless to stop it.

Ahead in the distance, an old wooden bridge crosses a wadi. Victoria scrambles down the bank to the dry riverbed, ignoring Mary and the lightning that flashes across the black sky overhead.

"Victoria! Don't! We aren't allowed to go past the bridge! It isn't safe! Don't you remember? There's been lion sightings. And hyenas. We're not allowed to come here by ourselves."

*"And hippos and dinosaurs too," Victoria laughs. "Come on, Mary. It's
the middle of the day. It's perfectly safe."*

*Before Mary can respond, a little voice pipes up. "Wait for me, Victoria!"
Her little sister Alexandra is just a few months past her sixth birthday.*

*Without another word, Alexandra climbs clumsily over the rocks, mak-
ing her way down to Victoria. Mary yells for them to stop, but Victoria
ignores her, takes her little sister by the hand and walks down the wadi
toward the bridge.*

*Overhead the sky blackens, and large raindrops kick up small plumes of
red dust. Thunder rolls, nearer now than before. Alexandra looks nervously up. "It's awfully close," she says, as the rain falls harder.*

*"Get out!" Mary screams a warning, but it's too late. A wall of water
boils down the riverbed, howling toward them.*

*Victoria gets to the side of the wadi. She drags Alexandra, slipping and
crying, up the bank. She holds onto a root with her left hand and holds
onto Alexandra in her right. They are almost out of the riverbed but then
the water hits them like a fist, like a scythe threshing wheat and Alexandra is ripped away, torn from Victoria's grasp. She screams once and disap-
pears into the churning brown and white spray.*

And then she is gone.

Peter Deng stood like a statue in the shadow of St. Josephine's Catholic Church. After waiting a minute or so to make sure he wasn't followed, Abena hurried over to join him.

He took the new resettlement form, tucked it into his ragged shirt
and told her that Victoria was healing well enough. His father was
still in the camp somewhere, but he'd only returned home briefly and
hadn't laid hands on any of them since. After no more than a minute
huddled together, the boy scampered away, promising to come back
in two more days with the completed paperwork.

Forty-eight hours later Peter returned. This time, their exchange
was quicker; in less than a minute, he handed Abena the carefully
folded form then was gone. By the time the diesel generator shut
down and the camp faded to black that night, Abena had read the ten

or so pages over and over and realized just how tragic Victoria's journey had been.

The woman's entire life was written down in small, carefully crafted script. Names, dates and events from her childhood in Rumbek to Ukiwa Refugee Camp, each properly placed in the correct box. Some of the details Abena knew from her sister's paperwork, but much of the information was new. And remarkable.

Why did you leave the country you fear returning to?

How did you leave the country you fear returning to?

What do you believe may happen to you, or the people in your application form, if you were to return to that country?

Who do you think will harm or mistreat you if you return to that country?

These last four boxes — the largest ones with instructions to add extra paper if needed — were the ones that broke Abena's heart.

Mary Deng's own form contained the same information, but it was factual, clinical, written down by a bureaucrat. Victoria's story? First person, devastatingly powerful in prose and eloquence. Invasion. Death. Flight. Rape. Each sad chapter of her life, built on top of the others. The last two boxes where Victoria listed her fears of going back to Sudan were the worst of all.

My husband is a commander in the SPLA. He has made it clear that we shall be returning to Sudan imminently where my seventeen-year-old son will be forced to join the SPLA. My daughter will be married to a guerrilla, as is custom. She is fourteen. I cannot let this happen.

I was forcibly married to my husband when I was a young girl, not much older than my own daughter is now. Since then I have been raped repeatedly, assaulted and beaten more times than I can remember. He has broken my bones, scarred my body, almost killed me. If we return to Sudan, there is no doubt in my mind that all of us will die. I cannot protect my children or myself in Ukiwa, but at least we are monitored by the UN. If we return to Sudan?

We too will disappear.

"I need another favour, Frank."

There was nothing else to do, nobody else to turn to. It had seemed so simple, so easy at the time, but Abena had been terribly naïve, hadn't thought things through, had no idea what her next step should be. Like it or not, McClune was the only person Abena could turn to.

"Favour?" He looked at her suspiciously. "And what might that be? Your favours are getting pretty expensive."

Abena passed him Victoria's paperwork. "Victoria Deng and her children. I need to find a way to get her to Canada with her sister, but I don't know what to do now."

McClune scanned the forms. "I should have fucking known. That's what she said to you, wasn't it? That little secret you exchanged before we left her place?"

"I didn't go back there," she said hurriedly, watching McClune's face drop. "Peter came to the school for the form and brought it back to me when Victoria completed it. I promise."

"Filling these papers doesn't mean shit. It's only one small step. That's why there's a process."

"*Process?*" The word sounded ugly. "How long will the *process* take until Victoria's accepted as a refugee?"

"First, the UNHCR needs to make sure she and her kids are who she says they are. Then there's an interview, where they'll try to verify the claims she made here. It's compelling stuff she wrote, I grant you, but it could all be complete bullshit, for all you know. You wouldn't believe the things people say to get out of here. If it were me, I'd lie through my teeth."

"Are you saying you don't believe Victoria's story?" Abena could not fathom that after meeting William Chol first-hand, McClune doubted this woman.

"Settle down, Walker. I believe her, but it's not me she has to convince. The UN will try to verify her story, and then if she clears that hurdle, her name and those of her kids are submitted to potential reception countries."

McClune read through the rest of the form before speaking again. "If they're lucky, one country or the other will consider them for resettlement, but at any time along the way, they can be denied, turned down, rejected. The great con, remember? The hope of hope? Some of these people have been waiting twenty years for resettlement, and those are the ones in the pipeline already."

"Twenty years? But Frank! You saw what happened. You read the form. Victoria's husband is going to take her children back to Sudan any day now. They don't have twenty *days*! I'm supposed to give Peter an update later this week. What am I going to say?"

"I don't know. Honestly, I don't. Not that it matters. You aren't going to do one damn thing more."

"Frank! Peter's going to be a soldier. And Alexandra?" The thought of what could happen to her if she were taken to Sudan horrified Abena.

"I don't know what you expect from me," McClune said defensively. "I found her sister, what more do you want?"

"That child in the picture, the one with the vulture? You told me that you'd stuck around here to help her. Do you remember that, or was that all just a bunch of booze-fuelled self-pity and bullshit?"

"Listen, Walker," McClune said, his temper climbing.

"No, you listen, Frank. That girl? The one in the Kevin Carter photo? She's gone, but Peter, Alexandra and Victoria are still here, and they need your help."

McClune, about to fire back, stopped and slumped back into his chair. "This is gonna cost me a lot more than a few bottles of Scotch, isn't it, Walker?"

Abena wrapped her arms around McClune's neck and hugged him tightly. "Really? You'll try?"

"No promises." McClune sounded as if he couldn't quite believe what he was saying himself. "It's a one-in-a-million shot — the craziest fucking thing I've ever heard."

"You're not acting like the cynic you pretend to be. Why are you going to help her?"

"I don't have a clue." McClune lit a cigarette despite Westshore's strict rules against smoking inside company buildings. "But if you figured out why you came to Africa, maybe it's time I did too."

27

EDWARD MBOYA LOOKED at McClune in astonishment. "You cannot be serious. Do you have any idea what you're asking me to do, McClune?"

"Forge official documents, conduct a fake interview, accept a resettlement application from a family that technically hasn't applied, find a way to get them to Canada and do it all within two weeks without alerting the Kenyan government or the SPLA. Does that pretty much sum it up, Eddy?"

"My apologies," Mboya said, not bothering to correct McClune about his name, "you understand perfectly. Now I understand your previous preoccupation with the other Sudanese woman as well. Sisters. You're planning a family reunion."

"Something like that."

"I wonder if Chief Inspector Obanda would be as interested in this family as you are. Kenyan jails are full of foreigners, McClune. Your charm and white skin won't keep you out of one if you're caught."

"No, but this might." It would take more than whisky to convince Mboya to do this task and McClune was prepared. He placed a roll of American dollars on the counter. Five hundred dollars in twenties, held together with a thick elastic band.

It was a great deal of money; two months' salary for a Kenyan clerk, even for one like Mboya with a year of college and a job with the United Nations.

"You're the gatekeeper, Eddy. Stamps, signatures — you can do it and you know you can. Make it an urgent case, move it through the system and earn yourself some pocket money. The UN and the chief inspector need never know. What do you say?"

Mboya stared at the cash, his breath quickening. A few bottles of booze was one thing, part of daily life in Africa, but a bribe of this magnitude was something else entirely. Risky. Dangerous.

Tempting.

If Mboya reported him to either Chief Inspector Obanda or the camp director, there was no doubt McClune would stare out through the bars of a cell for a substantial amount of time.

"It *might* be possible," Mboya said, "but there would be additional costs involved; assistance required from other people. This is risky enough without any unforeseen . . . complications."

McClune had anticipated the response. Another thick roll of twenties appeared. "Five hundred more. Is that enough to assist with any such 'complications'?"

It certainly seemed to be. Mboya pocketed both rolls of cash. "You'll need pictures, McClune. Passport style for the files. I can't do anything without them."

"Pictures I can do. When do you want them?"

"The sooner the better. And be careful for both our sakes. If Obanda hears about this, I'll be fired. And if the SPLA learns what you're planning, McClune? Jail will be the least of your problems."

28

PETER ARRIVED IN the morning before school began. Abena gave him the small digital camera she'd obtained from McClune, quickly showing the boy how to use it. Three headshots of each, no smiles, features clearly visible. The boy took the camera then vanished, promising to be back at the end of the day.

True to his word, Peter returned just after one, hiding in the shadows of the church, waiting for the students to leave. When Abena was alone, he sprinted to the school and passed over the camera. Abena turned it on and scrolled through the pictures quickly.

Three pictures of each of the Dengs were on the memory card, headshots taken just as McClune had instructed, with a sheet hung against the wall of their house for a backdrop.

Victoria's wounds were healing slowly by the looks of things. The ugly gash on her face was red and raw, still held together with McClune's stitches. The bruising around her eyes had gone down, but the image served as a reminder of the dangers faced by Victoria and her family as long as they remained in Ukiwa.

Abena organized another meeting. In two weeks, Peter would return, hopefully to hear good news. He hugged her, smiled then darted away.

Ten minutes later, McClune arrived. Without a word, Abena climbed into the Land Rover and gave him the camera. Peter had done his job. Now it was McClune's turn to work a miracle. Abena had no idea how he planned on helping the Dengs get out of the camp and he refused to answer any of her questions on the subject.

"You're better off not knowing in case things go south," he said cryptically, popping the clutch, speeding back to the administrative compound. "Don't ask me again."

29

CHIEF INSPECTOR BENJAMIN OBANDA took the call at his desk, a battered, metal piece of furniture in his office on the main floor of the Kenya National Police Ukiwa Headquarters. As well as Obanda's office, the building contained barracks for more than a dozen constables, an armoury and several cells used to hold drunks and addicts until they sobered up, or more serious criminals until they could be transported to jails farther south.

Obanda listened carefully, the earpiece pressed tightly against the side of his head. When the call ended, he placed the receiver back into its cradle, straightened out his blue beret and walked briskly from his office, past the blue-and-yellow police flag that hung above the door.

Utumishi kwa Wote. Service to all.

While the National Police service's motto, printed neatly under the crossed spears and shield on the flag, may have been true in a general sense, Chief Inspector Benjamin Obanda's service and loyalty lay closer to some than others.

Obanda strode purposefully into the lobby, giving a cursory nod to the young constable at the front desk, who sprang to his feet and saluted his commanding officer.

"Do you need a ride, Sir?" The constable, a twenty-year-old recruit fresh from the Kenya Police College in Kiganjo, was also Obanda's driver, tasked with taking him to functions, unofficial meetings with his contacts in the camp or to the brothels in Ukiwa town when the mood struck either the chief inspector or the camp director himself.

"Not now."

It was a short walk to the administration building, one he'd done countless times in the eight years Obanda had commanded the Ukiwa detachment. He reached the main doors in less than five minutes and walked wordlessly past the receptionist toward Angara's office.

Most people in Ukiwa needed an appointment to see Richard Angara. Some waited days, even weeks. Not so for Chief Inspector Obanda. He climbed the stairs to Angara's office, knocked once on the heavy wood door then entered.

Angara looked up from his paperwork. "Yes?"

"Sir," Obanda said taking off his beret, standing ramrod straight before the director. "We have a problem."

30

"YOU'RE A MIRACLE worker, Eddy, you really are." It was a genuine compliment and McClune meant every word of it. Six days it had taken to move the Deng family through the system, a period nothing short of remarkable.

"It wasn't easy, McClune." The clerk spoke with a self-satisfied air. "Reports to write, interviews to falsify and forged documents to send along to the Canadian Visa Application Centre in Nairobi, with both risks and palms to grease every step along the way. Not easy at all."

"Favours and bribes, Eddy?"

"I have a friend who works there. The official policy is that they interview all potential resettlement cases themselves, but I provided enough information and incentives that they were willing to accept your family on my say-so alone. They've even indicated what city they will land in."

"Eddy, if you tell me they're going directly to Toronto I'm gonna kiss you."

Mboya's face soured at the prospect. "Luckily for me, they're going to Regina, wherever that is."

"Good enough, Eddy. Good enough."

McClune understood the process and was grateful beyond words for what Mboya had accomplished. Refugees were settled as evenly throughout the country as possible in small towns and big cities alike, through partnerships between the Government of Canada and thousands of churches, service clubs and private individuals.

Sometimes new arrivals stayed where they landed, but they had freedom of movement as soon as they stepped on Canadian soil and, as often as not, settled newcomers would very quickly travel from their original reception communities to cities across the country that had large enclaves of their own countrymen.

"When are they supposed to leave?"

From the smile of Mboya's face McClune could tell that the clerk was particularly proud of his work. "The injuries to the woman's face and the blood drops on the paper were very convincing. They lent a certain degree of credence to the claim that this was an exceptional situation. Life and death, utmost priority. *Immediate peril*, I told my contact, McClune. As such, they're being accepted as an emergency case."

"When?"

"Three days. Next Thursday at noon, your family is scheduled to appear at the Visa Centre on Muthangari Drive. The paperwork's been sent directly there; all that's left to do is the medical screening to make sure they're not carrying tuberculosis or other communicable diseases."

"Jesus! Pucker up, Eddy, you're getting a kiss anyway!" The news was above and beyond what McClune could have hoped for.

Mboya eyed McClune warily, not sure if McClune was serious or not. "Once they've been cleared by medical staff, they'll undergo a brief cultural orientation while their travel documents are being prepared at the embassy. If everything goes well, a week after they arrive at in Nairobi they'll be on a flight to Canada."

Instead of kissing Mboya, McClune gave him a big hug, one the clerk awkwardly endured. "Thank you, Eddy. Thank you."

McClune reached into his vest and took out an additional hundred dollars. "A bonus," he said. "You've more than earned it."

Five minutes later, McClune realized one very significant problem remained. Abena's next meeting with Peter wasn't scheduled for more than a week. By then, the Dengs were supposed to be boarding a plane. If they were going to get the family out in time, someone would have to go in and get them.

"It's a stupid idea. Not much of a plan at all, but time's short and there's nothing else I can think of," said McClune.

"I don't think it's stupid at all." Abena's joy at learning that Victoria and her children would very soon be on their way to Canada made the small risk she was about to take seem worthwhile. "You'll show me the gap in the fence?"

The *boma* that surrounded the compound was intimidating, but not without its flaws. It was built to keep out rioters and terrorists, but if you knew where to look, there were gaps that let individuals sneak back and forth between the compound and the bulk of the camp.

McClune had slipped through the *boma* himself a hundred times for one reason or the other, but there was no way he could pass the message onto the Dengs himself. McClune would be far too visible, and word of his visit would reach many ears in a very short time.

It had to be Abena. She'd passed unnoticed in the dress and head scarf before, and would need to do so again if Victoria, Peter and Alexandra had any hope of reaching Nairobi and the world beyond.

The message she would carry was as simple as McClune's plan. Tomorrow afternoon, two hours or so before sunset when the aid workers in the camp were wrapping up their business, the Dengs were to walk to the eastern edge of the camp until they came to the dirt road that circled Ukiwa.

McClune had arranged for a friend of his to pick them up — a friend with a vehicle that wouldn't be searched by the guards at the checkpoint. A vehicle driven by a friend who would take them all the way to Nairobi with a day to spare, in case of some unexpected delay along the way.

McClune refused to say who this person was, but it was someone he promised Abena could trust to take the Dengs directly to Nairobi. Once there, they would be safe from William Chol and his plans to return them to Sudan.

The best part was that no one would know where they'd gone, even Richard Angara. Even if the camp director had access to the UNHCR or the Canadian government records, records that would show three recently accepted Sudanese refugees in Ukiwa Camp bound for Regina, Saskatchewan, he would be powerless to stop them.

Angara and Chol might even suspect Abena and Frank's hand in this, but there would be no proof they were involved in the Dengs' sudden departure. After all, people disappeared from Ukiwa all the time. The plan, such as it was, might just work — as long as Abena was not seen.

"Just be careful, for God's sake, Walker," McClune said, before leaving her room.

"I will."

Abena hugged McClune, a gesture made more frequently and easier over the past week. "Thank you, Frank. It will work out fine," she promised. "Nobody will see me."

"They better not. I'm out of favours and cash so if you get caught, I've got no way to bail you out."

31

"YOU CAN'T BE SERIOUS, Abena! You're not really going back in there, are you?" Abena could have kicked herself. Frank was clear that nobody was to know. He'd be furious that Denise Martinez had found out so quickly.

McClune and Abena had been spending a considerable amount of time in each other's company recently. That wasn't the sort of thing that went unnoticed in Ukiwa. Denise had gone to Abena's room unannounced with a bottle of wine, a knowing smile and many questions, but before she could ask any of them she saw the old dress and headscarf in Abena's hands and knew instantly what she was planning to do. Thoughts of an illicit office romance between her friend and McClune quickly faded from her mind.

"You can't tell anyone, Denise, I mean it."

"Of course I won't, but why are you doing this? Haven't you taken enough risks for that family?"

"I'm just going to see Victoria and the kids to make sure they're OK," Abena said, and not very convincingly, she feared.

Denise knew about Mary Deng, of course. Abena had also told her what William had done to Victoria, and how Frank and she had helped, but she knew nothing about their plan to get the family out of Ukiwa. On that point, McClune had been insistent.

"When are you going?"

"In a few minutes. Just to check up on them, that's all," Abena said. "In and out."

"And you'll be careful? You don't want any more problems."

"I will, I promise." Abena looked at her watch nervously. She had to leave now if she were going to get the message to Victoria and return before the sun sets.

"You better be," Denise said, as Abena stuffed the dress and scarf into a plastic bag and walked out of the room, "because I don't have a good feeling about this."

The break in the *boma* was at the northern edge of the administrative compound, between the Red Cross and the Jesuit Refugee Service headquarters.

It was around 4:15 when Abena ducked behind a modular building, put on the dress and head scarf and ran toward the small opening in the thorn tree branches.

The gap was no more than two feet high; a rabbit hole, one well used, judging by the track worn in the damp red dust, Abena noticed. She crawled on hands and knees, squeezing past the spiny branches and the rusting razor wire.

She emerged on the other side, brushed the sticky mud off her dress and adjusted the scarf. Ukiwa Refugee Camp began a kilometre or so to the north. In the distance, figures moved here and there, but nobody was close, and Abena felt certain no one saw her step out from the behind the *boma*.

The sun hung in the cloud-filled sky above the dun-coloured mountains to the west. It had rained again this afternoon and water pooled in the low-lying parts of the camp. Distinguishable landmarks were few in the sprawling expanse, and Abena's knowledge of the place, even after several months, was limited to her small school and the path to the Dengs' house.

"You'll slip through here," McClune had said in a quick meeting less than two hours ago. He'd indicated on a map of the camp the location of the hole in the fence. "The main road runs two hundred metres to the west. Avoid it or the guard and the checkpoint will see you. Stay in the scrub, keep the mountains on your left shoulder and walk until you reach the camp."

McClune pointed to several black dots on the map. "Food distribution centre, Red Cross medical clinic, water tanks, your school. That's your trail of breadcrumbs, Walker. It shouldn't take any more than forty-five minutes steady walking to get to their house. Half an hour or so to make sure her asshole husband isn't around, a minute for you to pass the message on and forty-five minutes to get back."

"That's not a lot of time, is it?"

"It is not. Sundown's at 6:28. No moon tonight. Cloudy skies. By 6:30, it'll be dark as shit and there's no way you'll be able to find your way back here. And that will be the least of your problems. The camp will be empty of aid workers, of police, of any help whatsoever. Bad men do bad things in the dark on the other side of this fence, and there are a lot of them about. Two hours max, Walker. Don't get lost. Don't be late."

Time was short. It was almost four-thirty; in ninety minutes, the first stars of the evening would emerge, hidden tonight by the clouds. Fifteen minutes later, it would be night. Less than two hours. Abena had no time to waste. She drew the scarf close around her face and, imitating the stooped posture and bowed heads of the refugee women, shuffled off toward Ukiwa.

For a terrifying moment Abena was lost in the overwhelming sameness of the place: the cookie-cutter mud houses, the gaunt, pulled faces of the women stirring mush in the same battered metal pots, the same children, ragged, unattended, kicking soccer balls made of rags and twine.

Then Abena saw the Red Cross clinic, a low brick building with the familiar red-and-white flag hanging limply in the still air. She collected herself, willed her heart to slow down, as she walked toward the large metal water tanks in the distance, her next landmark on the trail to Victoria Deng.

By five o'clock Abena was in familiar territory. She reached her school, forlorn and lonely, the wooden tables and benches faded and cracked, the tarp above them tattered. McClune had been meaning to replace it, but for the last little while he'd been busy with other priorities.

Fifteen minutes later, Abena stood on the street across from the Dengs' small mud hut. The place was quiet and still. The door was shut; no cooking fire burned outside. Five, ten, fifteen minutes passed with no movement, no signs of life. Abena was struck by the sudden, horrible thought that Peter and his sister had already gone, dragged back to Sudan and to the war by William Chol.

The door opened. Alexandra Deng, water jug in hand, stepped out into the street, off to one of the several distribution centres in the camp. It was the perfect opportunity. Abena strode quickly to intercept the girl, picturing Victoria's eyes lighting up with joy when she heard the good news. Mission accomplished, she would return to the compound, slipping through the *boma* with just enough daylight remaining to find her way back.

But she had to make contact first. "Alexandra," she whispered, crossing the street, closing in on the girl. "I have some news for your mother."

32

DENISE MARTINEZ LAY in bed, half-asleep, glass of red wine dangling from her hand when the door exploded off its hinges and her room filled with armed police officers. It happened so quickly, so violently, she didn't have time to scream before Chief Inspector Benjamin Obanda swiped his massive arm across the surface of her desk, sending a half-empty bottle flying to the ground shattering, its contents leaking out like blood onto the walls and the linoleum floor.

"Abena Walker! Where is she?" Obanda bellowed, although he barely managed to suppress a grin. Overwhelming a target with shock and awe was a technique he'd learned well from a SWAT team commander from the Dallas Police Department who'd been seconded to help train the Kenya Police a few years back.

Nobody was more surprised than Benjamin Obanda that the American teacher had flouted the command to stay away from the Sudanese woman and her children. Normally, Obanda wouldn't care less if a foreigner took a special interest in a refugee family, but this refugee woman was married to a man with very lucrative ties to the camp director — and to himself.

Their Sudanese friend had been most insistent that the Canadian teacher stay away from his wife, and was quite displeased that, despite the official warning, Abena was seen just the other week, huddled with the woman's son at her school, planning God knows what.

There were even rumours — unproven to be sure, but easy enough to believe — that the teacher and that boot-scuffing, smart-mouthed *mzungu* Frank McClune had been inside the woman's house, tending to her injuries after a domestic disturbance with her husband. Private, domestic business. No concern of his, and certainly not of the Westerners.

Obanda also knew that the SPLA came and went from Ukiwa, across the porous border his country shared with Sudan, going back and forth with weapons, hard currency and all manner of valuable things. He knew this because Chol paid the camp director a large sum to turn a blind eye to his activities. Obanda in turn got his cut of the *rushwa* as well, and he was furious that this Canadian busybody was jeopardizing it.

Chol wasn't the only one with a network within Ukiwa. Obanda had his own resources in both the camp and the compound, resources he'd paid to keep an eye on Abena Walker.

Most recently, his spies had watched the woman leave the Westshore buildings, sneaking suspiciously about until she disappeared behind a building, through the *boma*, and out of the compound, her footprints disappearing in the mud beyond.

Obanda had mobilized his network within the camp immediately, but nobody had seen any sign of the teacher. True, she was black and thus less conspicuous than the typical aid worker, but she was still a Westerner, and Westerners, black or not, tended to stand out in Ukiwa. As of yet, however, his people had not been successful in finding her, and so Obanda had been forced to resort to other measures. Measures like this.

The chief inspector slammed his beefy hand down onto the table and glowered at Denise, who was petrified. "Alcohol's forbidden in Ukiwa. This is enough to get you deported unless you decide in the next five seconds to be a little more . . . helpful."

"She's in the camp," Denise whimpered. "She said she was going to visit a friend."

Obanda was most pleased with himself: the teacher had crumbled and would now answer any question put to her.

This was good. The odds were high Walker was making her way to the Sudanese woman, and he had assets in place there, but the Canadian seemed smart enough to have made alternative plans, and any intelligence Obanda could gather on the Walker woman would help his men, already waiting inside the camp, to find her.

"Where?"

"I don't know, really, I don't."

Obanda believed her. She'd pissed herself with fear, he noticed, and was crying. No way was the woman lying to him.

"What was she wearing?" Obanda demanded, gathering information like the good police officer he was.

"A floral print dress, green scarf. She wanted to look like she lived in the camp. Like she was a . . ."

"Refugee. Clever girl." Obanda took out his own cellphone, spun on his heels and left the room, already dialling a number. The other officers followed smartly in his wake, leaving Denise Martinez to her tears.

No sooner had they left when Denise picked herself up from the floor, sprinted toward the main Westshore administration building and threw open McClune's door.

Denise Martinez, face raw from crying and with fear stamped all over it, nearly fell into the office. "Frank," she said before bursting into tears again. "Abena's in trouble and it's all my fault."

33

ALEXANDRA. Something had happened to her. Victoria knew it when she heard her scream outside on the streets, the noise rising above the voices of men, loud and commanding, shouting in Kiswahili. She threw open her door, panic rising in her chest. United Nations camp or not, Ukiwa was not a safe place for women, for girls.

But it was not Alexandra who was in trouble. Across the street, the Kenya Police had a woman in custody, her arms twisted roughly behind her back. Victoria couldn't see her face, but Alexandra seemed to know this woman and frantically tried to help her but was pushed roughly away by a police officer.

The woman fell to the ground, losing her head scarf as a policeman clumsily pulled her back to her feet and dragged her to a waiting truck. Then Victoria knew. It was the teacher. Abena. Her friend. "Victoria! There's something I need to tell you!" But before Victoria heard what Abena had to say, she was shoved into the back of the truck, the door slammed shut.

"Get the fuck back, you Sudanese bitch!" a policeman said, pointing his gun at Victoria's chest.

The gun didn't bother her, nor did his insults. Such words had lost power over Victoria years ago. More times in her life than she could remember, men had aimed any number of weapons at her: rifles, pistols, knives, their *uumes*, their fists. None scared her, not anymore.

Abena had come to give Victoria news of her sister or the resettlement application, and Victoria needed to know. "What did she say?" she asked Alexandra. "Why was she here?"

"I don't know. She wouldn't tell me, she wanted to talk to you. I was coming to get you when those men came out of nowhere." From inside the truck Abena shouted out to Victoria, but she couldn't hear her words over the yelling and the clatter of the engine.

The truck drove away, thick red mud spraying in an arc from the spinning tires. And then Abena vanished, taken by the police as surely as the flood had taken Victoria Deng's little sister and the bullets her father.

"I'll ask you one more time," Obanda thundered. "What were you planning to do with that woman?"

The interrogation room seemed claustrophobic, and with Obanda towering over her, Abena struggled to give an acceptable excuse.

"I heard she'd been hurt and I just went to see if she was all right, to check up on her." Abena hoped that this would satisfy him. Her shackled hands ached from the metal cuffs and her ears hurt from the shouting.

"And how did you know about *that*?" Obanda asked sharply.

Abena winced. She didn't want to get anyone else in trouble, but there was no way around it now. "Peter. He came to see me at the school. He told me that his mother had been beaten up by that man — his father — and I wanted to see if she was OK, if there was anything I could do for her. It wasn't his fault," she added quickly. "He was just scared."

"The boy," Obanda said. "How many times did you meet with him?"

Abena lied, convincingly, she hoped. "Just once. After his mother was beaten up."

"Only the one time? Are you sure?" Obanda leaned toward her, his voice dropping.

Abena swallowed before speaking. "Just once."

"Are you telling me that you never saw her after that?"

"Not since I had that problem with her husband."

"Neither you nor Frank McClune? You are sure?"

"Apart from today? Never."

Abena was terrified of the man and was surprised she hadn't collapsed into a ball, telling Obanda everything that she'd done. Perhaps six months ago Abena would have done just that, but she was no longer the same person she had been back in Vancouver.

"Never?" Obanda repeated. And then Abena knew. Growing up, she was always good at reading people, and she read the chief inspector now: Obanda knew some things, but not as much as she'd feared. He was fishing.

"Never."

To crumple now, to give Victoria up to men like Obanda and Chol? Abena wouldn't be that person. There was still a possibility that Frank could do something to help, but that chance would evaporate like rain on a hot afternoon if she said anything about resettlement to the police.

After a fruitless hour, Obanda gave up in disgust. He left Abena alone in the interrogation room until a young police constable came in, unlocked her hands and took her to a large room down the hallway, secured with a heavy steel door.

Inside the windowless room, lit by a bare bulb that hung from a wire in the centre of the ceiling, was a series of jail cells. With little ceremony, the constable shoved Abena inside one of them then slammed the door with a loud click. In the next cell was an old man. Somali, Abena thought, though it was hard to tell as he lay sprawled on a hard cot, stinking of alcohol and his own excrement.

For a while, Abena feared he was dead, but as she stared at him through the rusted bars, contemplating whether to call a constable to come and check on the man, he moved his half-bald head, coughed a bit then fell back asleep.

Abena didn't know the time. The police had taken her watch and shoes, although she still wore the dress, now dirty and soiled from the mud outside Victoria's house. The scarf was gone though, confiscated on the chance Abena would contemplate hanging herself with it to avoid Kenyan justice.

Her cell was small, no more than six by ten feet in all, empty except for the metal cot and plastic bucket in the corner, the purpose of which was painfully clear from the smell. Abena lay down on the bed and somehow managed to fall fitfully asleep, drifting until she was jarred awake by the ringing sound of metal hitting metal.

She opened her eyes. Camp Director Richard Angara, dressed in a crisp white suit, waited outside her cell. Roger Hughes stood beside him. Neither seemed very happy. "I thought our expectations were made very clear," Hughes said. "You were to stick to your teaching, keep out of internal camp affairs and not risk damaging our relation-ship with the Kenyan government. I have no choice but to terminate your contract immediately,"

"But Roger, she'd been beaten up, she needed help." Abena tried to explain herself but was quickly cut off by Angara.

"Ms. Walker, that's enough," Angara said tersely. "You have been placed under arrest, suspended from working in Ukiwa Refugee Camp and an order has been made for your deportation. You've done enough mischief in my camp." Without another word, Angara de-parted, leaving Abena alone with the drunk in the adjacent cell and her former boss.

"I am very disappointed in you, Abena."

"For helping people? Isn't that why we're here in the first place?"

Hughes ignored the retort. "Your actions have seriously jeopar-dized our position with the Kenyan government. It took every ounce of persuasion I had to allow our other teachers to continue working. I can't believe that you would continue contacting that woman after you were given specific orders against it."

Hughes straightened up his tie and walked to the door. "Goodbye, Ms. Walker. I wish it had worked out better."

"When am I going home?" she asked.

"Home?" Hughes' reply was cold, a small smile creasing his thin lips as he spoke. "You're in the custody of the Kenya Police, Ms. Walker. You know what these people are like, it could be months before they get organized enough to ship you home."

"Roger," Abena pleaded. "You can't leave me here! You could do something, could get me out, couldn't you?"

"Yes, I suppose I could," Hughes said as the metal door slammed behind him. "If I wanted."

34

"WELL, WALKER? Are you going to spend the rest of the day loung-
ing around in bed, or do you want to do something productive?"

"Frank?" Abena struggled to sit up from the hard cot, her body
sore, her brain groggy and disoriented. McClune stood outside the
cell, leaning against the bars, an unlit cigarette dangling from his lips.

"You sound disappointed. Expecting somebody more handsome to
come and bail you out?"

"Bail me out?" Yesterday Hughes had said that she could be in jail
for months. "What time is it?"

"A little before six. Now get up and let's go — unless you'd prefer to
stay here."

"No, sorry, I'm coming," she said, slowly getting to her feet. "I don't
understand. I thought . . ."

"You'd be stuck in here until God knows when?" McClune slipped
a wad of Kenyan shillings into the hand of the grinning police con-

stable who unlocked the door. "You might well have been, except for a little bird who told Hughes a team from Amnesty International was making a surprise visit to Ukiwa tomorrow." McClune lit his cigarette as they exited the police station.

Abena squinted, her eyes burning even in the veiled early morning sunlight that fought its way through the grey clouds overhead. She stumbled in a puddle. It had rained in the night and fresh pools of water dappled the ground.

They climbed into the Land Rover. "It would appear that neither Angara nor Hughes want to explain to the international community why a young Canadian aid worker was locked up in a Kenyan police station. Roger sent me to get you, though it killed him to ask. You're not off the hook completely, though," McClune added. "You've been put under house arrest at Westshore."

"Amnesty International. Are they really coming?"

"How the hell should I know? Most of the little birds I talk to are lying bastards, full of bullshit just like me. In any event, you're going to be a long way from here before Angara finds out either way." The Land Rover stopped in front of the Westshore dormitories. "Now get changed and meet me outside in five minutes."

"Why? I thought I was under house arrest."

"*Sometimes ordinary people do extraordinary things.* Do you remember when that refugee — when Victoria said that to you?"

"Yes, but I don't understand."

"Be outside in five minutes, Walker. But only if you want to do something pretty fucking extraordinary."

"Where are you going at this time of day?" the police officer guarding the road to Ukiwa asked McClune suspiciously.

"I need to fix up one of the schools," Abena heard him say from underneath the large canvas tarp stuffed in the back of the Land Rover where Frank had hidden her. "New roof. Surely, you've heard what happened. I have a replacement teacher coming next week and I have to get things ready."

The police officer grunted something unintelligible then waved McClune through. A few hundred metres up the road, McClune pulled over and Abena crawled out from underneath the canvas, her head covered in sweat, body sore from lying on the hard metal floor of the Land Rover.

"I thought I was going to suffocate," she said, gulping in the fresh air.

"And I thought you were going to sneeze or scream and get us caught. Good thing we were both wrong."

"How is this going to work, Frank?" she asked, watching the orange sun climb above the rounded brown bulk of an extinct volcano to the east. "It's too late to get them to Nairobi."

"It's *almost* too late," McClune corrected her. I've arranged a pickup just outside of Ukiwa town in an hour. They've got twenty-six hours to get to Nairobi; the timeline's tight but manageable."

"And what's your plan for getting the Dengs out of the camp?"

McClune looked sideways at Abena. "After the last time I thought you'd have figured out that planning isn't my strong suit."

"But you've thought of something?"

"I was originally going to ask Obanda to pick them up himself and drive them to the airport, but that probably won't work, so I'm down to plan B."

"Plan B?"

"Drive in, hide everyone under the tarp, drive out and pray the guard is stupid enough to let us through the checkpoint without looking. That's plan B unless you have a better idea?"

Abena did not. "And if her husband is at the house?"

"He won't be," Frank said confidently.

"And how do you know that?"

"Because that would require plan C — and I don't have a plan C."

"I'll start praying," Abena said. "It can't hurt."

"No, it can't," said McClune, passing the first mud huts of the camp. "Though I hope God listens to you, Walker; he hasn't heard my prayers for years."

McClune parked a hundred metres from Victoria's home. The sound of a vehicle in the camp at any time, especially this early in the morning, was a dead giveaway that Westerners — or the police were present. "What are we going to do?" Abena asked.

"Wait five minutes," he said, taking his pistol from the back of his pants. "If one of them doesn't come out, then I'll go in and get them."

"Do you think her husband's there?" Abena asked worriedly.

McClune pulled back the slide with a metallic click. "Who knows, but he won't be happy to see us if he is."

Four slow, anxious minutes ticked by. The street had started to wake as people up and down the dirt road emerged from their small mud shacks, on their way to the latrines or the water distribution centre. Some lit small fires to boil their breakfast porridge while others shuffled about. Movement was everywhere — except in the Deng's house.

"Time to move," whispered McClune.

Gun clenched tightly in his right hand, he was about to step out of the Land Rover when Abena grabbed his arm. "Wait. The door's opening."

Peter emerged from his house, barefooted, wearing a T-shirt and basketball shorts. He stood, stretched, yawned and walked slowly down the road toward the concrete latrines. Without waiting for McClune, Abena darted out of cover and closed the gap between her and the boy in ten seconds. "Peter!"

"Miss! My father's inside! You have to go; he'll kill you if he sees you here!"

"Are your mother and sister inside as well?" she whispered.

"Yes," the boy protested, "but my father is sleeping inside."

"Can you get them out without waking him?"

"Maybe, I'm not sure. He was drinking last night."

"Your last homework assignment, do you remember? If you could be any animal you wanted to be?"

"Yes, Miss, but I don't understand."

"Do you still want to be that eagle?" Abena asked.

"Yes, of course. Why?"

"Then go in there and get them right now. You've got one chance to fly your family as far away from here as you can."

35

PETER SHOOK VICTORIA gently awake. "What is it?" she murmured, pushing herself up from the ground. He said nothing, his eyes wide and fearful, and pointed instead to the door of their house, urging her out.

Chol slept beside her, snoring, stinking of the *chang'aa* he drank last night. He remained still as Victoria got to her feet and followed Peter outside, pushing their flimsy door quietly open. A lump rose in her throat when Victoria saw a woman standing outside her hut, a woman she'd never expected to see again.

"Victoria, you've been accepted to go to Canada just like your sister. Your plane leaves next week, but we have to get you to Nairobi now."

Victoria heard the words, but they didn't register, didn't make sense, and she struggled to understand. "Victoria!" Abena whispered, louder, more urgently. "If you want to go, we have to leave right now. Get your daughter, nothing else."

Victoria was rooted to the ground, frozen, but Peter moved quickly, slipping into the house and returning in seconds with his sister, groggy, rubbing the sleep from her eyes. The man, Frank McClune, waited across the street. He was not a person that scared easily, Victoria knew, but she saw the fear in his eyes and understood that this was serious business.

Victoria gathered her children to her, an arm around each one. She looked at Abena who nodded gently, reassuringly. Victoria trusted her, believed her, and although she would not yet dare hope that she would soon will be free, she was willing to put her faith in Abena Walker. After all, today was Tuesday.

A few minutes later, they crossed the dirt road and raced toward the Land Rover. Fifty metres away, then forty, and as the vehicle grew larger in front of Abena, she felt hope rising in her chest. Another fifteen seconds and they would be driving away from Ukiwa, mission accomplished.

Then a shot rang out. A cloud of dust kicked up beside Frank as William emerged unsteadily from the house, chest and feet bare, wearing just khaki trousers, his gun raised to fire again.

"Move!" shouted McClune, spinning around to face William. Abena watched in fear as he aimed his own pistol at the Sudanese man staggering toward them, still feeling the effects of the home-made booze, by the looks of him. McClune fired once, the bullet thudding into the house a few inches to the left of William, the sound of the shot echoing around the camp.

People screamed and fled into their homes and Abena knew that their hopes of a quick and quiet getaway had just evaporated. "Put your gun down!" McClune shouted. He fired again, putting the round closer this time, the bullet screaming past William's ear. "Put it down or the next one takes your fucking head off!"

William hesitated. McClune was less than twenty metres away, pistol now aimed directly at his head. Drunk or not, there was little doubt in Abena's mind that McClune would do what he said.

William must have felt the same way. Slowly, almost casually, he opened his hand. The pistol slid from his fingers, landing with a gentle thud on the ground.

"Kick it away from you," McClune ordered. William complied, booting the gun with his bare foot a few feet in front of him.

McClune advanced. Without taking his eyes off William, he bent down, picked up the discarded weapon and threw it back toward the Land Rover, out of William's reach.

William sneered at McClune, the men not much more than two metres apart. "What are you going to do now? Kill me and take my wife and children away to be your servants?"

On William's neck, Abena's Africa-shaped pendant glittered. Mc-Clune grabbed the chain and ripped it from his throat. "The only thing I'm going to take from you is this."

"Peter! No!"

The shout came from behind. McClune backed up, glancing quickly over his shoulder to see that Peter had picked up the discarded pistol and was hurrying over, rage burning in his eyes.

"I'll kill you!" the boy screamed, brushing past McClune, hand trembling as he pointed the weapon at his father's head.

William laughed, his hands held out toward his son. "Do it!"

"No, kid," said McClune. "He's not worth it."

"What's wrong with you?" taunted William. "You cry like a woman! Pull the trigger!"

"Don't do this," Victoria said as the boy's fingers tightened, his left hand angrily wiping away the tears streaking down his face, over the still scabby wound his father had inflicted. "This is not who I raised you to be."

"*Aboi*! Coward!" William spread his arms like Christ on the cross. "Shoot! Where are your balls?"

Victoria stepped toward her son and now stood directly beside him, her hand around his waist, staring at her husband. "You don't own my children," she said calmly. "And you don't own me."

Peter's hand shook, the gun aimed at his father. "Go ahead. Pull the trigger," William sneered. "Be a man. Be like me."

Slowly, Peter Deng wrapped his left arm around his mother, and lowered the gun. "I will never be like you."

His own weapon still on target, McClune eased over beside Peter and took the pistol from his hand. "Get in the Land Rover," McClune said. "It's time we got the hell out of here."

"We're not going to have time to get to town, so you're going to have to meet us as close to the gate as you can," McClune said to whoever he was talking to on his cellphone. "When? Right about fucking now would be when!"

Victoria and her children were in the back seat of the Land Rover as McClune hurtled through the camp. Speed was essential; experience had shown that if the Kenyan authorities didn't already know about what just happened, they'd find out soon enough. After he exchanged shots with Chol, the plan to sneak the Dengs out quietly was null and void. Subterfuge was out.

The morning sky darkened as thick black clouds rolled over Ukiwa. McClune flew recklessly down the road, large raindrops pelting the vehicle. "What are we going to do, Frank?" Abena asked as the checkpoint appeared in the distance ahead.

"Plan C. Drive really fucking fast," he said. "And when we get to the gate, we're gonna duck, hold on to our asses and hope the cop on duty is a bad shot."

36

THE VIOLENT JANGLE of the phone woke up Constable Charles Omandi so quickly he almost fell out of his chair. Normally, Omandi wouldn't be sleeping on duty, but it had been a slow morning in the wooden sentry house guarding the road to Ukiwa Refugee Camp. The weather was awful, keeping most of the Westerners in the compound. No aid trucks were due for at least a week, and there'd been no traffic on the road at all for the past hour except for the *mzungu* who had gone in to fix up one of the schools.

"Yes?" Omandi said groggily into the receiver. The message was short, but it snapped the young police man from Malindi quickly to attention. "Yes, Sir," he said. "They won't pass. I promise."

It was the chief inspector himself, sounding as angry as a hive of bees. A shooting in the camp, a kidnapping, a suspect vehicle most likely heading his way, driven by the same white man he'd admitted into the camp earlier. Adrenaline rushed through Omandi as he fumbled for his AK-47. He was the one who had allowed McClune into the camp, the chief inspector had reminded him, so he had damn well better be the one to stop him — and his passengers.

Shoot on sight. Reinforcements would be arriving any second from the police station, but until help arrived, Constable Charles Omandi was all there was to save the honour of the Kenya Police — and to fulfill Obanda's order.

The young officer heard an approaching engine a few moments later, and then he saw the Land Rover cresting the top of a small hill up the road, barrelling toward him.

Omandi stood in front of the lowered barrier and waited, heart pounding, fingers drumming anxiously on the stock of the automatic rifle. Omandi had never fired his gun at a live target. He had gone through the obligatory training on the shooting range, of course, but rounds were expensive, budgets tight and his experience with the gun limited. Omandi was nervous, but the young constable knew the cost of failing to stop the oncoming vehicle. He knew what Angara and Obanda did to those who failed them and needed no further motivation.

The young constable was a long way from home and he missed his mother. He missed Malindi, missed the salty, azure waters of the Indian Ocean, missed the bone-white sand of the shore and the smell of frying fish in the open-air restaurants on the city's seafront. If he screwed things up in Ukiwa, Omandi knew he would never earn a transfer back to the coast. Most likely he'd end up hunting heavily armed bandits and terrorists in the lawless, snake-infested scrub along the Somali border, and as bad as Turkana Province was, the northwest corner of the country was a cakewalk compared to the northeast. He would not fail in this.

Through the driving rain, Omandi watched the Land Rover close in. He raised his gun, flicked off the safety and waited.

37

FROM THE BACK SEAT, Victoria saw the policeman fire. The first bullets missed, but then the officer squeezed the trigger again, the air filling with gunfire. Bullets slammed into the Land Rover. The windshield exploded, showering them with shards of glass. Smoke puffed up from underneath the hood.

"Keep your heads down!" screamed McClune. Abena watched as they approached the checkpoint, flying full speed toward the policeman and the heavy iron barrier blocking the red-mud road.

Victoria saw McClune look to the sides of the road, no doubt contemplating their chances if he went off-road, but the ditches were deep and full of muddy water, and Victoria knew that he would not find safe passage there.

"Stop!" Victoria shouted.

"Are you crazy? Not on your life!"

"I said stop. Nobody will die because of me."

"Fuck!" McClune slammed on the brakes, the Land Rover stuttering to a stop not twenty metres from the gatehouse.

The lone police officer's rifle was pointed right at them, and although Victoria was close enough to see the fear in his eyes and his trembling hands, he did not shoot. Not yet in any event.

She was right, Victoria. There was no way around, and to carry on meant hitting the heavy barrier, flipping over, being thrown from the vehicle — if they were even still alive by then. The first time he shot, either the policeman missed them deliberately or was too far away to hit his target. At this distance? A child could kill them all.

"What the hell do you think you're doing" Victoria heard McClune say as she climbed out from the back of the Land Rover, brushing away the protests from her son and daughter who begged her to remain. "Are you crazy? Get back here!" McClune cried.

But Victoria did not.

Instead, she walked slowly, purposely, toward the police officer and his rifle.

"Stop where you are!" The officer was a very young man, Victoria could see, scarcely older than Peter. "Stop or I'll shoot you!" he commanded.

But Victoria did not.

Calmly, as if she were out on a stroll on a country lane, Victoria approached. Another few strides and Victoria stood directly in front of the man. She ignored the black hole of the rifle barrel and looked into his wide eyes instead. "What is your name?" she asked.

"Constable Omandi of the Kenya National Police. I order you to raise your hands and surrender. All of you!" he added, waving his gun toward the Land Rover. In the wooden guardhouse a radio crackled. Omandi and Victoria ignored it.

"My name is Victoria Deng." Victoria looked to the Land Rover. "Those are my children, Peter and Alexandra, and my friends Abena and Frank."

It was the first time Victoria had called McClune by name, the first time she had used the word "friend" in reference to the Westerner. But he was, she knew. He'd helped heal her, had stopped

William as well. Frank McClune had saved her life twice, most likely.

"I said surrender!" The young constable seemed as if he would wet himself with fear.

But Victoria did not.

"What should I call you?"

"Charles," the policeman stammered. As he spoke he lowered the gun, ever so slightly.

"It is a pleasure to meet you, Charles."

McClune and Abena listened in stunned silence as Victoria talked to the man who just a moment ago nearly killed them all.

"Please, you must surrender." This time it was not spoken like a command. Instead, Constable Charles Omandi nearly begged Victoria to obey him.

But Victoria did not.

Omandi wanted to go back to Malindi. He wanted to taste his mother's cooking, wanted to smell the salt and the spices of home, to walk barefoot on the sands. He wanted to see his younger brothers and sisters, still living at home, still going to school.

All he had to do was stop a pathetic refugee and her family, along with a law-breaking *mzungu* aid worker and a woman. A light squeeze of the trigger, and all five would be cut down. Charles Omandi would be a hero. A commendation guaranteed. Promotion possible. Transfer to the coast looked upon favourably in six months or so.

"Put up your hands." His voice shook even more.

But Victoria did not.

Victoria turned to the iron barrier. At one time, it had been red, but most of the paint had flaked off and now the thing was stained and rusty. A large counterweight with a handle was at one end, the operation of the barrier easy to see, easy to do.

"Charles," Victoria asked. "Do you have children?"

Omandi did not and told her so. He was just nineteen after all. "One day you will," Victoria said. "And I'd like to think that when you do, and if the time were to come when they needed help, someone would be there to look after them."

Jacob Bok. He'd said those words, or close enough, a lifetime ago when Victoria and the other lost children arrived at a small village on the banks of the Nile. She hadn't thought about that day for years. Until now.

Victoria continued to speak, her voice soft like a gentle breeze. "I am going to open this gate. You can help my children by not stopping us."

The police officer was very alarmed now. "No! You are going to surrender!"

But Victoria did not.

"I am going to open this gate and the only way you will be able to stop me is to kill me."

Omandi was near tears. He could not let them escape, but to kill a woman in front of her children? He tried to aim his rifle at Victoria, but his hands shook so badly he could barely hold onto the gun.

In the Land Rover McClune reached for his own weapon. Abena grabbed hold of him, pushing his arm down so the police officer couldn't see the gun. The last thing they wanted was to hurt this boy, but both time and options were rapidly running out.

A desperate Omandi tried to regain charge of a situation that had spun out of control. He thought of his own mother, of her disappointment at a dishonourable discharge from the police force, of his chosen career ending in a hearing or a dismissal.

Omandi looked at Victoria. His mother was about the same age as this Sudanese woman. He looked to the Land Rover — not at the Westerners but the two children in the back, staring fearfully at him. "Please," he begged one last time. "Please stop."

But Victoria did not.

Instead, she walked past the young constable. Frozen in place, Omandi watched as Victoria leaned down onto the counterweight. With a gentle squeak, the iron bar lifted into the air. In the Land Rover, McClune flipped off the safety of his pistol. Behind him, Alexandra cried.

"Move away right now or I will shoot you!" Omandi was hysterical. The ramifications of what was happening, of what would happen to him in the very near future front and foremost in his mind. He would be dismissed for sure, possibly court-martialled for failing to obey orders.

But to shoot an unarmed woman? To kill two children and the Westerners? What would his mother think about that?

"Please, move away from the gate! I won't ask again. Move away or I will shoot!"

But Victoria did not.

And to Abena's great surprise, neither did Omandi.

"I'll be damned," said McClune.

Victoria held her breath as McClune slipped the Land Rover into first gear, and it inched forward toward the now open gate, then through it.

"Thank you, Charles," Victoria said as she lowered the gate, turned away and climbed in. McClune stepped on the gas and drove away.

38

THE LAND ROVER slid wildly on the slick road, fishtailing and drifting before McClune wrestled it under control. "Is everyone OK?" he shouted.

In the back of the vehicle, Victoria, Alexandra and Peter bounced around like a ship in rough seas, looking terrified but otherwise unhurt. "Yes. You?"

"Peachy," he replied. "I wish I could say the same about our ride." The engine raced erratically, and the temperature gauge spiked dangerously high. It was steam that poured from underneath the hood, the radiator punctured by a bullet.

The Land Rover lurched hard to the left and ground to a stop. "Walker, look at the front tire." When she did, Abena understood the reason for his concern. The tire was flat, another casualty of the gunfire.

McClune drove on. On three good tires and a metal rim, they flew past the entrance to the administrative compound, now swarming with police. The gate opened, and through the widening gap, Abena saw more police pickup trucks and Land Cruisers, lights flashing blue, stuffed full of heavily armed men. "Frank? They're going to catch us any minute."

At the best of times, McClune's old Land Rover would not have been able to outrun the powerful police vehicles. Now, running on three wheels and with a punctured radiator, it would be lucky to make it another kilometre.

Ahead, a white van appeared, racing down the road toward them, driving almost as recklessly as McClune. "About time," McClune said, slamming on the brakes, turning the Land Rover sideways on the narrow dirt road, and drifting to a stop. He pulled Victoria and her children out of the back, helping the dazed woman to her feet. "It looks like you might make your flight to Canada, after all."

Abena almost cried with happiness when David Ndereba's smiling face leaned out of the open window of Westshore's white Toyota van.

"You took your time," said McClune, sliding open the van's passenger door.

"Elephants on the road," Ndereba said. "What do you do?" He smiled widely when he saw Abena. "I hear you have done some very good things in Africa, after all. I'm proud of you, Abena."

"You told me once you solved problems," Abena said. "We've given you a big one, I'm afraid."

Ndereba laughed. "Nothing I can't handle."

"David here will take the three of you to Nairobi," said McClune. "You have an appointment with Canadian officials tomorrow and after that, a long flight to Regina, God willing."

"Regina?" The word was new and strange to Victoria. "Is that anywhere near Toronto?"

"Nowhere even close, but after a few months you'll be able to move to Toronto or wherever you want. Vancouver even."

Victoria hugged him, then turned to Abena. "Vancouver; that is your city, isn't it?"

"Yes," Abena said. "Frank's too, once upon a time."

"It sounds like a good place." Victoria put her arms on McClune's shoulders. "Thank you, Frank McClune. I will never forget what you did for me — for us. You are a good man. You saved my life twice."

"I don't think my boss would agree with your assessment of my character right about now. And for what it's worth," he added, "it was you who saved mine."

A wailing siren rose on the air behind them. "Hurry, please," said Ndereba. "We don't have a great deal of time. There aren't any road-blocks in town yet, but that will change very quickly."

"Abena." Victoria's eyes glistened with tears. "I don't have the words to thank you."

They embraced, both crying freely.

"I'll come and see you sometime when you get to Regina," said Abena.

"Thank you, Miss Abena," said Peter, his hand extended.

Abena ignored his arm and hugged the boy. "An A plus, Peter, you earned an A plus."

"I'm sorry, Miss? I don't understand what you mean."

"Your homework assignment. You're the best eagle I've ever seen."

The police sirens grew louder.

"We have to leave now," Ndereba warned.

"You look after your brother," Abena said, embracing Alexandra quickly.

"I always do," the girl replied before getting into the van to join her mother and brother.

"They're going to be looking for you," said McClune as Ndereba started the engine and gingerly turned the van around on the narrow road.

"Don't worry. I've an uncle in Ukiwa; I'll borrow his car for the drive to Nairobi."

"Just don't eat the chicken if you stop for lunch in Sigor," Abena told Victoria as they pulled away. "It won't agree with you, believe me!"

Ndereba sped off, disappearing as the road turned sharply to the right several hundred metres away. McClune reached into the Land Rover, took out the keys and threw them into the ditch.

"Nobody's getting past here for at least a half-hour," he said with satisfaction. "That should be enough time for David to get to town. I think this is yours," he said as he reached back into the glovebox, showing Abena the necklace he'd torn from William Chol's neck.

"Thank you." Abena took the pendant and broken chain and clutched them against her chest. She'd never thought she'd see it again and her heart sang at the sight.

"My mother gave it to me when I was little. Oh my God! My mother! What's she going to think, Frank? I promised I wouldn't embarrass her, but look what I've done."

"I don't think she'd be embarrassed at all," McClune assured Abena. "She'd be proud. I'd say Victoria was right; you did something very extraordinary here."

"We both did." Abena watched as the first police pickup truck pulled up. "Frank. The little girl in the picture and that woman in Rwanda?"

"What about them?"

Abena wrapped her arm around his waist. "I think they'd be proud of you too."

Half a dozen armed police officers poured out of the pickup truck, guns aimed. "Stay calm," McClune whispered as they raised their hands. "This won't be much fun." Four police officers threw Abena and McClune to the mud, twisting them onto their bellies, pulling their arms roughly behind their backs, handcuffing them.

Abena's face was pressed into the muck, her mouth filling with dirty water and mud. She couldn't breathe and, despite McClune's warning to keep her wits, Abena panicked and thrashed around desperately until two sets of strong hands pulled her up and set her roughly down against the side of a police pickup.

McClune was sitting beside her, looking like hell. His face and hair were sopping wet and filthy. Blood ran freely from his nose, dripping onto the ground, mixing with the rainwater.

"Let me do the talking," he said. "The cops are plenty mad already and we don't want to give them any more reasons to kill us than we already have."

Abena managed a weak grin. "You think you doing the talking will calm them down?" Another police vehicle, one of at least ten more, drove up, stopping mere inches from McClune's feet. Chief Inspector Obanda stepped out of the passenger seat and, in one quick motion, strode over to McClune and kicked him hard in the ribs, knocking him over. "I said you needed to tread more carefully. It seems you didn't listen."

McClune grunted with pain as he rolled onto his back to face Obanda. "And I said you needed to take better care of that uniform, Benjie. Look at those boots. Scuffed again. Guess I'm not the only one who isn't so good at listening." Obanda roared in anger and kicked McClune again, this time in his face. McClune's neck snapped back, blood flying.

"Frank!" Abena screamed, certain that McClune had been killed. She nearly wept with relief when after just a few seconds of lying prostrate on the ground he struggled back up.

"Not very good at taking my own advice, am I?" he wheezed, blood running from both a split lip and a thoroughly broken nose.

"Sir! We can't move it!"

Abena strained her neck to see several officers straining to push McClune's shot-up Land Rover off the road. "Then drive around the damn thing!" Obanda screamed, as if he were talking to imbeciles.

"Sir, we can't," protested one of the men. "We tried, but the ground's too wet. Look."

A police pickup truck had indeed attempted to drive through the ditch to get around McClune's stricken vehicle but had quickly sunk to its axles in the soupy morass.

"Where are the keys? Tell me!" Obanda ordered.

"Somewhere in there," McClune said, his bloodied head pointing toward the ditch. "I'd be careful about going after them, though. I think I saw a crocodile."

"Chief Inspector Obanda! No!" Obanda had lined up, knee cocked, ready to land another kick to McClune's head when he was stopped cold by Richard Angara's order.

Abena hadn't seen the camp director arrive, but there he was, impeccably dressed in a white suit with a matching safari hat and brown leather shoes, picking his way carefully through the sludge-filled road. Obanda was frothing at the mouth. "I'm going to kill this son of a bitch with my bare hands!" he swore as Angara approached.

"No, you're not," Angara replied tersely. "Too many questions will be asked if you do."

"But Sir! Our associate was very clear what he wanted to happen to the *mzungus* and the Sudanese woman."

"*Kuwa na utulivu!*" Angara raised his voice louder than Abena had heard it before. "Be quiet! I run this camp — not the SPLA, no matter what they may think!"

Angara leaned over McClune as Obanda reluctantly stepped aside. "Who was driving that van, Mr. McClune, and where is it going?"

"Mario Andretti?" Frank replied. "Off to Daytona Beach?"

"Very well." Angara turned to Abena. "Ms. Walker, perhaps you will show a little more common sense than Mr. McClune and kindly tell me."

"I don't know who Mario Andretti is," Abena said. "But if Frank says it was him, it probably was."

"Told you," grinned Frank. Angara's cheek twitched slightly, and for a second Abena thought that, despite his previous order, Angara would unleash Obanda on them both. Instead, he shook his head sadly.

"Very well. I see your reputation for obstinacy and rule-breaking is well earned. No matter. We'll have our wayward Sudanese guests back in the camp by nightfall with or without your help."

"Take them into custody," Angara ordered. "Ms. Walker won't be the only *mzungu* leaving Kenya because of this." Hands still trussed up firmly behind their backs, McClune and Abena were trundled into the back of the nearest police Land Cruiser.

252 / David Starr

"What's going to happen next, Frank?" Abena asked worriedly.

"I'd say about three weeks in a Kenyan jail, maybe two if Amnesty International really does show up, followed by a quiet deportation when the dust settles."

"And after we get sent home? I can't imagine Westshore will be willing to write us reference letters, do you?"

"I've been thinking about that," McClune said. "It's been a long time for me, but perhaps we can both go back to UBC."

David Ndereba drove deftly away from the chaos in the camp, with Victoria and her children nervously watching out the rear window. After a quick stop in Ukiwa town to exchange vehicles, they hurried south — Ndereba driving all through the night to get them to Nairobi, with little more than half an hour to spare. Victoria was amazed that he could find his way through this warren of streets and buildings. Neither Victoria nor her children had seen such a place, full of towers that reached so high into the sky.

"This is the Visa Application Centre," Ndereba explained as they pulled up to a concrete building. "They're expecting you." Victoria stepped out of the car and stretched. Thunder pealed overhead. The rain fell in sheets. Victoria was in no hurry to move, to get under shelter. The rain was cool and refreshing and she raised her hands to the sky, letting it cascade down upon her. Overhead a large bird, an eagle perhaps, soared lazily through the sky.

"Look, Mama," said Alexandra, pointing to the ground. Red mud flowed from their feet, running away like a river of blood. "The rain is washing away the dust from the camp!"

"It is," Victoria said, hugging her children tightly, "and so much more than that."

Epilogue

HE SEEMED PUZZLED by their files, the headmaster. Over the years, Victoria had learned to deal with men like him, people to whom she was just a number or a piece of paper in a thin folder.

The bureaucrats, United Nations officials or Western aid workers she knew in Africa, they were the same as this man, obsessed with paper, with files. Except, perhaps, for two.

"Sudan, Ethiopia and Kenya?" he said quizzically, looking at the travel documents she was issued in Nairobi. "Strange, but they seem to be in order. So what nationality are you and your children, Ms. Deng?"

What could Victoria Deng say to that?

She explained that, despite her children's differing countries of birth, they were all Sudanese. Dinka by blood. Then she said as best she could that sometimes, things as simple as your name or your country can be complicated in Africa.

He responded uncomfortably.

"Sorry about the questions, but we've got to be careful with foreigners, especially since the World Trade Center disaster in the States. Besides, we don't get a lot of refugees here."

Victoria nodded deferentially and smiled. That was the best way to deal with government men, to not make them feel stupid, she had learned. She said that she understood then assured him the documents were authentic, issued by the Canadian government officials in Kenya, who confirmed both her parentage and the fact that the three of them were no threat to the security of North America, even after September 11, 2001.

Victoria's answers seemed satisfactory. The headmaster signed the registration forms, accepting the children into the school. Victoria exhaled, not even realizing she'd been holding her breath. After all that had happened, she wouldn't have thought she'd be nervous, but she had been in Canada only a short time now and still felt as if she were living in a dream. She gathered herself then asked if Peter and Alexandra could start school right away.

"I'm sorry, but not today," the headmaster told her. "Like I said, we've never had any refugee students before. Some schools here have but not us. It's going to take a few days to find appropriate classes for your children."

Despite her best efforts to be polite, Victoria very nearly lost her temper. Not that that would have surprised her father. She had changed a great deal since that last day she saw him, but at times, the girl she once was found her way back.

"My children speak Dinka, Arabic, English and Kiswahili, and can read and write in two of those languages. Appropriate classes? English, mathematics, history and whatever else Canadian children study in this school would be more than appropriate."

The headmaster realized he'd offended her again and apologized. This was new. Victoria had not seen a man in his position say sorry before. "Just policy. Paperwork. Hope you understand. Bring the children back next Monday. We'll get them started then."

Victoria told him Monday was fine. She had a great deal of experience with both paperwork and waiting and could afford to be a little patient still. It had been twenty years, after all. What were a few more days?

The rain pattered against the window. Outside, the trees disappeared in the fog. Hidden in the mist, they seemed more like ghosts, like skeletons, their stems thin and frail compared to the baobabs. But she should expect to find great differences between Africa and Canada, they had told Victoria in Nairobi, so she supposed that went for trees as well as everything else.

"Terrible weather today," he said, but her thoughts had drifted a long way from the headmaster. Victoria hardly heard the man speak as she stared out the window.

"The rain, I mean," he said again, bringing her mind back to the here and the now. "Being from Africa you must not get a lot of it, droughts and all. Probably quite the treat for you. Here on the West Coast? We get nothing but the wet stuff from now until April. You'll soon get pretty sick of it."

"I used to feel the same way about rain," Victoria said, "until a friend taught me something very different about it."

"A friend?" he asked curiously. "A Kenyan? From the refugee camp?"

"No," Victoria said, her heart swelling. "A Canadian, from Vancouver. She is the reason we left Regina. She said we would like it here."

"Well, isn't that something," the headmaster replied, half-listening as he focused on the paperwork. "A smart friend too. You think rain is bad, you should see snow. Six months of winter out in the Prairies? No thanks. You got out just in time."

He put down his pen. "Registration's complete." He shook Victoria's hand, her small fingers swallowed up by his meaty palm. "I have to tell you that it's kind of exciting for us too. Like I said, you're our first refugee family."

Victoria looked over the headmaster's shoulder, through his window to the entryway outside. A woman with a rounded face, jagged white scar visible on her cheek, was approaching the main entrance of the school. Her skin was much lighter than Victoria's, taking its colour from a long dead great-grandfather who'd once travelled across Africa from Nigeria to Sudan with the British Colonial Army.

She wasn't alone. Two nervous-looking girls, with new dresses, shoes and backpacks walked hand in hand with the woman, each a carbon copy of their mother.

Victoria broke into a wide smile as they reached the front door of the school. "If you think one refugee family is exciting," she said, "let me introduce you to your second."

AUTHOR'S NOTE &
ACKNOWLEDGEMENTS

Like Joyful Tears is a work of fiction based on recent history. Some characters are inspired in part by real-life people.

As an educator and writer, I have had the privilege of working with the refugee and newcomer community for well over a decade. I wrote my first book, *From Bombs to Books* (2011), to chronicle the journeys and celebrate the courage of families from Sudan, Congo, Syria, Somalia, Afghanistan, Iraq and other regions of the world where conflict forced them from their homes. That opportunity has been one of the most profound personal and professional experiences of my life.

It is a tragedy of our modern world that refugees in increasing numbers seek safety in the West, and in doing so face vilification for fleeing political and military violence and economic hardship, in part created by the very countries where they seek sanctuary. Many do not make it. They die by the thousands in the Sahara Desert, the Mexican wilderness or on the Mediterranean, forgotten and unknown. It is my hope that by giving names, stories and context to the people in this novel that we can begin to see past the numbers and the headlines to understand the common humanity we share with those who seek refuge.

258 / David Starr

This novel would not exist without the wisdom and help of many people. The lives and experiences of Mambo Masinda, Haval Ahmed, Qasim Abdulle and Latifa Jawansheer were critical in helping me understand the perspectives and lived experiences of refugee families. In particular, the stories shared by Rose David and Amel Madut, two remarkable "sisters in struggle," were invaluable to this novel and I cannot thank them enough. I would also like to thank my wife Sharon and my family for their love and support and for giving me the gift of time to write. I am also very grateful for the support of Ron and Veronica Hatch for their belief in this project, and for publishing books that matter. Thanks as well to Meagan Dyer for her work on the manuscript. I would like to note that Arabic, Dinka and Kiswahili phrases have been used in the book when appropriate. Any mistakes in their use are the author's alone.

Author royalties from the sales of this book are shared with Rose David and Amel Madut as well as two remarkable charities. Canada Scores Vancouver, founded by Jon Lutz, provides soccer, literacy and leadership opportunities to vulnerable youth in Metro Vancouver, including many who come from a refugee and immigrant background. The Obakki Foundation, started by Treana Peake, helps communities in South Sudan, Cameroon and Uganda fund freshwater wells, education, and agricultural and vocational opportunities, as well as medical care. To learn more or to support either of these charities, visit www.obakkifoundation.org and www.canadascores.org.

ABOUT THE AUTHOR

David Starr is a prize-winning author of six previous books, including *From Bombs to Books*, which chronicles the stories of refugee children and their families coming to B.C. *The Insider's Guide to K–12 Education in B.C.* is a resource guide for parents about the B.C. school system. David grew up in Fort St. James in northern British Columbia, and he now lives in Greater Vancouver with his wife, four children and a dog named Buster. He is one of the UBC Faculty of Education's Top 100 Graduates and is proud to be principal at Terry Fox Secondary School in Port Coquitlam, B.C. For further information and readings availability, visit www.davidstarr.org.

MARQUIS

Québec, Canada